A Taxonomy of Love

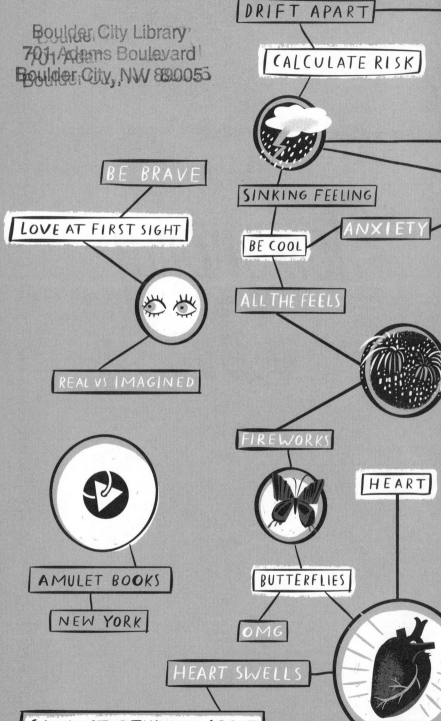

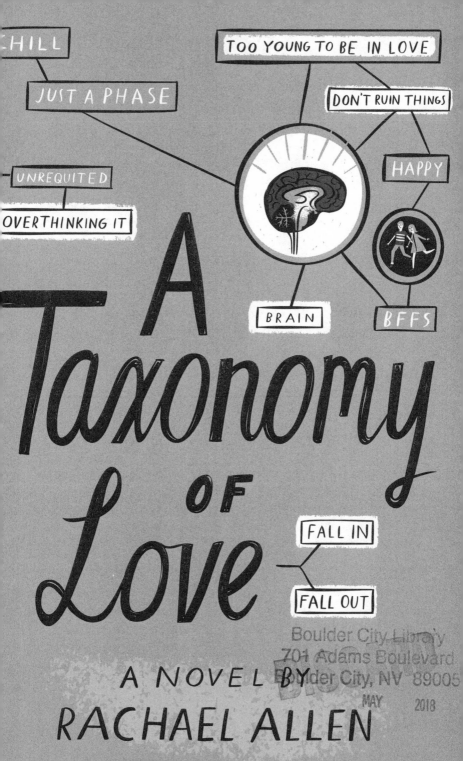

CHILL

JUST A PHASE

TOO YOUNG TO BE IN LOVE

DON'T RUIN THINGS

HAPPY

UNREQUITED

OVERTHINKING IT

BRAIN

BFFS

A

Taxonomy

OF

Love

FALL IN

FALL OUT

A NOVEL BY

RACHAEL ALLEN

Cataloging-in-Publication Data has been applied
for and may be obtained from the Library of Congress.
ISBN 978-1-4197-2541-8

Text copyright © 2018 Rachael Allen
Book design by Alyssa Nassner

Printed and bound in U.S.A.
10 9 8 7 6 5 4 3 2 1

Amulet Books are available at special discounts when purchased
in quantity for premiums and promotions as well as fundraising or
educational use. Special editions can also be created to specification.
For details, contact specialsales@abramsbooks.com or the address below.

ABRAMS The Art of Books
195 Broadway, New York, NY 10007
abramsbooks.com

*To Susan, for believing,
and to Zack, for everything*

Prologue

Two important things happened the summer I turned thirteen.

Hope moved in next door.

Mrs. Laver assigned a summer project on taxonomy.

The goal: Photograph twenty distinct kinds of insects and classify them by drawing their taxonomies.

The best part was when I found this devil scorpion carrying fourteen milky-white baby scorpions on her back. They looked just like her, except light colored and in miniature: miniature pinchers, threadlike legs, bodies smaller than her stinger.

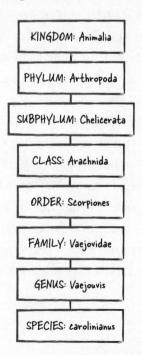

KINGDOM: Animalia

PHYLUM: Arthropoda

SUBPHYLUM: Chelicerata

CLASS: Arachnida

ORDER: Scorpiones

FAMILY: Vaejovidae

GENUS: Vaejouvis

SPECIES: carolinianus

Looking at the world that way really made sense to me. Because you have all the scorpions together on one branch, with their pinchers and their segmented tails with the stingers on the end. And if you go up a branch, you get the Arachnida class, which maybe surprises you at first because spiders and scorpions don't seem that much alike, but then you realize they're both invertebrates with eight segmented legs. And if you keep going up and up, you can see how every living organism is the same, but also how they're different, and also how many degrees of different. You can see how everything fits together.

After the project was over, I started doodling taxonomies here and there—usually funny, goofy stuff. But before I knew it, I was drawing them all the time. Some people don't like labels and things, but I think they can help you understand yourself. Sometimes. Like if you've been acting really weird and you can't help it and the doctor finally tells you that you have Tourette's syndrome. It's more than labels and words. It's an *aha* moment and an explanation and a plan. Labels like that can lift the weight off your shoulders.

I guess that's why I've always liked classifying people and things, even if it's just figuring out which creature on a Magic: The Gathering card is the most like my terrifying P.E. teacher. And these taxonomies, I mean, they could be even better than the Magic cards. Maybe I could finally figure out why I see things so differently from everybody else. Maybe I could use it to understand why girls always seem to like my big brother so much. Maybe I could use it to understand *everything*.

Part One

13 years old

A TAXONOMY OF GIRLS WHO MAKE IT DIFFICULT TO CONCENTRATE ON MATH HOMEWORK

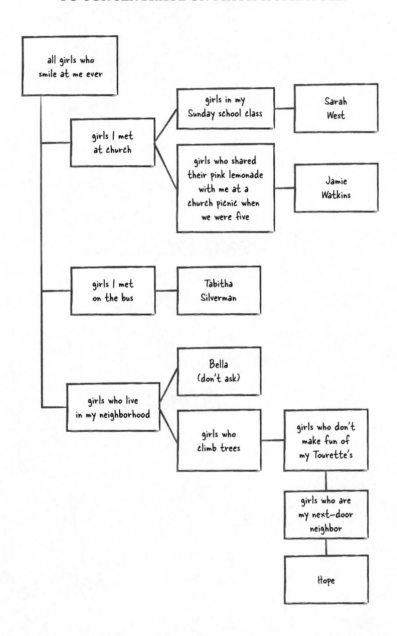

My new next-door neighbor, Hope Birdsong, has magical powers, I'm, like, 80 percent sure of it.

Fact: She makes bullies twice her size cower in fear (which suggests mind control, or at the very least, otherworldly bravery).

Fact: Her hair smells like honeysuckles in spring, and she has the entire world tacked to the walls of her bedroom.

Fact: Did you miss the part where her name is Hope Birdsong? Ordinary people don't have names like that.

Given all this information, I should have happiness shooting out of my pores. There's just one problem.

Fact: Hope Birdsong will never, ever, EVER love me back.

I blame the cookies.

At any given time, there's a 35 percent chance my stepmom is baking cookies. Some days, the cookies feel like more than just baked goods—like they're harbingers of awesomeness. Other days, they're just really freaking delicious.

Pam is working on another batch of Peanut Butter Blossoms when I hear a great big engine yawn to a stop next door. Before they can get their doors open, I'm peering through the blinds, fingers crossed by my side that there will be kids coming out of the moving van and that they won't be a bunch of Neanderthals like my big brother, Dean, and all his friends. I wait and wish. The graphic of carnivorous plants splashed on the side of the truck seems like a very good sign.

Let him be the kind of kid who likes Minecraft and spy gear more than punching people.

Let him think camping is the best way to spend a Friday night.

Let him—

And I never get to finish that thought because the door opens, and out jumps *her.*

"Spencer, what are you looking at?" asks Pam.

Some things can stun you into absolute honesty. "The most beautiful girl I've ever seen."

"Oh, yeah? What does she look like?"

You can hear the amusement in her voice, and it's pretty cool of her not to make fun of me. In fact, Pam is mostly a pretty cool stepmom, except when she does weird stuff like freak out and buy an industrial amount of cleaning products just because I told her I pee in the shower. Like everyone else doesn't.

"She has white hair," I finally manage to say.

Pam looks up from where she's rinsing a bowl. "You mean blonde?"

"Uh-uh. *White.*" It's practically glowing. It reminds me of fiber optics.

I watch in wonder as she frolics around the yard with a German shepherd that is halfway between a dog and a puppy.

"Hope!" yells a voice from the house, and she runs inside.

Hope. Of course that's her name.

The oven beeps.

"Do you think we should take some cookies to our new neighbors?" asks my stepmom.

YES! Yes, that is the best idea in the history of good ideas! Yes, I should do it right now because Hope has been gone for six whole seconds and I'm already starting to go through withdrawal! My mouth is open, but nothing comes out. The one slippery, life-changing word I need hovers cruelly out of reach.

And at exactly that moment, I hear my brother's voice behind me. "Who's that chick with the white hair?"

Hope! I turn, and there she is in her yard again.

"Boys. Welcome cookies?" Pam holds up the gleaming plate, and she is looking right at me, but my jaw has spontaneously wired itself shut. Not Dean's. He swoops past and plucks the plate right out of the air, plucks the confidence right out of my chest. He had to have seen me trying to say yes. My feelings were so big, they were bubbling against the ceiling and leaking out the open window. He had to have noticed.

I watch—seething—as that a-hole skips up the stairs of the Birdsongs' front porch and into Hope's heart.

It should have been my hand clanking the anchor-shaped door-knocker the Rackhams left behind.

It should have been my eyes eating up her smile and beaming it back.

It should have been me.

I'm still kind of moping about it the next day. Pam suggests I go over and introduce myself—no way—and then she says if I keep making that face, she's going to take me over there herself and make me shake hands with everyone in their family, so I decide it's time to get out of the house. ASAP.

I escape to the mudroom and try to figure out what to do next. I guess I could see if Mimi—that's my grandma—wants to go hiking. I glance out the window at the apartment over the garage where Mimi's lived ever since Grandaddy died six years ago. The light is on, so she's probably home. I can't help glancing at Hope's house, too, but I don't see her, and anyway, I need to stop being pathetic.

I shake my head and grab my hiking boots. I do not expect to find a caterpillar lurking behind them.

"Well, hi there, little guy. How'd you get inside?"

He's brown with a bright sunny green patch that covers his entire back like a blanket, except for dead center, where there's a small brown circle that looks like it's meant for a miniature rider. I do not pick him up. A saddleback sting is worse than ten bees. Those little tufts that cover the horns on his head and tail and look like they'd be oh-so-fun to pet? They are poison-filled barbs.

I can't resist, though, so I touch my index finger to the soft skin of the caterpillar's saddle. He rears back his head and tail, body curving into a *U*. *The petting zoo is closed today, my friend.* I jerk my hand away. I'm pretty sure he's glaring at me.

"Hey, Spencer. Whatcha doing?" My dad sweeps in and sits on the bench across from me.

"Oh, well, I just found this caterpillar."

He squints at it. "Huh. Funny little guy. Listen, Dean and I are fixing to go to the cabins to make some repairs. You'd probably rather stay here and catch caterpillars, though. Right?"

He doesn't really look at me while he's talking, busy pulling on his tennis shoes without bothering to untie and retie the laces.

"Oh, um. Yeah." The last time I tried to help out at the cabins, there was an unfortunate incident involving a staple gun.

"Thought so." He touches the top of my baseball cap. "See you, buddy."

(Everything you need to know about my dad: One time he sliced his leg with a chain saw while he was cutting down trees, and he took a shower AND made himself a BLT sandwich before driving himself to the hospital.)

I go grab a piece of printer paper and gently prod the caterpillar onto it with the tip of a work glove. Dean rushes in and squeezes his feet into his already-laced-up shoes.

"Crap, I forgot my hat." He runs back downstairs to his bedroom.

I look down at my unlaced boots. I wonder if everyone puts on their shoes the same way except me. Maybe my mom doesn't. Maybe she drinks skim milk with her Chinese takeout, even though everyone else thinks it's gross. But I don't know. I haven't actually seen her since I was five.

I carry the saddleback outside on his paper stretcher. You can tell it's summer just from the noises. Kids yelling and laughing, and the sound of a basketball echoing against the asphalt. For some reason, the raucous pick-up game across the street makes me feel more alone than ever.

Then I realize I'm not. Alone, I mean.

Hope is standing on her front porch, empty cookie plate clutched against her chest. And the expression on her face, well, I'm pretty sure it matches the one I was just wearing.

Dean slams the door behind me. Hope turns toward the sound. Sees me. Waves. She's walking down the stairs. This could be my shot. I have approximately twelve seconds to think of a stunning introduction. Something that will make me seem worldly. Cool. Mysterious.

"This is my brother, Spencer. He's playing with a caterpillar." Not that.

But she smiles. "Hi, I'm Hope."

"Hi," I say. And then I tic. It's just a shrug, probably my least embarrassing tic, but now all I can think about is whether I seem nonchalant or deranged. My tic-shrug isn't the same as my real shrug. When I tic, it looks like my shoulders are connected to a piece of string, and someone decided it would be fun to give me a yank.

Hope doesn't seem to notice even when I tic-shrug a couple more times. I'm not ready to put her on the Kids Who Don't Make Fun of Me list, but we'll call her a solid maybe. "I, um, brought your plate back. The cookies were really good. Thanks."

I reach my hand out, but Dean snags the plate first (again). His hand brushes against Hope's, and her cheeks turn pink. I hate my brother. I mean, I really hate him.

"Dean!" my dad bellows from the truck. "Let's go."

"See ya." He cocks his head at Hope and shoves the plate against my chest like he's doing a football handoff.

I guess I expected Hope to leave after that, because it surprises me when she stays standing in front of me.

"So, what grade are you gonna be in?" she asks.

"Seventh."

"Me, too!"

I am thinking this is possibly the best news I've received all summer, when a woman with the most toned arms I have ever seen emerges from Hope's house.

"You ready to go to the farmers' market?"

"Sure," Hope calls over her shoulder. She smiles at me. "I'll see you around, okay?"

"Sure. Definitely." I am proud of myself because I manage to say it as she walks away instead of after she's already in her car.

A couple of the basketball guys stare at her as she goes. I can already see it happening. They'll assimilate her right into the fold, and that will be the end of it. I upgrade the chance she'll be making fun of me by next week from maybe to probable.

But then I notice her watching them as her mom drives away. She's making that face again. The lost one.

I downgrade from probable to maybe not at all.

CHAPTER
2

FYI, when someone says they'll see you around and then doesn't show their face for four whole days, you can bet they are calling you Caterpillar Boy to any and everyone.

Dean just left for baseball camp, so I'm in the den playing whatever games I like for as long as I like because he isn't there stealing the controller and giving me ultimate wedgies. It is a land of aliens and car thieves and zombies, and I am king, and I could play forever. Or just for the next ten minutes, because the king could really use a Mountain Dew break.

I'm walking back from the kitchen, drink in hand, when there's a knock at the door, and I happen to answer (read: am forced to by Pam).

It's her.

I'm tempted to shut the door and open it again just to make sure, but I don't want to seem weird, so instead I stare at her awkwardly and wonder if her hair is made of sunlight.

"Hey, do you want to come outside?" she asks.

Yes, I say. Except inside my head and not with my mouth.

No, no, no, no, no. Not again. Is this what it's going to be like every time I see her? My teeth sticking like someone superglued them together and my tongue falling down the back of my throat? I make a guttural, choking-type noise. Hope looks at me like she's wondering if I have some kind of brain damage.

"Do. You. Want. To. Come. Outside?" She flashes me a reassuring smile. The porch fans spin in lazy circles, also known as The Speed That Sends Hypnotizing Ripples Through Hair.

"Sure," I say, relieved that I no longer seem to have lockjaw. And then my shoulders twitch upward in a tic. Not a big one, but she must have seen it. Except she doesn't react. Maybe she thought it was just the regular kind of shrug. Maybe my tic-shrug isn't as different as I think it is.

And then I'm thinking about my tics, and Hope noticing my tics, and the tan lines painted across her collarbones, and whether she noticed me noticing the tan lines, and holy balls, my nose itches . . . *Do it. Just do it. You'll feel so much better.* There are freaking fire ants crawling around inside my nose and tickling me with their scritchy-scratchy feet, and all I have to do is sniff, and they'll all go away.

Hope is watching me.

Don't. Tic.

I have to!

Don't.

But the ants. I NEED TO TIC SO BAD, I—

Sniiiiff.

The relaxation is instant. I think this might be what my dad feels like when he sneaks behind the woodpile with a cigar. Except I'm also flooded with this tremendous sense of accomplishment, like at the cellular level. Releasing a suppressed tic makes me feel like I have just climbed a mountain, and all is right with the world.

I follow Hope down the stairs, hoping she doesn't notice that sniff or the two that come after.

I tic a lot (dozens of times a day? hundreds?), but it definitely happens more when I'm anxious. And maybe I notice it more when I'm anxious? Probably both.

"Where are we going?" I ask.

"I was gonna go climb trees. You wanna come?"

OMGPANCAKES, IS THIS REAL LIFE??? "Yes."

I trail behind her, feet shuffling, mind spinning. I do this thing—okay, it's dorky, but I have this deck of Magic cards, and I tape people's names onto the cards based on what they're like (not the valuable ones, *obviously*). I don't know, I feel like it helps me get a handle on people or something. It started this one time when I threw up when we were hunting. Dad and Dean were laughing, and I was like, Minotaurs, the both of you! And if I had to guess for Hope, I'd say she's a Satyr Grovedancer or maybe some kind of dryad. I've been wrong in the past (when Dad first started dating Pam, I thought for sure she was a mountain troll). But there's the hair, the name, and then the tree climbing. No human middle-school girl wants to spend her Saturdays climbing trees. They've all received the standard-fun lobotomy by now and started acting like Bella Fontaine across the street. Bella divides her time between obsessing over boys, making fun of people like me, and plotting middle school domination via text message, and she is most decidedly not a dryad, though I could be convinced she's a harpy.

"I found this grove of perfect climbing trees out past the cul-de-sac that way." She points into the distance, her chin jutting out in a regal kind of way. It's a strong chin for a girl, with just a hint of a cleft.

"Yeah! I know that place. Those are pecan trees."

"They are? That's so cool!"

"I know! In the fall we pick them, and Pam makes pies."

Making homemade everything is Pam's hobby (obsession). Pies, pickles, sourdough bread, peach-habañero salsa, bacon jam. BACON. JAM. I tell Hope about all the awesome stuff you can find in our food closet, which she seems to think is called a pantry, and also about how homemade pickles taste nothing like store-bought.

"I'm telling you, these pickles will completely change the way you see pickles."

"That's cool that you get along with your stepmom," she says.

"Oh, yeah. Pam's awesome."

(Everything you need to know about Pam: She's the one who puts the pictures on Pinterest that make other women freak out and reassess their abilities as wives/mothers/hot-glue-gun operators. Except she doesn't do it on purpose. She just genuinely loves hot-gluing stuff to other stuff.)

Hope asks me what middle school is like here, and I tell her a version that makes me sound 20 percent cooler.

"Is it weird having to make new friends all over again?" I ask. "You probably had a ton of friends at your old school."

"Oh, sure. Um, tons." She eyes the basketball goal at the end of the street.

Our words ping back and forth as we leave the road and wade through briars and Queen Anne's lace. I hold back a branch so Hope can pass, in what I feel is a supremely suave and gentlemanly move, and then I sniff for what must be one time too many because Hope says, "Do you have a cold?"

"Oh, uh, yeah." And then I pause. I don't want to do it. But I don't have the kind of Tourette's syndrome where I get to decide when and if I tell people. One fountain of verbal tics spews out, and people know *something's* going on with me, even if they don't know exactly what. And then I get the "What's wrong with you?" or the more polite, "Are you okay?" while giving me a concerned look that really means, "What's wrong with you?" I can't stand to hear her say that, so I rip off the Band-Aid. "Well, no. Well, I have Tourette's syndrome."

I wait for her to lean away—that's what 97 percent of people do when I tell them. Their eyes might be smiling, and their mouths might be saying nice things, but their bodies betray the truth: a primal urge to get away in case my weirdness is catching.

"What's it like?" she asks. She leans forward as she says it.

It's such a small thing, but in that moment, I am eleven feet tall.

I swing myself up into the nearest pecan tree, and she swings right up beside me. "I don't yell out the F-word all the time or anything. I just, you know, sniff or shrug, and sometimes I want to repeat a word someone says. Like, over and over again. Like, I can't not do it."

She nods like she doesn't know what to say and keeps climbing.

"Anyway, it's not like it's a big deal or anything." Tic-sniff. Except that it is because I am totally embarrassing myself in front of a girl I like.

Hope sits on a branch and swings her legs, and I perch on one across from her. She grabs a handful of hard, green pods.

"So these are going to turn into pecans?"

"Yep. Pecans." And then my Tourette's brain decides it really hates me because it latches on to the word "pecans," and I. Can't. Stop. Saying. It. *Pecans.* Only I'm saying it like "pee-cans" because apparently I'm as southern as Mimi today.

"PEE-CANS." If I can just keep my mouth—"PEE-CANS." Ugh. I keep repeating it at a half-shout volume. My voice echoes through the grove of pecans, which I am currently not feeling so fond of. This is why I have to bring a washcloth whenever I go to the movies. I wish I could stuff something in my mouth right now. I try covering it with my fingers.

"PEEE-CNNS." Well, that's just great.

"You really can't stop it?" She's looking right at me. I'm used to people staring, but only for a second, just long enough to put me in a Box for People Who Shouldn't Be Looked At or Spoken To. Then they turn away like they haven't seen me at all. This is different.

"Nope." Except I think I maybe finally have stopped, but I don't want to fixate on it for too long and tempt it to come back, so I try to empty my mind of the word and rush to talk about the first thing I can think of. "But I went to Tourette's camp this summer—I just got back last week, actually—and I got to meet other people who have it and share coping mechanisms and stuff." Oh, man, I have to stop this ship from sinking. "I met Sophie there."

"Sophie?" The sunlight streaming through the leaves hits her face, and she wrinkles her nose.

Yes! Sophie! Sophie is cool! Let's run with this Sophie idea!

"Yeah. Soph's great. We message each other, like, every day."

See? Sophie's a girl, and she likes me. You could like me, too.

"Oh." She climbs higher, and I can't see her face. "Well, that's great. Um, so, Dean. Does he have a girlfriend?"

Something falls out of the tree and splats against the rocks below. My heart. I'm pretty sure it's my heart.

Lie! Lie! Lie! "No," I say (truthfully—ugh). "He doesn't."

Before she can do something terrible like ask me to ask him if he thinks she's pretty, I say, "I'm gonna try another tree." I've climbed as far as I can get in this one.

I pick my way to the lowest branch and hang by my fingers before falling the rest of the way to the ground. Before I can catch my balance, there are hands turning me around and pushing me against the trunk. I have a moment of complete and total disorienting fear, but I manage to stay upright. I look up. And up. And up. Into the face of Ethan Wells and two of his Sasquatch-size friends. How did I not know they were here? I guess I didn't hear them over the sound of my still-breaking heart.

Ethan's face gets so close I think it's going to eat mine. "What's up, Spencer?"

"Dean's at baseball camp," I say, as fast as I can. No Dean was supposed to mean two whole weeks with no towel-whips, no pants-ings, no stop-hitting-yourself. No purple nurples from Dean's friends who seem to spend every waking moment waiting for me to walk around corners. It was going to be a glorious preview of this fall, when they'll all start their first year of high school and I'll be in seventh grade by myself.

The Sasquatches grin. "Yeah. Big brother's not here to protect you now," says the taller one.

Dean? Protect me? I'm still trying to process the validity of that statement when Ethan says, "We weren't looking for Dean. We were looking for you."

"Me?" I sniff and try to play it off by wiping my nose.

"Yeah, you. Have you been looking in my girlfriend's window?"

"What? No." Tic-shrug.

"You sure? Because you're shrugging like you don't know." He smirks like he's the master of all things funny. The Sasquatches snicker.

"No. I swear." I wouldn't get within twenty feet of that she-cow.

"You're lying. Bella saw you with your binoculars pointed at her window, you creepy little pervert."

Oh, crap. "I wasn't. There was a red-headed woodpecker in the tree by her house. I was watching it store grasshoppers in the cracks in the bark."

"A woodpecker. Riiight. Well, just in case you get any ideas, I think we're gonna have to teach you a lesson about bird-watching." He cracks his knuckles. My skin winces. I can't believe Hope is going to see this. "Say you're sorry. Say you're sorry for watching her change."

And then I reach that familiar point where I just can't take it anymore. "Into what? A gargoyle?"

I'm pushed back against the tree. "What did you say?" They converge over me—a three-headed Cerberus—and I wonder if beatings work like muscle memory, because I can feel the bruises waiting to form. Ethan's hands dig into my shoulders. My outbursts always feel like they're worth it until the first punch. I wish I could blame them on the Tourette's, but this is 100 percent my own stupidity.

"Listen here, mother scratcher." Hope swings down from a branch and lands beside me with a soft thump. "My boy Spencer doesn't give a crap about seeing your girlfriend in her training bra."

Ethan's fist is frozen in midair like this is a movie, and if you only hit play, you'd see the part where he breaks my nose.

Hope seizes the opportunity to remove my face from the line of fire. The Sasquatches watch with stupider-than-usual looks on their faces, their knuckles and brains completely immobilized. I wait for Ethan's punching muscles to start working again. Hope pops each of her fingers all in a row. Is she scared? She sure doesn't seem scared. Ethan seems a little scared.

"We're going to my house for a snack," she continues. "And if you know what's good for you, you won't follow us because my mom's the only female firefighter in Peach Valley."

This is no ordinary girl. This is the Queen of Badassery. And apparently it runs in the family.

Hope leads the way, and I trail behind her in a daze, wondering how it is that I'm still alive.

"Cheese and Fries, Spence, did you have to say that thing about his girlfriend being a gargoyle? It's like you want to get beat."

Spence. She called me Spence. "You don't know Ethan. He's going to beat the crap out of me anyway, so I might as well make it worth it."

She looks at me like all my cells have shifted and now I'm something else. "Huh. I like your style, Spence."

"Thanks." If she keeps calling me that, I'm going to walk into a tree.

Hope's compliment puts me in such a happy haze that I barely notice anything during the rest of the walk through the woods, even when we clomp across her back deck, even when she grabs two string cheeses from the fridge. But then she throws open the door to her bedroom, and I feel like I have extra nerve endings and extra eyes, compound ones, with thirty thousand facets like a dragonfly. Because this room—I've never seen any-thing like it.

Photos of people and animals, like the kind you might see in *National Geographic*, are tacked from one end of the room to the other. Hot-air balloons next to a polar bear next to the Eiffel Tower. A canyon made of ice fractals. Tibetan monks holding the biggest horns I've ever seen. A map of the world that takes up half of one wall, and another one of the United States up over her desk. And then other maps, smaller ones, like the one of the Caribbean by her window. I shuffle closer and notice a purple pin shaped like the letter *J* sticking out of Haiti.

"What's this?" I ask.

"It's for Janie, my sister. Last month, she was in South Africa, and now she's in Haiti." She taps the *J*, but I don't know her well enough to read the face she's making. "She left nine weeks ago. It's the longest we've ever been apart." She shakes her shoulders back and forth like that will get rid of the seriousness. "But it's okay. We've been messaging at night and sending each other postcards. And look! She draws pictures for me." She points at a woman with her arms wrapped around her daughter; a crowded market; two little boys holding hands in front of the wreckage left by a storm. The drawings are beautiful, but the faces—I feel like I've had a *Matrix*-style mind dump of everything they've ever lived.

"Wow. The faces . . . " It's all I can manage.

Hope nods. "I know."

"So she's an artist?"

"Nope. That's just something she does. She's over there on this project installing solar panels. Like, at hospitals and schools and stuff? She works for this foundation, and she's going to get to help all these people and travel all over the world." She throws her arms wide and does a half-twirl. "And someday I'm going to travel all over the world, too. Mom said I should plan a trip whenever Janie's out of town—to help with missing her and stuff." She gestures to a map. "So, here's the one I'm planning to Haiti. We're gonna see the Citadelle and the ruins of the palace of Sans-Souci. And the caves! You wouldn't believe the caves in Haiti." Her fingers skim across the map like water bugs, landing for a second on each place she's drawn a cave icon. "And Janie and I are going to hike through all of them. Or do you think that's overdoing it?"

"No way. I think it's a great idea." She beams, and I wrack my brain for something exciting enough to interest a girl who plans cave tours of Haiti. I'm still wracking as she moves on to the map she planned while Janie was in South Africa. And there's Madagascar, practically blinking at me, and it hits me. "Madagascar has some of the coolest bugs in the world!"

Hope pauses mid-sentence. Smooth. Real smooth. But then she smiles. "It does?"

I take this as a sign that I should plow ahead. "Oh yeah. I mean, I know that's not the same thing as South Africa, but maybe you guys might have a chance to go there, too, and they have the most beautiful butterflies, well, moths, actually, Madagascan sunset moths, and their wings are all kinds of pinks and greens and oranges. And the coolest thing is, their wings don't even have any pigment. It's, like, these micro-ribbons that are all woven together, and the light refracts off of them." *Did I really just tell her about the micro-*

ribbons? I should stop, I really should. But the insect facts keep pouring out of me. "And there's these spiders—Darwin's bark spiders—and they make some of the biggest webs in the world, like eighty feet wide, and they're stronger than steel or titanium or even Kevlar." I am struck with the sudden realization that I've gone overboard and finish with, "If you're into that."

It takes hours for her to react. My shoes put down roots, and dust gathers on my shoulders. *Oh, man, she must be thinking this is so lame. Do girls even like spiders? At least I led with the moths. But—*

"Yeah. Yeah, that could be really cool." And I can tell she means it.

I grin like an idiot. "Yeah?"

"Yeah. I wish more people got that excited about stuff."

She's grinning back, and I can't look at her, so instead I look at the map over her desk and notice there is a blue *H*. "So, I guess this is you?"

"Yeah. Mine's pretty much always stuck here in Georgia." She sighs. "But there's so many places I want to go. See?"

She points to a piece of butcher paper that rolls from the ceiling to the floor. There have to be at least a hundred cities scrawled on it.

"We're going to go to all of these together. You know, some-day. And all these other pins—those are the places we've already gone." She sweeps her hand over the map where a bunch of purple pins and also some blue ones speckle the United States. "Janie's are the purple ones. I've got the blue."

I touch a blue pin in New Orleans and think about how Hope has been there. "It's so cool," I say, almost to myself.

She looks at me like she's sizing me up and what she sees passes the test. She rummages around in a desk drawer and places a box of pins in my hand. It feels like she's giving me the keys to another world.

"You can be yellow."

Hey Janie!

How are things in Haiti? We're good here, but it's so weird living in a new house without you. Everything's different.

I met our next-door neighbors. There's this guy Spencer. He's my age. We climbed trees today. He's really cool, but I think he has a girlfriend named Sophie. Anyway, I let him be a part of our trip-planning thing. I hope you don't care? Also, his big brother, Dean, is so seriously cute, even though he kind of acts like a jerk when his friends are around.

Write back soon! Miss you!

Hope

Aug 10, 10:59 PM

Janie: YOU MET A BOY!!!
Hope: i see you got my postcard
Janie: Um, yeah. Which means you have known for days, maybe even weeks, about this boy.
Janie: Make that BOYS!
Janie: There are two of them!
Janie: How can you sit on a secret like that when you know I'm starving for news?
Hope: he's just a boy
Janie: I don't believe you.
Hope: :/
Hope: anyway, he has a girlfriend, so forget it
Janie: So not going to forget it.
Janie: Hey, what about the hot brother? Does he have a girlfriend?
Hope: he's 2 years older than me. high schoolers don't like 7th graders. he thinks i'm a kid
Janie: You are a kid. Stay away from high school boys.
Hope: janie! you promised you'd never go mom on me!
Janie: Sorry.
Hope: s'okay. do you mind that i let spencer in our travel club thing?
Janie: Nope, totally fine with it! Although . . .
Hope: what . . . ?
Janie: He WILL need to go through a rigorous initiation process. Walk a fence post blindfolded. Pledge an oath of fealty. Drink the blood of a yak.
Hope: EWWWWW. weirdo *throws up all over laptop*

26

Janie: That's why you love me.

Hope: i think he'll be good. he really likes exploring. he took me to all the best spots in the neighborhood

Hope: there's a grove of pecan trees perfect for climbing

Hope: and a big giant rock, like bigger than our driveway

Hope: and a dry creek bed where we're going to build a place to hang out. oh! and a waterfall!

Janie: !!!

Hope: just a little one, but still!

Hope: we're going to make a dam there so it turns into a fish pond at the bottom

Janie: That sounds great! And he sounds great. I'm so glad you made a good "friend."

Hope: not even gonna respond to that

Janie: Sorry! I can't help myself where boys are concerned!

Janie: And speaking of boys . . .

Hope: boys! what boys?!

Janie: Oh, now you want to talk about boys.

Hope. well, duh. if they're your boys. especially if they're cute and/or have accents

Janie: His name's Jonathan, and he's amazing.

Hope: accent?

Janie: Nope. He's from Seattle.

Hope: cute?

Janie: Very. The guy's got abs for days, and these eyes that just, like, sear into you.

Hope: :D

Hope: how'd you meet?

Janie: He works for the foundation too, in Pediatric Drug Access. He's super smart. Total hotshot.

Hope: very cool

Janie: Right? Pretty much every girl at work wanted him. I think he actually dated quite a few of them before I got there. Anyway, he's still in South Africa, and I'm still in Haiti for the next two months, which means I haven't seen him in FOREVER. And did I mention he is AMAZING??

Hope: that's awesome :)

Janie: Thanks <3 I can't wait to see him again, but I'm also really busy here, so it's not like I'm sitting around all pathetic and mopey. I've made a ton of new friends.

Hope: oh, yeah, i loved the pics you sent of your team and the solar panels. and the pictures you drew, especially the one of the little boys holding hands. that's my favorite.

Janie: Thanks. I'll send you more soon.

11:18 PM

Janie: You still there?

Hope: yeah

Janie: You need to get to bed?

Hope: in a little bit. i don't want to say bye yet

Janie: Me neither.

Janie: But we are running out of things to talk about.

Janie: Hmmm . . .

Janie: What are you doing? Right. Now.

Hope: sitting on my window seat with the window open and leaning against the screen. there's some kind of flower growing up the trellis

Janie: Pretty.

Hope: jasmine, maybe?

Hope: it smells really amazing

Hope: well, when i can smell it

Janie: :)

Hope: i wish you had gotten to see the new house

Janie: Me too.

Hope: i can't imagine starting a new school year without you. how am i supposed to get dressed in the morning???

Janie: By sending me pics of any and all outfits.

Hope: i don't know if i'm looking forward to it. i'm worried i'll be Luna Lovegood again. plus, there's this girl across the street, Bella Fontaine, who's an 8th grader and also a real Bring In The Cheese Haters. <— That's an acronym.

Janie: *snort*

Hope: oh! the wind started blowing, and i can smell the flowers again

Hope: i keep pushing my face against the screen trying to smell them better

Hope: it would be really bad if i pushed too hard and fell out. i wonder who would miss me. do you ever think about stuff like that? like, am i ever going to do anything that matters or makes a big difference in the world?

Hope: sorry that's weird

Janie: Are you kidding? You do good things for people every day. And I love that you think about things like this, but also don't get too hung up on stuff like your place in the world just yet. You're just getting started.

Hope: ok.

Hope: thanks :)

Janie: And Hope?

Hope: yeah?

Janie: I would miss you. Every second. Of every day.

Hope: i would miss you every second too

Part Two

14 years old

A TAXONOMY OF ALMOSTS

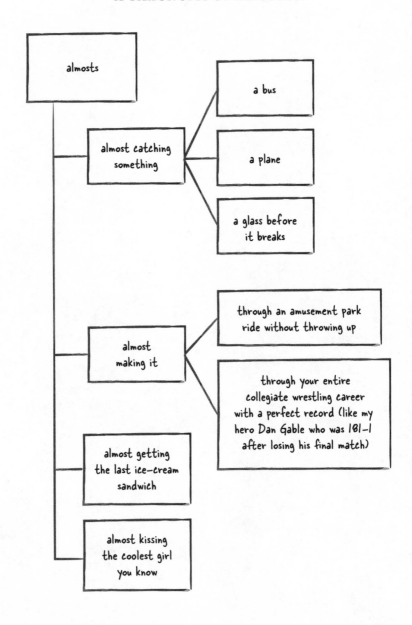

CHAPTER

3

Fact: Janie Birdsong has been here for five days, and my brother is already a lovesick, sniveling mess.

"Are they back yet? I think I hear a car." Dean pings from window to window like a puppy. Hope and Janie went out to get groceries over an hour ago, and I think he has been counting down the minutes.

I snicker, but I kind of feel bad for the guy. Having a crush on a Birdsong sister is no joke.

I flip through my Magic cards. "Do we think Janie is more of an Elf Warrior or a Pixie Queen?"

"I dunno." He pushes aside a curtain. "I really thought I heard something."

"I'm also getting a bit of a Charging Badger vibe."

Dean waves his hand like he's swatting away a mosquito. "Dude, grow up. Nobody cares about your stupid Magic cards."

Before I can say anything back, there's the unmistakable crunch of tires on gravel. A silver Honda Civic pulls up by the cabin down the dirt road from ours. My family has a couple hundred acres that start at our house and spread across fields and forests to a man-made pond and two wooden cabins that my grandaddy built with his own hands. He and Mimi used to live out here, and it's always where we spend the week of Fourth of July. Only this year we invited the Birdsongs. So, it's like we're still next-door neighbors, only now we're on vacation.

Dean's already outside, hovering. "Oh, cool! You got peach tea. Did you go to Granger's? The tea's unbelievable, right?"

I swear, if Janie said she thought it sucked, he'd be all, "Me, too!" But she confirms that peach tea is, in fact, the nectar of the southern gods, so no one has to renounce their heritage or anything. Dean helps them bring in their bags, and as fun as it would be to just watch and mentally mock him, I go over and help, too. As I pick up a gallon of milk, my head jerks to the side in a tic. It's a new one. We always joke at camp about catching each other's tics and taking them home. Not that it works that way, but sometimes it feels like it. I'm always worried I'll catch one of the swearing ones. Echoing is bad enough because sometimes it looks like I'm making fun of people.

"So," Janie says as she shoves the empty canvas grocery bags into the cabinet under the sink. "What are we gonna do? Go canoeing? Wrestle a bear? I need to be fully indoctrinated in your cabin ways."

"Hmmm . . ." I look at my brother. It has to be just right. My head jerks to the side a few times. "Four-wheelers?"

He nods decisively. "Four-wheelers."

Dean and I tear off to the garage like little kids because the Raptor is newer and faster. We have a butt war over the seat (Dean wins—jerk), and then we drive the four-wheelers up the hill and to the dirt road between the cabins where the girls are waiting. Dean is in front of me, trying a little too hard to look like some kind of dark and mysterious motorcycle gang leader, if you ask me. He comes to a stop in front of the girls and rakes a hand through his blond hair.

Janie claps her hands together. "Oh! I love ATVs! We rode them in South Africa."

My brother looks slightly crestfallen that this isn't her first rodeo.

I try to figure out a nonobvious way to make sure Hope and I end up on the same four-wheeler.

"How fast do they go?" Janie asks.

Dean's bravado recovers quickly. "I bet I could hit seventy if we had a good straightaway."

(He has never gone over thirty-five.)

"And I don't want to brag, but I got the fast one, so you should ride with me."

Janie shrugs. "Okay."

Which means Hope is with me. I don't grin maniacally or pump my fist in the air, so I feel like I'm doing a pretty good job of being cool about it.

She steps up beside my four-wheeler. "So, how does this work?"

"You can sit behind me." I gesture to the part of the seat I'm not sitting on. She puts her foot in the footrest and swings her other leg over. The insides of her legs are pressed against the outsides of mine.

"Okay," she says.

"Okay. So." For a second, I forget everything I know about riding four-wheelers. "So, there's bars. These, um, bars by your legs here." I point to them. "And you can hold on there. But it's kind of awkward, so if we get to going fast or make any sharp turns, you can, um, you can hold on to me."

"Should I be worried?"

"What?"

Hope taps the sticker under the handlebars.

"Oh." My heart rate returns to normal. The sticker has a sixteen with a circle around it and a line through it that says: Operating this ATV if you are under the age of sixteen increases your chance of severe injury or death.

"Nah, we're okay. I've been driving this thing for years. And my tics ease up a lot when I'm driving, too."

And then it's almost like my stepmom can smell that our lives are about to be in danger, because she pokes her head out of the screen door. "You better be wearing helmets," she calls.

We both groan.

"Aw, come on. It's like ninety degrees," says Dean.

"I don't care and neither does traumatic brain injury. Wear your helmets."

She goes back inside without bothering to watch us, because she knows what's going to happen next: We put on our helmets. (Grudgingly.) We give one to Hope and Janie, too. And then we're off.

Hope holds on to the bars, and I ease on the gas, gradually picking up speed. Dean guns it so that Janie has no choice but to wrap her arms around him. I roll my eyes.

Hope laughs behind me. "THIS IS AMAZING! How fast are we going? It feels like we're flying! It's got to be, like—"

"Fourteen miles an hour."

"What?! That can't be right. Seriously, I think your gauge is broken and we're actually going, like, sixty-five."

"I know. It's crazy, right?" I yell because it's harder to hear the person in front over the sound of the engine (like a lawn-mower on steroids). "It's too bumpy out here to go really fast, but just wait'll I get her up to eighteen."

We follow the path as it cuts through pine forests and fields of yellow and violet wildflowers. It's been a while since it rained last, and the four-wheelers kick up clouds of red dirt that sting our eyes and throats. I can't follow too closely behind Dean because if I do, we will literally be eating his dust. Plus, it's kind of nice being alone with Hope. I point things out to her: brambles of wild blackberries, the creek where Dean and I used to catch crawdads and pan for gold, tree stands that hang from trees every now and then like deranged Christmas ornaments. They look like someone stapled a chair or a tiny platform to a tree and then hung a ladder off the bottom. They're for sitting in and shooting at deer. Mostly, they're pretty simple, but my dad has this one that is basically a tree house for grown-ups. He and Dean built it so they could hunt better, but it seems like whenever Pam sends me to get them for lunch, all they're doing is eating beef jerky and laughing.

Hope points at something black and round. "Is that a trash can?"

"It's a rain catcher. The deer hang around here more when they don't have to go too far for water."

"So, you attract the deer here with water, and then you shoot them?" Even though she's sitting behind me, I can tell she's wrinkling her nose.

"Well, it's illegal to have them within so many yards of a tree stand because that's just like shooting fish in a barrel."

"Oh."

"My dad's really big on following all the rules about hunting and safety and stuff."

She's silent behind me. I tic-sniff several times.

"And it's not like he and Dean are just killing for sport. We eat everything they bring home."

"It's fine, Spence."

"Okay."

I don't know why I feel so defensive. I don't even like hunting. My dad runs the hunting and outdoor supply store off 75. My grandaddy owned it, and his grandaddy owned it, and someday Dean is going to own it. But only after he goes to college on a baseball scholarship like the kind my dad dreamed of getting before he tore his shoulder.

I focus on steering the four-wheeler down into a small creek bed and up the hill on the other side. It's not the easiest thing, and I feel Hope's arms squeeze around me quick. Today is possibly the best day of my life.

We stop a few times to get off the four-wheelers so we can look at things. Old wells that are half-filled in with dirt but could still reach water if you dug them out. The remains of a row of Depression-era shacks.

Hope and Janie zip together every time the engines stop. *Did you see those wild hog tracks? Can you believe how hot the seat gets after a few minutes? Are you checking your phone AGAIN?*

Janie flushes and shoves her phone in her back pocket. "I was just checking to see whether Max got my last e-mail. We haven't talked in—"

"A few days. *I know.*" Hope rolls her eyes.

"Well, things were kind of tense when I left because I spent my last night in South Africa with my friends, so I just want to make sure we're good."

"Mmm-hmm." Hope walks in the other direction, lips buttoned up tight.

Janie comes over and stands next to me while I'm looking at

what's left of a building foundation. "So, you used to come here all the time as kids?"

I nod. Even though she smiles at me a lot, she makes me nervous. I want so badly for her to like me.

Dean jumps in. "Oh, yeah. Spencer and I used to scavenge what's left of these shacks for glass bottles and other little stuff like that." He talks and talks and talks and talks.

Hope is still inspecting a rock in the foundation with something like wonder.

"Hey, there's a grove of beech trees up the hill right there," I say. "You wanna go see them?"

"Sure."

We walk away from where Dean is still regaling Janie with stories of our youth.

There's a tree to our right. Its pale trunk is dappled with gray like a pony, and the branches spread skyward with a kind of queenly magnificence.

"You can tell they're beech trees because of their smooth gray bark," I say. "They're the best trees to carve in."

We get to the top and I lead her to the biggest one, the oldest, the mother of all beech trees. It is covered in writing. "See those initials?" I say. "Those are my great-great-uncle Clint's. He was born in 1890."

Hope traces the CB with her fingers.

I point at another set. "And here's my mom and dad." I lower my voice. "We don't really point them out if Pam's around."

Hope smiles her secret-keeping smile.

"And here's Dean. And my granddaddy. And me." I tap the SB at waist level that stands for Spencer Barton.

Hope's eyes travel up and down the trunk. She grins. "You literally have a family tree."

I grin back. "You want to put your initials in it?"

She shakes her head. "No way. Your stepmom's not even on it." She surveys the grove. "But maybe we could start our own tree."

So we pick one. A skinny beech with young green leaves and a trunk that's only as big around as a can of soup. I take out my pocketknife and carve an SB and then Hope carves an HB. There's no plus sign or heart or anything, but I like how our initials look next to each other.

"Hey, Spence, where does your mom live?" Hope is looking at the sky when she asks me.

"I don't know."

We never really talk about my mom. Well, I never bring her up, and Hope has always politely steered around her, even though I suspect she's always wanted to ask me questions.

"She's a singer," I finally say. "My parents met and fell in love at a show of hers in Athens. She had to run away from home to be a singer, so I don't even know if I have, like, grandparents or uncles or anything."

"What was she like?"

A slow smile settles over my face. "The best. She used to take us in the bathroom at restaurants just before my dad hit the point where he'd get grumpy and yell, and we'd have these bathroom dance parties where we'd get all our sillies out so we could behave at the table."

Hope grins.

"And we look alike. Dark hair and dark brown eyes." Sometimes I think that's why Dean is my dad's favorite. He can't stand the look of me. "And Mimi says we act kind of alike, too. She says we're dreamers." My breath catches, because I remember it isn't just the good things we share. "She didn't fit here, either."

Hope touches my shoulder. "Spence, you—"

Dean and Janie start yelling for us, so I don't get to find out what Hope was going to say. I take the knife from her and tuck it in my pocket fast, because I don't need to guess how long Dean would tease me about carving our initials into a tree (for all eternity, it's a given).

"One sec!" Hope calls back.

She moves down the hill in short flying leaps, each time grabbing a new tree to steady herself against the steepness. She pauses in front of a tree trunk almost entirely covered in skinny white mushrooms, and I stop short so I don't run into her.

She turns. "We don't have to tell anyone," she says. "About the initials." It's almost like a question.

Her secret-keeping smile comes back, and it makes me think there are other things she wants to do and not tell anyone about.

"No, of course not."

I shove my helmet on as soon as we get back to the four-wheelers because I can feel my face getting hot.

"Hey, do you wanna try driving?" I ask.

"YES."

I teach her how to push the gas with her thumb and how the brakes are just like bicycle ones. After a few jerky starts, she gets the hang of it. And after a few more minutes, she *really* gets the hang of it.

"I AM THE QUEEN OF THE WILDERNESS!!!" she yells as she races up an easy hill. Then, when we get to the top, she says, "Ruh-roh."

There are some pretty steep drops here, and on the other side of the dry creek bed, lots of places where you have to do a sharp climb or slalom around some trees.

"Oh. I kind of forgot this is one of the trickiest places to ride," I say.

Dean sputters up beside her. "You might not be able to handle it," he says.

He takes off down the hill with a wild animal yell. Janie had her arms around him before, but now she's slamming against him with every bump.

A fact about Janie: Her boobs. They are massive. And I'm pretty sure my brother's back is now intimately acquainted with their topography.

Hope turns her head. "Do you think I can handle it?"

I lower my voice. "You got this. Go easy on the downhills, shift your weight opposite the turns and obstacles, and lean forward and speed up to gain momentum on the uphills. And, um, I should probably put my arms around you this time."

"Okay," she says.

She gets so still, statue still, while she's waiting for me to do it. It's all very precarious. Not the terrain, Hope handles that like a boss. The part where I have to figure out where to put my hands. Definitely not anywhere near her boobs, but I can't go too low, either. There is not a lot of space to work with, people!

I settle on somewhere over her belly button, but her body is still soft in a way that feels dangerous.

Sometimes my head will tic-jerk to the side or my shoulders will shrug, but I work really hard to keep my hands still on her stomach. It's kind of a relief when we stop again and I can let go of her. I hop off the four-wheeler and pull off my helmet. So does Hope, except she does it with a victory dance. I slap her a double high five. Janie unwraps herself from my brother so she can do the same. Really, Dean is the only one who isn't in on this little celebration.

"I'll just be a minute," he says. "I need to check this pressure gauge."

Yeah, right. The pressure gauge in his pants. He's awkwardly hunched over the front of the four-wheeler, and it couldn't be more obvious what he's hiding. Well, to me, anyway. The girls actually don't seem to notice, even though it takes a full five minutes before he decides the "pressure gauge" has been adequately checked.

Hope and Janie and I are already walking around the slave cemetery. The sun filters through the leaves, but it feels like it's casting shadows instead of light. It makes us speak in hushed voices.

In front of me is a scooped-out hollow in the ground, all covered in grass and leaves. To the left and right are a few more hollows, forming a row. They're graves. Over time, they've sunk a few inches lower than the rest of the ground. There are other rows, sometimes with as many as six graves, sometimes only three, depending on how much space there is between the trees. Every now and then, they're marked with stones. Not the big headstones with writing and stuff. Just gray rocks the size of a cantaloupe or a large shoe.

"I can't believe there are slaves buried here," Hope whispers. "And it really wasn't that long ago."

"I know," I say. A hundred and fifty years. I try to figure out how many great-great-grandparents it would take to count back until I got to someone who was alive when people still actually BOUGHT AND SOLD other people. It makes me sick just thinking about it.

"What were they here for?" asks Janie. "I mean, do you know what they did while they were here?"

"There were some fields a few miles from here. Cotton, I think. But they weren't our fields," I rush to say. "I mean, my family didn't own the land way back then."

I guess I just can't stand her wondering.

"One time I found an arrowhead in front of this tree," I say. "It's crazy to think there're four-wheeler paths on top of old lumber roads by Depression-era shacks near a slave cemetery in a grove of trees where a Cherokee family maybe used to live. There's so much history stacked in layers on one plot of land."

Hope steps closer to me, like it'll help her see all the overlapping histories I'm seeing. "It makes you wonder what sorts of things you'll leave behind. And what the people a hundred years in the future will be thinking about you."

"Yeah," I say.

"You guys give me hope for the future, you know that?" says Janie.

Dean, who desperately needs to turn this into yet another opportunity to show off in front of Janie, starts talking in this weird, deep, serious voice. "Oh, yeah. I think it's really important to take everything we can from history, so we don't repeat the same mistakes in the future. The land can tell us so much." He kneels and touches a headstone dramatically. "These graves can tell us so much."

I mean, jeez, you'd think he went back in time and abolished slavery himself. Does he really think Janie's going to buy any of that? I hazard a glance at Hope. She is giving him extreme side-eye.

It makes me feel like doing something bold. And stupid. "Hey, Dean, remember the time you and Tater—that's our cousin, Tater—tried to dig up one of the graves?"

Janie's face blanches white as a beech tree. "You dug up one of the graves?"

Dean looks like he may just murder me when we get home (if he can hold off that long), but Hope is snickering into her fist, so I press on. "They started to, but they got all scared because it was getting dark, so they stopped before they could finish. And when they came home, they were covered in chigger bites." I pause for dramatic emphasis. "Do you know what a chigger is?"

Dean shakes his head sharply. His eyes have gone full Minotaur, but every wedgie he's ever given me is playing in my head, and there's nothing I can do. "It's this teeny-tiny red bug that drills a hole in your skin and uses its saliva enzymes to break up your cells from the inside out so it can slurp up the skin-cell juice like soup."

Janie looks like she swallowed a slug. "That is the second most disgusting thing I've ever heard," she says. "The first being disrupting the final resting places of people who were treated as less than human."

"I was—" starts Dean, but I cut him off.

"So, anyway, they come home covered with bites, and Pam said it was God punishing them, and Mimi said they better go out to the yard and pick a switch because God may be done with them but she wasn't. And they went and picked the smallest, thinnest ones they could find, which is a rookie move because everyone knows the small ones lash your skin up the most. They couldn't sit down for a week."

Hope's eyes bulge. "Your parents really hit you like that?"

I shrug self-consciously. "I mean, yeah. But only if we do really bad stuff. So, like, not very often or anything. People, uh, don't do that in Decatur?"

"Definitely not."

I've been looking at Hope during most of the story, but now that it's over, I finally remember to look at my brother. And I realize I am in for probably the worst and most painful revenge ever devised. He probably won't beat the crap out of me. At least, not here in front of Janie and everything. But sometime. Soon. My demise is imminent.

He forces the scariest fake smile ever onto his face. "It was really stupid and wrong, and I'm really embarrassed I did it," he says.

Then, he turns and gets on his four-wheeler and cranks the engine.

That's it? Janie really is a miracle worker. I mean, I know I'm in for it later, but still.

Hope moves past Dean to get to the other four-wheeler, but he grabs her arm.

"Hey, Hope, ride with me on the way back." He raises his eyebrows at me when he says it.

"Um, okay." She sits behind him on the four-wheeler and the insides of her legs touch the outsides of his.

Janie bounces onto my four-wheeler behind me. "I'm glad I get a chance to hang out with you," she says. "Hope talks about you all the time."

"Really?"

"Yeah. It sounds like you're a pretty great friend."

Friend. "Thanks."

Up ahead of us, Dean guns the engine so Hope has to press herself tight against him.

Everything is different. I can feel it even before Dean squeals to a stop beside me. Before Hope pulls off her helmet and shakes out her corn-silk hair. They're both laughing at some joke that's just for them, and he holds out his hand to help her down, and when she takes it, there it is. A dazed, dreamy look settles over her face, and she hangs on a second too long, and I think now would be a good time to go flush myself down the toilet. For the rest of the day, she giggles whenever he calls her Birdsong.

I don't get it. I don't get why one minute it feels like Hope is maybe starting to like me, but then one four-wheeler ride with my brother is enough to turn it all upside down. I wish it was easier to make sense of the world.

I go to my room and pull out a notebook. I guess if I had to throw some labels on me and Hope and categorize our relationship like so many devil scorpions, this is what it would look like:

A TAXONOMY OF HOPE AND SPENCER

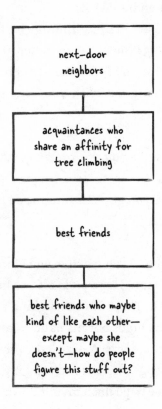

What I Want to Be When I Grow Up

By: Hope Birdsong

I fall in love with countries the way other people fall in love
with people. So does my sister. It must have come hardwired
into our DNA. We hear about a place we want to go to and have
to learn everything about it, become consumed with it, until
I swear I know exactly what crêpes Suzette tastes like even
though I've never been to France. Until I feel the winds from
the Mediterranean calling to me in my sleep.

I want to have adventures that I'll never forget. I want
to snorkel in the Great Barrier Reef, and I want to go to
every continent, even Antarctica. I want to watch the great
wildebeest migration across the Serengeti, cruise down the
Amazon in a riverboat. I want to walk the entire Appalachian
Trail, all 2189.2 miles of it, and maybe someday even swim/
bike/run the Hawaiian IRONMAN Triathlon.

My mom says I was born in the wrong time period because
I should have been an explorer like Marco Polo or one of those
other guys. People say everything's been discovered nowadays,
but they're wrong. You don't have to be the first to see
something for it to count. If you can see it differently, if you
can make other people see it differently, if you can leave a
mark and change something for the better, that all counts,
too.

Because it's not just the things I want to do, it's the
people I want to help. Sometimes I care about them so much
it hurts. The kids who don't learn to read because they
don't have a single book at home, and the babies in developing
countries who die of measles because they don't have access

to vaccinations. When I see pictures and read stories, I can't just forget. I turn them over and over and over inside my head, and sometimes I feel like the knowing could swallow me whole. But it never does. Because I know my big sister is out there, doing things—big things—that could maybe someday fix stuff.

So, what do I want to be when I grow up? I want to be my sister. I want to see everything there is to see. I want to change the world.

CHAPTER 4

"Janie, you are SO annoying." Hope stomps into the living room of the cabin where the Birdsongs are staying, carrying an empty pitcher.

Janie looks up from her book, her nose scrunched in irritation. "*What?*"

Hope brandishes the pitcher. "Is there any more peach tea?"

Janie takes a sheepish sip of the peach tea she's holding. "Oh. Sorry!" she says.

"It's fine," says Hope, but her eye-roll says that it isn't really.

Janie holds out her glass. "Do you want some?"

"I said it was fine," Hope grumbles.

She goes to the fridge to get something else. I follow.

She lowers her voice. "She always manages to get the last one of everything. It's a dark gift."

"Kind of like your dark gift for always spilling stuff on my shirts when you borrow them!" Janie yells from the other room.

Hope sticks her tongue out at her when we come back with our (barely tolerable, might as well be poisoned) root beer.

She told me this would happen. For the first six days, they'd be falling all over each other with excitement, but by the seventh, that feeling of missing each other would wear off, and they would become capable of annoying each other like normal siblings.

Her idea of normal siblings is still a heck of a lot more kumbaya than mine.

I'm just finishing my root beer when I get a text from Pam:

```
Hi Spencer,
Come home and pack for camp!
Love, Pam
```

She always writes them like that, like it's a mini–e-mail or something.

I look at Hope, who is making huffy noises into her empty root beer bottle, and Janie, who is turning the pages of her book with audible vehemence, and decide that writing my name on all my boxers in Sharpie is a super critical task that I should be performing, like, right now.

"Okay, see you guys," I say awkwardly quick and rush out the door.

As soon as I enter the Barton cabin, I am greeted by Dean. With a headlock.

Speaking of annoying siblings.

"Hey, Spencer, I wanna try some new wrestling moves." He clamps his armpit tighter against the back of my head. He smells terrible.

"Yeah, well, I don't."

I try to pull my head out. I'm tired of being his practice dummy. Plus, I can't stop thinking about the dazed way Hope was looking at him after their four-wheeler ride.

"Well, I didn't want you to tell Janie all kinds of embarrassing crap about me, but sometimes we don't get what we want." He keeps squeezing.

"I'm serious," I say.

"Keep it down," snaps my dad. "I'm watching a game."

He goes back to Braves vs. Mets.

I manage to get my head free, but Dean attaches himself to my leg, safe in the knowledge that I can't cry out under threat of meeting Dad's wrath (which goes from a nine to an eleven any time the Braves are playing the Mets).

He drops me to the ground using one of the fancy moves his coach taught him. He's going for the pin. I could give up. If I let him pin me, I can go upstairs like I want.

But I am so over this crap.

I fight back. Hard. I am ferocious. I am a praying mantis. A black spitting thicktail scorpion. An entire swarm of killer bees. He is not going to pin me. Never again. I slip out of his hold like I'm slathered in baby oil. Fast as a dragonfly. I snake my forearm under his neck and lock it with my other arm and use the momentum to throw him off me. Fear flashes in his eyes. Just for a moment, but long enough for me to know. He's scared I might win.

His fear is my adrenaline. Knowing that, it's huge. It changes everything. We're no longer playing our specified battle roles. Dean: offense. Spencer: defense. I am attacking the crap out of him, and I. Just. Might. Win.

I go for his leg, and I've got him, I can feel it. If I can just twist his arm a little more. Shift my weight by a couple degrees. Crap. He jerks out of it. And before I can get him again, we're crashing into an end table. The one that holds my dad's beer during games. I wait for the beer and my dad's temper to come crashing down on my head.

They don't. In fact, my hair is refreshingly beer-free. And my dad, he's smiling at me.

"Where did you learn to do that?" The smile melts into his voice.

I duck my head. "I don't know. I guess I must have picked up a few things from Dean."

He shakes his head like he's still working on believing what he saw. "It's more than that. You've got a hunger. You're small, too. It's hard to find guys like you. Are you going out for wrestling this year? You'd be a natural."

"You actually would," Dean agrees. He doesn't even seem pissed that I almost pinned him. "I could work with you on your moves and stuff."

"Next year," I say. "They don't have wrestling in eighth grade. But I could do it next year."

Did I just say that? I've never even thought about wrestling, but the way my dad is looking at me, with his arms crossed and his chest puffed up—it has never happened before, and I don't want it to end.

CHAPTER 5

We eat our Fourth of July feast outside on two wooden picnic tables pushed together. Hot dogs and hamburgers, corn on the cob, chips with salsa, and two kinds of guacamole because Pam and Mimi almost had a throwdown over cilantro. (Personally, I think it tastes like soap, but there was no way I was putting my foot in that.)

I spoon some guac onto my plate, sneakily so as not to trigger the apocalypse. Hope's dad goes for more pimento cheese dip.

"This dip is delicious. Where did you get it?"

Pam grins. "I made it myself."

"Okay, you have to tell me your secret."

They jump into a conversation on cooking that sounds like it could last the whole night. On the other end of the table, Mimi fans herself with her napkin.

"It is hot as *Hades* out here, don't y'all think? Lord, and they say global warming is a myth." She takes another sip of sweet tea. "Whew. So, Janie. Spencer tells me you've been in South Africa for the past year. I want to hear all about it."

(Everything you need to know about Mimi: She was the first female reporter for the Macon *Telegraph* at a time when working was something women down here simply did not do. She also claims to be the first Democrat in all of Peach Valley, though I haven't fact-checked that one.)

Mimi trains her reporter eyes on Janie and asks her every question under the sun about South Africa, the foundation, and her work. Janie gushes about how excited she is to go to work every day, how her next project is going to revolutionize access to health care. My head jerks to the side a bunch of times while she talks, but everyone lets the conversation flow right around my tics like water, even Janie, who seems totally used to them even though she hasn't been around me that long.

"Well, that's just wonderful," says Mimi.

Mrs. Birdsong squeezes Janie's shoulder. "We're really proud of her." She beams at Janie for a second before putting her other arm around Hope. "And, of course, we're proud of our Hope, too. She's next."

Hope feigns shyness, but her grin could light up the world.

"I can't wait for you to come and visit," says Janie, touching Hope's hand. "Everyone at my work would love you, especially Max."

"And who's Max?" asks Mimi.

"He's my new boyfriend," says Janie.

Dean wrinkles his nose and picks at the chili on his fourth hot dog. She's twenty-three years old, dude. It wasn't going to happen anyway. But Dean's girl logic is very simple: I like her, therefore I will go for her.

"I thought Jonathan was your new boyfriend," says Mrs. Birdsong.

"That was her last new boyfriend," says Mr. Birdsong across the table. "Max is her new new boyfriend."

Janie rolls her eyes. "You know, not *everyone* meets their soul mate when they're fifteen years old. I don't even think I would have wanted to. You've got so much to figure out still."

Janie keeps talking about life and figuring things out. Dean seems less than interested.

"Psst. Hey, Birdsong, think fast." He launches a tortilla chip at Hope, and she giggles.

The plan was to eat as the sky fades to orange-pink-purple-black, and then set off fireworks. My brother and I can't wait that long. We were antsy at pink, and have completely lost the ability to sit still by purple. If you saw the set of fireworks my dad bought at Big Zack's, you'd understand. This thing is the mother lode, and really, it's not our fault that he didn't think to hide it somewhere better than the garage.

"C'mon, Dad." Dean bounces on his bench. "C'mon. C'mon. C'mon. C'mon."

"Pleeeeease," I add.

It's like we're seven years old, only infinitely better because now we're old enough to touch all the really dangerous stuff.

"They're gonna be on you like ducks on a June bug until you say yes," says Mimi.

A wise woman, that Mimi.

"Fine," he eventually tells us, and we high-five each other and race off before he can change his mind.

We return with seventy-two megatons of firework glory and grins that threaten to break our faces in half. We are ready to set the entire world ablaze. First, some bottle rockets, staking them into the soft ground, lighting the fuse, then sprinting away before they shoot up over the lake and explode in red and blue starbursts. Something about the whistling noise they make when they cut through the air makes me feel like I'm the one soaring.

Hope's German shepherd is freaking out and trying to

clamber under our bench. Hope calls a cease-fire to the festivities so she can lead Eponine inside by the collar and tuck her into her anti-firework bunker aka the bathroom.

Roman candles are up next.

"I don't like you boys holding them in your hands," yells Pam. "People have gotten their fingers blown off doing that."

Thankfully, my father is a man of compromise. "Just keep them pointed at the lake and make sure to count the shots," he calls.

The Birdsongs let Hope and Janie light some, too. On the off chance that something goes wrong, we do have a member of the Peach Valley Fire Department sitting at our picnic table.

Hope lights sparklers and writes her name in the air.

A fact about girls: They become 200 percent more beautiful when playing with sparklers.

The sky is full-black now, and you can see every star, even the tired ones. Hope lets her sparkler lead her like a flashlight to a tree at the edge of the water.

"Hey, Spencer, come look at the moon. They said it's supposed to be a supermoon tonight."

I run over to where she's found a gap in the trees, and the moon is shining like a beacon.

"It's seven percent brighter and fourteen percent larger," I say.

"Um, cool."

Crap, maybe she just wanted to talk about how pretty it is. We stand there and watch it, while our sparklers trail smoke whispers behind us. When they burn down to the nubs, the darkness wraps itself around us so thick I can't even see the grass at our feet. We've wandered too far away from the house lights. I'm tic-shrugging like a mofo, but I don't think she can see it.

"It's so dark out here," Hope says.

She shifts her weight to her other foot, and the movement makes her shoulder brush against mine. She doesn't pull it away. I don't pull away, either.

"I know," I say. "It feels like there could be anything out there right now, and we wouldn't even know."

It's the kind of darkness that hides clandestine meetings and portals to another world. The kind where anything could happen.

Like a first kiss draped in shadows.

Or your stepmom yelling that she needs you to run inside and get some paper plates so she can cut the dessert. Even though I happen to love the angel food cake/whipped cream/ blueberries/strawberries American flag she makes every year, I'm like, *Now? Really?*

"Spencer!"

"I'm going!"

I run up the stairs of the cabin, leaving behind Hope and the feeling I've missed yet another shot. Or maybe I'm just imagining things. I saw the way she looked at Dean after we rode four-wheelers. And this morning when we were hanging out on the dock. And at dinner. I decide to take my frustration out on random items that I bang around while searching for the plates.

Hope appears in the doorway. "Mimi sent me to get forks."

"Oh, hey. I'm having trouble finding the paper plates." I set down a jar of apple butter (gently) and step back from the shelves to give them one more scan. Hope stands in front of me and helps me look. Right in front of me. This closet is barely wide enough for two people. If I moved forward, even an inch, my chest would be touching her back.

Hope steps backward. More than an inch. How do people do things like look for plates while touching other people because I am finding it very difficult? I take a breath and my chest moves up and down her back. She takes a breath, and the same thing happens in reverse. I mean, I could just stay in the food closet like this all night.

She turns around so we're face-to-face. "So, you're leaving tomorrow, huh?"

"Yeah." Holy crap, I don't think our lips have ever been this close together. I can't believe this is happening. She's choosing me instead of Dean. That's what this means, right?

"It's going to be so boring without you here."

"Yeah?"

"Yeah." She crosses her arms over her chest like she's pretend mad. "I'm pretty jealous that I'll be stuck here with Bella while you're having all kinds of fun with s'mores and canoes and stuff."

I want to make her laugh with a well-timed joke about poison ivy. Instead I say, "I wish you were coming with me." I lean closer.

"Me, too." So does she.

But then she hesitates. "And Sophie? She'll be there, too, right?"

I feel like there is maybe not enough air in here because I am having trouble thinking. "Um. Well, yeah. She goes every year. Our cabins always have this epic prank war."

"Right," she says, nodding her head like she's figuring things out. "And you'll be together. At camp."

"Well, yeah." I mean, no. I don't know what I'm saying, but if it stops her from doing whatever it is she's about to do, it has to be the wrong thing.

And then she's standing super super close. She reaches out. For the back of my neck? To kiss me? I am paralyzed as her hand brushes the top of my shoulder and grabs something on the shelf behind me.

"The plates. They're right here, behind your head."

SPENCER AND DEAN PRO/CON LIST

Okay, I'm not saying I like either of them
or both of them, but if I did . . .

SPENCER

PROS
- Loves running, hiking, and camping
- Kind
- Can be serious

CONS
- I still can't figure out if that girl Sophie is his
  girlfriend and I don't want to ask
- He's kind of weird sometimes

DEAN

PROS
- Awesome arm muscles
- Smart
- Makes me laugh
- My stomach feels funny whenever he talks to me

CONS
- I don't like when he makes fun of people
- He dug up a slave grave, and how
  much has he really changed?
- He's always with all these girls and they're
  all so much cooler/older/prettier/blah
- My stomach feels funny whenever he talks to me

Part Three

15 years old

A TAXONOMY OF TRAITORS

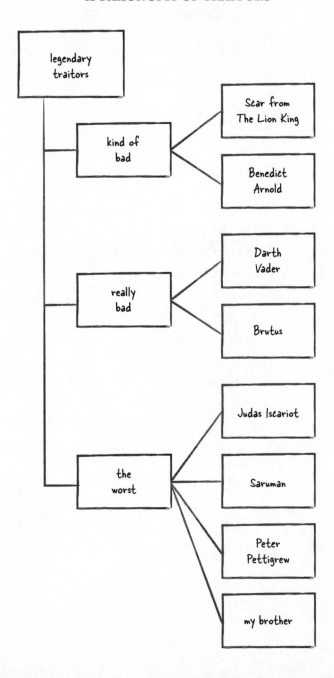

CHAPTER 6

Fact: Full-body tics suck.

It didn't hurt the first time. It does now. I wait for it like I'm waiting for my own execution, the moment when the skin over my ribs and hipbone feels so warm that I can't fight it anymore. My body snaps to the side, feels like it's snapping in half. My hip tries to slap my ribcage a vicious high five, and my head bobbles with the aftershock. And it hurts. Neck, back, abs, everything. I'm sore all over.

I'm putting my hands on the table to steady myself when my body whips in the opposite direction, not once, but twice. And the second one is a real beast. I rub the back of my neck as I work my way back to a sitting position in my chair. Both Pam and Mimi are watching me with their best Concerned Mom Faces.

"So, I guess that's why I'm taking this, huh?" I attempt a grin, but neither of them laughs at my feeble joke.

The pill sits on the place mat in front of me. It's the color of lichen and mint-chocolate-chip ice cream, pistachios and luna moth wings, with the medication name chiseled into one side and "25 mg" on the other.

"Let me get you some water," says Pam. It makes moms feel better when they're doing something.

She fills a glass and sets it beside the pill.

"There you go."

"Thanks."

And we're back to the tag-team staredown. I now know what the lightning bug on the inside of the jar feels like.

"You know this is because we feel like there's no other option," says Pam.

"I know."

I get how scary this is for them. The full-body tics are so intense, they thought for sure I was having seizures when they started up a few weeks ago. And we've talked the subject of me and meds into the ground. My brain is still developing, Mimi says. My body is a temple, Pam says. But the tics were so bad I couldn't get to sleep at night, even with my weighted blanket, and they came at me in tornado bursts that left me feeling like I'd been in a car accident without a seat belt. Then one day Pam found me crying on the floor of my room, wadded up in a ball of pain, and everyone got on the meds train real quick after that.

I take a big gulp of water and hold it in my mouth. Then I push the pill in between my lips and swish it to the back so it's floating right over my throat. And I swallow. I sure hope this works—they don't make drugs specifically for Tourette's syndrome, so it's kind of a toss-up, and the doctor said it could take a while to find something that works for me.

Mimi pats my hand. Pam nods her head and says, "Okay, then."

And I have another tic. A full-on spring-loaded convulsion.

"Oh," says Pam.

"Well, it's not like it was going to be immediate," I say.

"Of course not," says Mimi, and I don't miss the look she

shoots Pam across the table. "So, listen. You tell us if you feel sick or anything, okay, honey bear? Any side effects at all."

Pam nods furiously. "I've been reading all the Tourette's-mom forums, and sometimes kids will get on the wrong meds and do really terrifying things, like try to jump off the roof."

She puts her hand to my forehead, like it's a scientifically proven way to gauge roof-jumping tendencies.

"I'm not going to jump off the roof," I say.

They go back to eyeing me like I'm some kind of petri dish project. Again.

"Okay, I'm gonna go see if Hope wants to ride bikes or play basketball or something."

Anything. I would do anything to get out of here before I drown in sympathetic scrutiny. I wave my way out the door before either of them can think of a reason to keep me.

I know I'm lucky to have Pam, but whenever she goes all supermom, it makes me wonder about my real mom. I used to try to Google her and stuff, but I could never find her. I don't know. Maybe she goes by a stage name.

I wish I could remember more about what she was like. Dean told me she was a Manic Pixie Dream Girl, which I guess means she turned Dad's world upside down by making him shoplift cotton candy or dance around in the rain or something. That's what happens in the movies, anyway. But the movies don't ever take you out past the Happily Ever After. They don't show you what happens next.

Apparently, Manic Pixie Dream Girls aren't built for dinner on the table at five or car-pool lines or small-town gossip. Or kids. So they have to choose, I guess. Tamp down all the light inside them and be everything for everyone else with smiles that never reach their eyes. Or tear themselves in half so they can fly away and keep their souls.

I want to think it tore my mom to pieces to leave us, even if I can barely remember any of it. I know it must have been hard. But I'm glad she chose to keep her soul, I really am. I like to imagine her somewhere happy. So, I'm fine with it. Really. I'm totally good. Better than good—I'm great.

When I find Hope, she's in her garage, sitting by her bike and lacing up her shoes.

"It's like you can read minds," I say.

She grins and puts two fingers to her temples. "I sense that you want to ride to the Citgo with me and get a slushie."

"You sense right."

She stands, and I'm struck all over again by the fact that my nose only comes up to her chin now. When did she get so tall? She pulls at her tank top, where it's suddenly tight across her boobs. Probably about the same time she got those.

I shake my head like I'm trying to get water out of my ears and run back home for my own bike. The tics don't harass me nearly as much when I'm riding, so this slushie mission is going to be a relief on multiple levels. (Plus, slushies!)

As I wheel my bike up to Hope, she asks, "You okay, Spence?"

I'm going to tell her about the meds, but for now, I just want to be around my friend and not think about anything that has to do with me and my tics.

"Yeah. I'm great."

We pedal off down the street together, and every now and then, I'll have a tic that makes my bike swerve, but they mostly stay inside the threshold of pest territory. Hope's right there beside me, just like every other day this summer. We go hiking or swimming or to the movies, but we're always together. So, how come we're not *together*? Maybe it's because neither of us has the guts to ask. Maybe it's because she's waiting for me to do it. Could it really be that easy? If that's all it takes, I mean, maybe I should try it. Like now.

As soon as we come to a complete stop, I go for it.

"Hey, Hope?" I say all cool-like as I nudge my kickstand into place with my foot.

She pulls off her helmet and sets it on her seat. "Yeah?"

"I was thinking, I mean, we hang out, like, all the time. And we're really good friends, and we both like each other a lot." Her eyes get big, but I keep going. "So, do you think we should—"

"Race each other to the slushie machine right now?! HECK YES, I DO."

She sprints inside, and I don't know what else to do, so I tear inside after her.

Aug 14, 1:47 PM

Hope: guess what!!!

Aug 14, 1:49 PM

Hope: JANIE! where are yoooouuuu?

Aug 14, 1:54 PM

**Hope: i don't care if you're there or not! i'm too
excited!**
**Hope: i'm going to a party this guy Mikey is
throwing. AND he's in high school AND there will be
all kinds of hot high school boys there!**
**Hope: (like the kind i will be going to school with
in 2 weeks!)**
**Hope: AND (can you believe there's another AND?!)
it's a pool party, so i'm wearing my new bathing
suit. the red bikini that i didn't want to buy but
you kind of made me? yeah, that one**
**Hope: and yes, i'll be careful. and no, i don't
actually know this guy, but Dean does, and Pam is
making him take Spencer, and of course Spencer
asked me**
**Hope: Dean's actually kind of pissed about the
whole thing**
Hope: but whatevs, high school pool party!!!

Aug 14, 3:58 PM

Janie: HOPE!!! I need details, and I need them NOW! Hurry up and get home!

Aug 14, 4:00 PM

Janie: No, for real, I have the most killer headache, and the only cure is fancy high school pool party stories! (Probably wouldn't hold up scientifically or whatever, but I swear, it would make me feel at least 76% better.)

Aug 14, 4:33 PM

Janie: This is so unfair! I'm tempted to call you, but I keep reminding myself that it costs ALL THE MONEY.

Aug 14, 5:41 PM

Janie: Are you killed?

Aug 14, 5:43 PM

Janie: No, but seriously, that swimsuit is lethal. If some poor guy looked at you without sunglasses, your hotness may have melted out his eyes, and you're probably at the hospital right now.

Sitting by his bedside and holding his hand while
the doctors explain there's simply nothing they can
do when a person is THAT HOT.
Janie: Okay, you really need to come home soon
because I've lost what little sanity I had left and
have resorted to telling myself outlandish stories
in your absence.

Aug 14, 10:06 PM

Hope: THIS BATHING SUIT!!!
Janie: OH THANK GOODNESS!!!
**Hope: ohmygosh, Janie, it was just like in Grease
when Sandra Dee turns into Sandy, and everyone
is all "Holy crap. Check her out in those leather
pants."**
**Hope: there were all these guys flirting with me,
and i totally felt like a different person**
**Hope: and Dean was all, "Hey, Hope. Cute bathing
suit."**
Hope: Hey. Hope. Cute bathing suit.
Hope: can you believe it???
**Hope: he never calls me Hope. he always says
Birdsong. i'm pretty sure it means something**
Janie: Do you like Dean?
**Hope: i mean, he's Dean. every girl likes Dean. i
just never thought he'd ever like me**
Janie: You didn't exactly answer my question.
**Hope: well. yeah. yeah, i guess i do like him,
okay?**

Hope: there was this time at the party when Spencer seemed more interested in the bugs caught in the leaf trap than being at an actual party and these guys were making fun of him and Dean made them lay off. he can actually be kind of nice

Hope: whatever. it doesn't even matter

Janie: Don't be like that. I'm sorry for being judgey.

Hope: it's not that. it's just, Dean flirted with me, yeah, but he also flirted with like 18 other girls at that party

Janie: 18?!

Hope: okay, more like 4, but it felt like 18

Janie: Whew. But still, gross.

Hope: yeah, and like, sometimes i see girls in the bushes outside their house at night, and they'll knock on the window and Dean will let them in. he's kind of the biggest player in school

Janie: Hope . . .

Hope: but he's not a bad guy! i mean, he never lies to any of those girls or anything. he always says he doesn't want a girlfriend. but the thing is, i do want a boyfriend. so, this whole thing is probably stupid, and i should just stay away from him, i know, but what if i can't? what if he really likes me? what am i supposed to do?

Janie: Just be you.

Hope: be yourself? that's your big advice? i could have gotten that from Dad, and at least it would have come with a cookie

Janie: Oh, man, I miss Dad's chocolate chip cookies.

Janie: But that's not the point. Focus! What I mean is, there are things that you want and things that you are. And maybe Dean can live up to those things and maybe he can't, but don't go changing them for him. Just be you. And if it doesn't work out, then it wasn't meant to be.

Hope: huh

Hope: you know sometimes you can be pretty awesome?

Janie: I know, right? I feel all meta.

Hope: why do i get the feeling you're about to go all big head on me?

Janie: What? Just because I'm the Dalai Lama of dating.

Hope: omg. i knew it

Janie: And have the answers to all of life's mysteries.

Hope: -_-

Janie: I really should have my own advice column.

Janie: Or maybe a podcast.

Hope: i'm going now

Janie: Wait!

Janie: Write me a letter and tell me anything else that happens!

Hope: i will

Janie: You can address it to: Janie Birdsong, Relationship Guru Extraordinaire

Hope: BYE Janie

Janie: And send me some of Dad's cookies too!

CHAPTER
7
♥

I guess the pills are working. I stopped having the full-body tics, anyway. But they didn't stop me from shouting out "cheeseburger" like a total lame-ass last period.

I need to go to the nurse's office to take my midday meds, so I have to book it there and then to World History, but I manage to slide into the desk next to Hope right as class starts. I don't even try to pay attention to Mr. Siegel's lecture on Nicholas and Alexandra. Instead, I doodle a taxonomy to the right of my history notes.

| kids that school sucks for | kids that have Tourette's | me |

Hope is being super nosy and trying to look over my shoulder. Sometimes I write funny taxonomies and pass them to her in class. I try to cover this one with my hand, but she makes me pass her my notebook. Mr. Siegel is oblivious. There's something about Rasputin that puts him in a rapture-like state.

Hope writes something and passes it back. Her hand touches mine when she passes the note, and I think about how she looked in this crazy-hot bathing suit at the party we crashed this past weekend, and then I think about wrestling statistics to help me stop thinking about how she looked in the red bathing suit.

I know I'm not the only one who noticed, and it scares me. But maybe it's better this way. Because, really, if she only picked me because she couldn't have Dean, that is maybe not the best thing. Not that she'd pick me either way. Not that anyone is going to pick me ever.

I look down at what she wrote me.

I don't know what to say back to that. Seriously, I could agonize over it forever, but the longer you take, the worse it looks, so I scrawl down a quick *Thanks*, plus a smiley face. (Dean says girls like those.)

Hope flips the page, and it looks like she's writing a full-on note. She glances up to the front to make sure Mr. Siegel is writing on the board before she passes the notebook back.

Hey Spence!
I'm planning a trip to Belize! Did I tell you Janie's in Belize now? ← Ha! It's funny because I've told you like 8 billion times.
Wanna help?

I grin. I don't even care that she's probably just trying to distract me.

YES.

I pass back the notebook.

Yay! Here's what I've got so far:
Visit a jaguar preserve.
See Mayan ruins.
Kayak an underground river. (About the underground
river—it goes through all these caves, and the ancient
Mayans used to live there, and there's still stairways and
terraces and altars and ceramic dinnerware. So cool!)
Oh, and we're definitely going scuba diving in the Great
Blue Hole.

Um, I think you have to have a license for that.

Details. We'll totally be licensed scuba divers by the time
we take this trip. Ahem. As I was saying before the paper was
so rudely ripped away from me, we can transport ourselves to
an entire underwater universe via 400 ft sinkhole. Doesn't
that sound like the coolest thing in the world?!

It would—if I didn't know there were giant prickly stick insects
in Australia that grow up to 8 inches long and release a chemical that
scares other bugs, but to people it smells like peanut butter.

Whoa. Whoa. Whoa. Are you trying to out-nerd me?

I'm not trying. It's just what's going to happen if you keep playing.

It.

Is.

On.

Did you know there's a lake in Australia that's Pepto-Bismol pink because of the algae that grow there?

Did you know there are voodoo wasps that bewitch caterpillars to take care of their babies?

What? I don't believe that.

100% fact.

Are you sure? Because it sounds like just the kind of thing one might make up if one desperately wanted to win a World Series of Facts Throwdown.

Are you questioning my honor? That hurts, man. Also—I think you're stalling.

How's this for stalling: In the wilds of Baños, Ecuador, there's a tree house that looks like it's about to fall over the edge of a cliff and into oblivion. And attached to one of the branches is the Swing at the End of the World. And if you're brave enough to hang your whole life on two pieces of rope and a board, you can fly out over a canyon AND an active volcano (if you don't die).
P.S.—Nailed it.

That is really cool. But possibly not as cool as a cicada that sleeps for 17 years under the ground and then mates for two weeks.

Aw! That's so romantic.

Wut.

17 years of sleep for two weeks of true love. ♡

You are such a girl.

Yeah . . . Obviously.

Anyway, I've been following a website that tracks them, and the next time a million of those suckers come bubbling out of the ground, I'm going to be there. (And you should come with. You know. For the romance.)

Definitely! But first—I have a competition to win. Did you know Hawaii has every color of beach sand (yellow, white, black, red, and GREEN) AND active lava flows AND at least 8 different climate zones so you could theoretically ski and snorkel in the same day?

I need active lava flows in my life. Also, green sand. Also also, did you know that driver ants have jaws so strong they stay locked even if they die or get ripped in half, and in some countries they use them as emergency sutures?

Okay, that is legit cool (and also legit GROSS). Legit cooler: there's this place in Turkey that looks like an ice palace made of terraces all stacked on top of each other, but really, it's not ice, it's minerals, and each terrace forms its own hot spring pool. How you doin' over there? Running out yet?

No! Did you know there are bees that can sniff out bombs? Or that there's a North American termite with a gun for a face?

That was totally two things you big, cheating cheater! But it's cool, because guess what? I know about a place in New Zealand called the Glowworm Grotto. You can only get there by taking a boat through a twisty, turny network of caves, but it's totally worth it, because inside, there are thousands of Arachnocampa luminosa shimmering overhead like mosquito-size stars. BOOM. *drops mic*

ARE YOU SERIOUS???

Yep.

How is it possible that you know something about bugs that I don't?

You have clearly underestimated me.

You can win this and all other games as long as you promise to tell me the exact location of this glowworm cave.

No worries. I got you, Spence :)

The bell rings, and I fold up the note and shove it in my pocket. Today still sucks, but I guess it sucks a whole lot less now.

Hey Janie!

How are things in Belize? I hope the cookies aren't totally disgusting by the time they reach you. Dad made a special batch just for you, and then Spencer helped me hermetically seal them or something. He also helped me plan the most amazing trip ever to Belize (see the back of this page).

Anyway, remember how I told you I'd tell you if anything happened with Dean? Um, something might have happened. I was just sitting on the back porch painting my toenails (because you know how Mom freaks out over the smell!), and Dean comes running down the stairs, and right before he opens the door to his car, he sees me. And it's like he completely forgets about whatever it was that was making him rush down the stairs, and he's got all the time in the world to stroll over and hop onto our porch railing, and say, "Well, hey, Hope. Whatcha doin'?"

So, I tell him I'm just doing my nails, and I try to go back to it, only now my hand's shaking so bad I totally screw up and get green polish on my pinky toe. And before I know what's happening, he jumps down next to me, and he's holding my foot (MY FOOT, JANIE!), and turning it this way and that, and saying how it's a real pretty color and it reminds him of pistachio ice cream. And then he takes his thumb and wipes the polish that got on my skin, like, "Oh, I help girls out with pedicures all the time. You know, whenever I'm not doing whatever it is that makes my abs look so awesome."

And he says, "Hey, I'm fixing to go to Riverside. You wanna go?"

And I'm all, "Ohmygosh, are they open today?!"

(Side note: Riverside Catfish is AMAZING. We're talking best-catfish-in-the-universe amazing. No, for real, I'd send you some with the cookies, but I'm like 80% sure catfish isn't meant for international travel. Anyway, Riverside's got this really sporadic schedule and you never know when they'll actually be open, so it's pretty much like, they announce they're open, and everyone in Peach Valley rushes there as fast as they possibly can.)

And I know it was a bad idea, but his hair was still wet from taking a shower, and he shook it like a puppy. I don't know why that got to me so bad, but it did, and all I could do was nod my head and get in his car. (Seriously, Janie, my brain was gone. I think I would have followed that boy off a cliff.)

So, we go there, and we're hanging out with all these other juniors, and they're interested in what I have to say, and laughing when I'm funny, and Dean keeps squeezing my knee under the table. And I feel dumb even writing this, but it kind of made me feel like a movie star or something. There. I said it. Feel free to e-mail me and tell me how pathetic I am. Also, feel free to remind me that we should drive by that place every single day the next time you visit because the catfish, OMG.

Just in case you're worried that someone deep-fried my brain, I DID NOT let him kiss me good night. Here is what happened instead:

Dean (turns off the car and waits like it's no big deal even though the seconds are stretching into eternity): I'm glad you came with me tonight.

And then he tugs at the belt loop of my shorts like he's being playful, but it was a total seduction move! And I almost fell for it! An important finding: Bench seats are so danger-ous! I was thisclose to letting him pull me all the way across the seat and kiss me.

Me (reminds self that mouth tastes like fish AND onion rings; finds the strength to push him away): I won't be like the girls I see at your window.

Dean: What girls?

Me (raises eyebrows like, "Hello. I'm your next-door neighbor. Do you really think I don't see?")

Dean (with the aw-shucks grin): Of course not. You're different.

Me (considers for an extra long time to make him sweat.): Prove it.

Dean: I'll do anything you want.

Me: If you want to see me, you come to my front door. I don't come through your window.

And you will be proud to know that I flounced out of his truck and up the steps of our house. Unfortunately, right as I was opening the front door, he had to call out, "Bye, Hope." And my insides melted like peach ice cream in July.

End dramatic reenactment.

So, as you can see, I'm in all kinds of trouble. Especially because he knocked on our door this morning and asked me to go to the movies with him, and I had no good reason to say no. Because I really do want to go, Janie. When we were alone in his truck, I don't know, he's different than I thought he was. He's really funny and, like, easy to be around.

Call/e-mail/write/message me, and talk some sense into me, okay?

I miss you like crazy!

Love,
Hope

P.S.—We haven't had a Skype movie date in forever! I'm feeling Chicago, but I could also be persuaded to watch West Side Story, so let me know! Also, I want to hear about your new boyfriend!

P.P.S.—I got your package last week. Thanks for the butterfly journal!

CHAPTER

8

I'm standing at the checkout line, typing in my code to pay for my chicken-finger meal and three skim milks, when I realize that Hope isn't at our table. She's perched next to Dean at a table full of juniors. I knew she went with him to get catfish or something, but I didn't know that meant she was *with him*. Well, until now.

It's finally over, I guess. I can take Hope out of the Maybe/Hopefully/Someday with Spencer column and file her under Girls Tainted by Dean. And it's worse than I ever thought it would be because I forgot to factor in the part where she's my only real friend. I stand there with my tray, every second that passes feeling like some huge horrible thing, a blinking sign over my head that reads *This guy is a loser with nowhere to sit.*

I could sit at our usual table. It's not like Hope and I were sitting there alone. But I don't really know any of the other people that well, and what if they were only tolerating me because of Hope?

I don't have a better idea, so I walk over and sit down. No one tries to stop me, which I take as a positive sign. No one really tries to talk to me, either, though. Which is fine. I just need to keep my head down and get through this day. I try to open my milk carton, but I guess my fingers are shaking because I almost spill it. I set down the milk and take a slow breath. Not at school. *Not here.* A few seconds pass, and a guy sits down next to me. He's in Hope's chair, but I'm guessing she won't be back for it anytime soon. I've seen him before. I think his name is—

"Hi. I'm Paul."

Yeah, that's it.

"I'm Spencer."

Well, that wasn't so terrible.

"Are you in Mr. Byers's class first period?" he asks. His voice is deep and gravelly for how skinny he is.

"Yeah. You, too?"

He nods, and things get awkwardly quiet for a minute, so I get to work on my chicken fingers, which suddenly seem edible again.

"So, you play Magic?" It's more of a statement than a question.

My hands freeze. How does he know?

"I saw a deck sticking out of your backpack yesterday."

I relax, but only marginally. Is he going to out me in front of the entire table? Get me banished? I wonder if he'd believe me if I said they weren't mine.

"I play, too," he says.

"Oh. Oh, well, cool."

"Not, like, at school, but if you ever want to hang out and bring your decks?"

"Yeah, that would be great." This guy is rapidly shooting to the top of my Potential New Friends for Spencer list.

"Cool." He grins, and I give him my number so he can text me, and we talk about Marvel movies for the rest of lunch.

First day without Hope, and I am owning this. I sit a little taller in my plastic chair. When the bell rings, Paul and I walk together to put away our trays. This could be really cool, this whole having-a-friend-who's-a-guy thing. Hope hates playing Magic. I had to trade her watching *High School Musical* AND *High School Musical 2* to get her to play last time. I can only handle so much Zac Efron.

I slide my tray onto the conveyor belt and back up. Well, I attempt to back up. There is a large mass standing behind me.

"Watch out." It's Ethan Wells. Ethan "I break people's faces and make small children piss themselves" Wells.

"Yeah, watch it, Twitch." His friend gives me a shove, but I stay standing.

I don't want to look like a loser in front of Paul, and my mouth shoots off before I can help myself. Not a tic, just pure, zero to sixty annoyance. "Dude, chill. It was an accident." And then, under my breath: "Lay off the 'roids."

The friend has better hearing than I anticipated. "Are you gonna take that?" he asks Ethan. And then when Ethan doesn't move: "E, seriously, are you gonna take that?"

Ethan looks back and forth between the two of us and sighs. He grabs his friend's tray and slowly peels the top piece of bread off what's left of a half-eaten PB&J. And then he claps me on the back. Not hard or anything, but the sandwich definitely sticks. "You should have kept your mouth shut," he says in a low voice.

Paul watches with wide eyes, but he's on the fringe—they don't know he's with me. And then Vice Principal Parks walks up.

"Boys, is everything okay here?"

I whip around so she can't see my back. Ethan and his friend paste on big ole grins. "Oh, sure, everything's fine."

Everybody scatters. School administration has that effect on people. Then the bell rings, and everybody scatters more. I duck into the bathroom to take off my shirt. By the time I come out, Paul is gone.

I know he had to get to class. The bell already rang. It probably has nothing to do with not wanting to be friends with a kid who has a target on his back (literally). I can probably expect a text from him inviting me to play Magic, oh, approximately never.

I spend the rest of the day wearing my undershirt, my polo with its peanut-butter badge of shame stowed safely in my backpack. I don't talk to anyone, and no one talks to me.

After school, I sneak up to the attic and look at pictures of my mom and wish I could just disappear. Or maybe jump out the window. I'm pretty high up. Ants can fall from practically any height and not die because they have a low terminal velocity or something. If I jumped, I don't think I'd be able to walk away.

I shake off the thought, and step away from the window. I go back to the photos of Mom and will them to pull me in. There's one of her at a church picnic—all these families, all the same, and then her. She pops out of every photo, more vibrant, *more alive* than all those regular people. Sometimes I think, *Well, of course she looks like that to you. She's your mom.* But other times, I know it's not just me. It's *her*. Her smile is too wild. The violet streaks in her dark brown hair scream, "I don't belong here."

I flip to another photo. This one is of my mom holding a guitar—which makes sense. Sometimes I think about her singing us to sleep, and I wonder if I'm really getting her voice right. In movies and stuff, they'll show a mom or dad leaving a kid, and whoever's left wants to protect them, so they hide all the letters and birthday cards the other parent is sending, until the big climactic scene where the kid finds out their missing parent really cared all along, and here are the years' worth of letters to prove it. They're so glad they weren't really abandoned, but also so very hurt that the other parent lied to them. You know what hurts worse than being lied to about the letters? The letters not existing at all. I used to tear the house apart trying to find them. And at first, when I couldn't find them, I thought it was okay. My dad was smart. He was burning them or trashing them before I could ever get to them. So I made sure to be the one to check the mail. Every day for a whole year, I opened the box and reached for a letter that never came.

How am I ever supposed to figure anything out when such a big piece of me is missing? I barely even knew her, but that didn't stop her from totally screwing me up. I kick the support beam in front of me like it's to blame for everything that's wrong with my life. Something falls from the rafters and clocks me in the head. After some swearing, I note that it is a big something (the knot on my head confirms). It is also a guitar-case something. And unlike everything else in this attic, it is completely devoid of dust. I don't understand and then I do, all at once. This is Mom's, and Dad keeps it here. Not only that, he takes care of it. He must, like, come up here and look at it and stuff. The guitar on the inside is beautiful, too. Old. Battered.

Before I know it, my cheeks are wet.

I hear footsteps on the attic ladder and rush to wipe my face. I wasn't, like, full-on crying, so hopefully it won't show. Hope appears at the opening to the attic and creaks her way across the warped floorboards to me.

My first thought: Thank goodness it's not Pam, because I didn't hide the guitar.

My second thought: She knows I've been crying. I can tell by the way her face is pinching together.

"Are you okay?" Her hand reaches for my shoulder, but I shrug it away.

"Dean's not up here."

She takes a step back. "I wasn't looking for Dean. I was looking for you."

I don't say anything, just start putting the photos back into boxes.

"I guess you already know we're going to the movies tonight." Dean might have mentioned it on the way home from school. She is actually wringing her hands now. I didn't know that was a thing people did in real life. "I'm still not even sure how it happened. Dean—he has this way of pulling people in. He's like the sun."

"Or a black hole."

Her mouth curves up in a half smile, and the atmosphere in the attic feels 80 percent less toxic.

Then she has to go and make the pity face. "I'm sorry, Spence."

"Why?" Why did she have to do that? Why couldn't we just pretend I never liked her? It's not like I ever told her. Now I'm permanently cast as the loser guy doomed to watch his brother date the girl he likes.

"Because." She gestures between us like that will explain everything. More hand-wringing.

My eyes narrow. "You know what? I think you should go."

Hope makes the I've-just-been-slapped face, but I don't stop there. "I'm busy with a lot of stuff right now, and I don't really want to talk about it. You should really just go and see *Dean*." I inject his name with as much scorn as possible.

Whatever spell that was holding her frozen breaks.

"Fine." She holds up her hands and backs away. "I was just trying to—forget it. Maybe I will go see Dean."

She climbs back down the ladder, stomping on each rung as she goes.

Part of me wishes I could get a do-over, and the other part of me knows I will always ruin it no matter how many chances I get.

Sep 28, 7:22 PM

Hope: are you around?
Janie: Yeah! What's up?
Hope: spencer and i had a fight
Janie: Aw, sweetie. What happened?
Hope: i started dating dean
Janie: Wait. WHAT?!
Hope: oh, right. you haven't gotten the cookies yet. details in the letter I just sent, but yeah, dean and i are going to see a movie, hence the fight
Hope: except that makes it sound like this is all my fault, which it totally isn't
Hope: it is all spencer
Hope: ALL OF IT

Sep 28, 7:26 PM

Hope: janie?
Janie: Sorry. I spaced out. It's really late here.
Hope: oh. well, um, that's okay.
Hope: i just wanted to talk to you about spencer. he's been acting so different lately and i'm really worried
Janie: Different how?
Hope: like really angry
Hope: and not just about me and dean, but like everything

Hope: and he says things that don't sound like him at all
Janie: Yikes. Is he, like, hanging out with different friends or something?
Hope: no, he has not taken up with the "wrong crowd"
Janie: I didn't say "wrong crowd."
Hope: you were thinking it
Hope: sigh.
Hope: i want to ask him about it but i'm worried that'll just make things worse
Hope: plus, i'm not talking to him right now
Janie: Ruh-roh. I do not envy him being on the other end of a Hope freeze-out.
Hope: i don't know what you're talking about
Janie: Puh-lease. Your freeze-outs are legendary.
Hope: well, he totally deserves this one!
Hope: i was trying to talk to him about stuff and he was all: why don't you go see dean?
Hope: and i get if he didn't want to talk but he was SO MEAN about it
Hope: he shouldn't have been that mean

Sep 28, 7:37 PM

Hope: right?

Sep 28, 7:39 PM

Hope: janie, are you there?

Janie: I must have spaced out again. I'm sorry. I keep doing that. Nolan's been making fun of me.

Hope: this is really important

Janie: I know. I'm really sorry. I just have a terrible headache. What if I call you tomorrow?

Hope: okay

Janie: Love you, Hope.

Hope: love you

CHAPTER 9

I need to talk to Hope so bad it feels like a splinter in my brain. I don't know if I can apologize to a known Dean Dater, but when I see her parents get in her mom's Jeep and pull out of their driveway, it's like my feet carry me over there on their own. I picture her snuggled under a blanket with the latest Laini Taylor book. In the kitchen feeding slivers of cheese to Eponine. Stretching for a run.

I do not picture her kissing my brother.

I'm bounding up the steps and about to touch the door handle, when I see them behind the screen door, standing in the middle of her living room, completely oblivious to the fact that I am frozen and can't look away.

It's the kind of kiss you don't expect anyone to see. A hungry, fly-across-the-room-the-second-the-parents-drive-away mauling of a kiss. I've never actually kissed anyone before, but of these things I am certain.

Dean's hands are running all over her—like her body is territory and everywhere he touches is a flag staked down that says *Claimed by Dean Barton*. Shoulders. Legs. The small of her back. Her perfect collarbones, his fingertips tracing the tan lines, like I've always daydreamed about doing. He traces them again, just on the right side this time, only his fingers don't stop when they hit her shirt. He runs them under the edge of her tank top where it scoops low across her chest. He moves by degrees, maybe because he's scared she'll stop him if he goes too fast. Maybe because her shirt is tight against her body and he's having trouble wedging his hand in there.

And then his whole hand is inside, cupping her, touching her. She moans into his mouth, and the sound of it, sweet merciful Lord, my body nearly explodes. Oh, man, what it would be like to have her moan like that because of something I did.

He kisses her jaw now, and her neck. Her eyes are closed. Her mouth half open. His kisses trail lower. Her collarbone. The top of one breast. And oh, holy crap, I manage to get myself together and turn my head away just as he pops her boob out of her shirt. It's the thing that really snaps me out of it. It's not okay for me to see that part of her unless she chooses to show it to me herself. I wouldn't even want to.

I sneak down off the porch. I also have to sneak back into my own house because Pam is doing some kind of craft project involving mason jars, and I'd rather not explain to my stepmom why I am comically hard right now. Ugh. I feel like I have no control over anything right now, even my own body.

When I finally get back to my room and get the door shut safely behind me, I'm shaking all over. An image of his hand down her shirt flashes in my mind, and I feel like there are holes in all of my important organs.

I wouldn't even know what to do.

If she was standing in my room right now in those cut-off shorts. Kissing me—an absolute mauling of a kiss.

I'd be lucky if I could remember how to breathe, let alone figure out where to put my hands. Dean gets all these girls without even trying. One after another after another, through the revolving door of his bedroom window. He has never wondered where to put his hands.

I try to imagine her now, but he's all I can see. Damn it! How does he ruin everything?

I'm not entirely sure how it happens, but I realize there is a crater-shaped hole in the wall in front of me and my hand hurts really effing bad. I'm gonna have a fun time explaining this one.

FROM: janie.m.birdsong@gmail.com
TO: hopetacular2000@gmail.com
DATE: Oct 11, 5:25 PM
SUBJECT: Good morning, Baltimore

Hey Hope!
Are you ready for our Skype movie date this Friday? I'm thinking *Hairspray*, circa 1988 or *Hairspray*, circa 2007. You pick!
Janie

P.S.—I'm so glad you and Spencer made up!

_____

FROM: hopetacular2000@gmail.com
TO: janie.m.birdsong@gmail.com
DATE: Oct 11, 6:58 PM
SUBJECT: Re: Good morning, Baltimore

Hey! I am so ready it's not even funny, and I choose John Travolta cross-dressing, OBVIOUSLY. (Side note: Can you believe this girl at school, Tabitha, thinks *Grease 2* is better than the original? WTH.)
And, thanks. I was so nervous, but everything turned out fine. I really feel like he listened to what I had to say.
Also! I have to tell you this thing that happened at school because it definitely can't wait till Friday. I think Spencer might be cool now. I mean, I don't care, and I don't think he cares (he's so angry lately, it's hard to tell). But maybe his dad cares. I don't know. It's complicated.
Anyway. So you know how Spencer sometimes gets stuck on

certain words? Well, we were in World History, and Mr. Siegel was talking to us about some European queen, and I guess her official title was Regina, only he wasn't saying it like "Ruh-gee-nuh." He was saying it like "vagina" but with an R. *Ruh-ji-nuh.* Can you imagine?! So everyone was trying not to laugh, and then finally, thankfully, he moved on to some war because war is like 80% of what you talk about in history class. And we were all SO relieved, and then out of nowhere, Spencer said, "Regina." Only he said it really loudly. And people snickered a little. And then he said it again. And again. And I knew it was just a tic, but everyone in class was laughing. Mr. Siegel asked him to stop it, and he kind of did for a minute, but then it was like I could see steam coming out of his ears, and he just kept saying it. And Mr. Siegel was all, "If you say that one more time, you're going to the office." And Spencer was all, "Mr. Siegel, you know I can't—REGINA." And all the guys that make fun of Spencer were laughing like crazy when he packed up his stuff. I thought it was going to get worse, like with them teasing him and stuff. But then at lunch, they came over to our table and kept slapping him on the back and telling him how "epic" it was. Oh, and they kept calling him "S-man." I'm telling you, it's a miracle I didn't puke all over my processed macaroni and cheese.

So yeah, AND THEN, Spencer tells me he's going to try out for wrestling. Like out of nowhere. I don't even know what this world is coming to. Oh, but guess what! I'm trying out for track this spring! Okay, gotta go because Dad is calling me for dinner!

XOXO,
Hope

CHAPTER 10

Hope and Dean are ruining everything that is good in this world. I'm minding my own business, going downstairs to play video games just like any other Saturday. Before I even make it to the last step, there they are, jumping apart on the couch. Dean wipes his face guiltily, and Hope is all, "You can stay." And I am like, "No fucking thank you," only without the F-bomb because I am totally cool with all this. Cool like an August day with no air-conditioning.

I go outside because at least I know they won't be there, but the den is definitely getting added to the map of Places That Could Be Contaminated with Make-Out Juices.

"Hey, Barton, c'mere. We need a fourth," yells Ethan.

He and his younger brother, Jace, and this guy Mikey are playing cornhole in Bella's front yard. I walk over, even though I know it's probably a bad idea. I think about asking them why Bella or her friend can't be their fourth, but decide against it.

"You know how to play, right?" says Ethan.

"Yeah."

Mikey glances toward my house before asking, "Can you play without spazzing out?"

I ignore him and pick up a beanbag. I'm on Ethan's team, and it's really pretty easy. You have to throw the beanbag and get it through a hole in a piece of wood. A bag on the board is one point. A bag through the hole is three.

Ethan and I tear Mikey and Jace to shreds.

"The spaz can play!" crows Ethan, slapping me a high five.

It's hard to know whether I've been complimented or insulted. I tic-sniff, and Mikey whispers something to the girls, and they snicker into their fists.

I try to shake it off and focus on the game. I already knew where Mikey fell on the Making Fun of Tourette's spectrum—this isn't a surprise. My next bag soars through the hole without even touching the sides. And apparently that is the thing that puts Mikey over the edge.

"I think Tourette's must give you secret cornhole-playing abilities," he says. On his next throw, he yells a cuss word at the top of his lungs. His beanbag sinks it. "Success!" he yells, holding his hands in the air like a goalpost.

And because it worked, he does it on every turn. And then Jace starts it up. And Ethan, too. The girls are laughing so hard, they can barely keep it together. I'm annoyed, but I'm trying not to show it, because that'll only make it worse. I hate how the swearing is what everyone thinks when they hear "Tourette's syndrome." I know, I know, it's what they always show in the movies because it's so freaking funny. But it sure doesn't feel funny right now. Mikey really hams it up, making his voice sound all unhinged and screwing his face up when he screams out F-bombs and C-bombs and basically every kind of bomb there is.

And then I rear my arm back to make a throw and, just as I'm letting go, he screams out a word that would make Pam drag him into the bathroom and shove a bar of soap in his mouth. It is not a coincidence. It is every. Single. Time. Ethan shakes his head, but he doesn't say anything. Mikey's eyes are mean, and the girls stop laughing. I start missing shots, but I don't want to give them the satisfaction of watching me have a meltdown, so I force myself to hold all my sharp edges together until the game is over. Then I make a weak excuse about needing to do something inside.

But I'm not okay the same way a powder keg or a gas leak is not okay.

My feet carry me to the office that doubles as my dad's trophy/weapon room and Pam's craft room. Pam is there, repurposing an old window.

She looks up from her work. "Hey, Spencer, how's it going?"

I shrug. "Okay."

"You feeling okay on your meds?" she asks, bringing us to a grand total of three for today. "Because we can always try something else if—"

"I'm *fine*. The all-over tics stopped. I don't want to talk about it, okay? I think I'm gonna get a snack." This is always a good idea when you don't know what else to do.

She eyes me for a second longer. "Well, I just made some coconut fudge. It's on the counter."

She brushes her hair out of her face and gets back to her project. I trek to the kitchen. Maybe if I eat my weight in coconut fudge, I won't feel like everything is conspiring to wreck me. Plus, the idea of Dean finding the empty pan is pretty appealing. The sound of giggles hits me before I turn the corner.

"Stop it. I don't like coconut!" Hope's voice sounds different. Softer or higher or something.

"This will change your mind about it, I promise."

Dean chases her mouth with a piece of fudge. She finally

accepts, taking a dainty bite so that her lips touch his fingers. He pops the rest of it in his mouth with a wink.

This is the horror that lurks between me and an entire tray of coconut fudge. This is what every day for the rest of my life is going to be like.

"Excuse me." I squeeze past and grab a piece of fudge, bumping Dean a little as I do because they haven't left me any room.

"What's your problem, man?"

"*Nothing.* Just. Do you guys have to be *everywhere*?"

I stomp out of the kitchen. I was managing a second ago, and now I feel like the world is exploding. But only inside my head, and it'll take every piece of me when it goes. I chew on my block of fudge, but it doesn't even taste good right now. What the fuck is wrong with my life that I can't enjoy coconut fudge?

"Spencer," Hope says in a mom voice.

I turn, and she's got her arms crossed over her chest like, "Didn't we just talk about this?" Dean and his stupid face are right behind her.

I throw up my hands. "I can't do this right now."

Everything is caving in. I don't want to be me anymore. I would give anything to get out of my brain for just one minute.

"Spence?" She's scared now. Uncertain.

Her voice comes to me through fog, and I see her like she's standing behind a shower curtain. I can't do this. I can't. I'd rather it all be over.

Pam joins Hope behind the shower curtain, wiping her hands on her pants. "Spencer, are you okay?"

I hate all the pity in their voices. Hate it.

"Everybody leave me alone! I just want to die!"

It seems like a good idea when I say it. The only idea. I walk straight to my dad's gun safe. Kick the wood-burning kit aside. Enter the combination. I can see it playing out inside my head. I turn the handle.

There are strong arms around me like iron bars, pulling me away, holding me back. I fight against my brother, but the guy's got at least forty pounds on me, and he's not going anywhere. He stays. And he stays. And he stays. And after a couple minutes, his arms stop feeling like a wrestling hold and start feeling a lot like a hug. I hug him back. I think I'm crying.

"I'm sorry. I'm so sorry."

"Don't worry about it, man. We're gonna figure this out."

And then Pam is there, closing the safe, joining the hug. Hope hugs me, too, so pretty much everyone is hugging and crying at this point. Everything is kind of a blur, and before I know it, I'm in the car, and Pam is whisking me to a special Saturday doctor's appointment.

"You don't have to do this," I say. "I feel fine. My tics are so much better."

"You're not fine. You haven't been fine for weeks. I don't want to hear it." She grips the steering wheel harder, and I know it's useless to argue.

When we get to the office, we have to wait until Dr. Davenport comes to open it up just for us. Pam explains what happened, while I sit there feeling embarrassed.

Dr. Davenport does not necessarily agree with her assessment. "You know, a lot of kids his age have these kinds of mood swings."

But Pam has already gone full-on Mama Bear. "Well, my kid doesn't. This isn't him, and you're going to find something else to give him so he can still be him."

The doctor agrees. (A wise decision if he values his life.)

꒳ ♥ ꒳

It takes eight days before I agree with Pam about the meds. Eight days when my tics get bigger and more frequent and the full-body tics start up again. But also eight days that make me feel like someone is slowly sucking the poison out of my soul. It was impossible for me to realize how bad things had gotten until things started to get better, and I could say, "Oh, wow, this is what life is supposed to feel like."

They're gonna try me on another med, but not until we're sure this one's out of my system. Pam already has big plans to watch me like a hawk. Not that she doesn't already.

I walk into the trophy/weapon/craft room, and try not to think about what happened there eight days ago. There's a new lock on the gun safe now, and it only opens with my dad's fingerprint. "I think I'm gonna go ride bikes, okay?"

Pam's hawk eyes switch on. "Are you sure?"

I haven't really left the house except to go to school since it happened. "I'm fine. I'll get Hope to go, too."

It's a lie. I'm still avoiding her, because I don't know what to say, but I don't have to tell Pam that.

Pam's eyes downgrade from hawk to peregrine falcon. "Okay. But come right back after. And call me if you get into trouble."

I hold in a sigh. "I will."

"Is your phone charged?"

"It's charged." I leave before she can think of anything else to ask, like if I know the number for 911.

I grab my bike from the garage and wheel it down my driveway. I'm about to hop on when I hear a voice from behind me.

"Hey!" Hope is running down her front stairs with a book in her hands. She was probably reading on her porch swing again.

"Hi." I scuff my toe against the asphalt.

"Do you maybe want company?" she asks.

I smile. "Slushies?"

"Slushies. Let me just get my shoes."

She starts back toward her house, but before she can get to the driveway, I call out, "Hope?"

She turns. "Yeah."

"Thanks for still being my friend. After, you know, everything."

Her eyes get kind of blinky and red. She comes over and gives me a hug, and she whispers, "We're always going to be friends."

March 4, 7:57 PM

Hope: AHHH!!! Only three more days till you get home!!! I can't believe you're bringing a boy this time! I can't wait to meet Nolan, and don't worry, I will totally help you out with Mom and Dad.

March 5, 11:18 PM

Hope: Two more days!!! We're going to eat catfish and go peach picking and watch every musical ever, and I'm so excited for you to meet Dean! I mean, I know you've already met Dean, but that was when he was hot, mysterious, and, okay, slightly douchey, Boy-Next-Door Dean, and now he's Boyfriend Dean, and you're going to love him, J, you really are.

March 7, 9:06 AM

Hope: I know you're on a plane now, and you can't see this, but I'm following your trip home because I can't. Freaking. Wait. I want to hear everything about Samoa!

March 7, 11:44 AM

Hope: We're in the car! On the way to Atlanta! To pick you up at the airport! There aren't enough exclamation points in the world to convey how

excited I am! But I'll try: !!!!!!!!!!!!!!!!!!!!!!!!!
!!!!!!!!!!!!!

March 7, 1:02 PM

Hope: We may or may not be waiting just past the
security checkpoint. With a huge, embarrassing
sign. And balloons. And Dad's cookies.

March 7, 1:26 PM

Hope: Squeee!!! Your plane just landed! Counting
down the minutes.

March 7, 2:11 PM

Hope: So . . . you're still not here. Did you miss
the part about the cookies because I really thought
that would do it?

March 7, 2:23 PM

Hope: C'mon, Janie. Throw some elbows. I want to
see you!

March 7, 2:39 PM

Hope: Oh my gosh, they're saying a woman collapsed
on your plane. That must have been so scary.

Hope: That's probably where you are. You're probably helping her.

March 7, 3:14 PM

Hope: Janie, just hurry up and get here, okay? I'm starting to get a bad feeling.

Some things that suck about funerals:

1) You have to be the center of attention during one of the worst days of your entire life. You have to talk to a bunch of people (most of whom you barely know), when really all you want is to be alone. But you can't because there's the after-thing at your house, and before that, the burial and the funeral and the receiving line and the wake.

2) And while we're on the subject, who the hell thought it would be a good idea to call it a wake? Because it's not like she's going to wake up. But every time someone says the word "wake," all I can think is, "Wouldn't it be the best thing in the world if she just woke up right now?"

3) Not being able to cry.

I know that sounds weird. All you do at funerals is cry.

I listened to a podcast one time about how different grieving is in other countries. In Haiti, they believe the dead are always with you—that people are a part of your story even after they die. They mourn their dead, fully, intensely, and then they celebrate them. The part I can't forget is this clip they played of women at a funeral. And these women, they were wailing. Not crying or even sobbing—this was something different from all that. These were air-rending, gut-clenching sounds. Shrieks with the power to rip through anything—air, hearts, the illusions we create to make ourselves feel better. These women were offering up an earnest sacrifice and grabbing clawfuls of solace in return.

It struck me that no one in America cries like that. Not even at funerals. And it struck me again at Janie's funeral. Maybe we should. Maybe being forced to stand up tall, all shiny haired and pink cheeked, and say profound, beautiful words about someone you can't find the will to function without, to be so fucking poetic in front of everybody—maybe all of that is a terrible idea. Maybe if we weren't trying so hard to stay strong, be cool, cry pretty, we'd all be a lot better off.

Now that she's gone, I think I'd much rather wipe my pretty tears, tear my speech in half, and scream at the heavens until my throat bleeds. The shocked church ladies would be thrown back against their pews, stapled by the arrows coming out of my mouth. They'd get how it feels.

4) People who think the Janie-size hole in my heart can be filled with casserole. Which brings me to why I started writing this in the first place: I can't do this. I can't sit downstairs with well-meaning people, who think casseroles and hugs can put any kind of dent in how I'm feeling. Who want to tell stories like they know anything about Janie, and who keep telling me how great my speech was at her funeral. I don't have the energy for their arm pats and hugs—to make them feel better by letting them feel like they're making me feel better.

So, I ditched. I grabbed the cheesiest-looking lasagna, and I carried the whole effing thing upstairs, and yes, I did see you, Mrs. Fontaine from across the street, and you can wipe that judgey look off your face. I locked my door and flopped on the floor of my closet (gently, because lasagna), and then I burst into tears because I realized I'd grabbed two spoons.

If Janie weren't dead, she'd think this was the best idea ever, and she'd be in this closet with me, stuffing lasagna in our faces and giggling like crazy about how this was so much better than being downstairs. That's when I decided to break out the notebook she got me for my fifteenth birthday. I still can't wrap my head around the fact that she won't be here for my sixteenth.

How can it be real that we'll never get to do stuff together again? A movie montage, like the kind from a cheesy *Lifetime* movie, plays in my head—Hope and Janie, the highlights. Singing into our hairbrushes while making terrible music videos, spending every second of summer at the community pool, watching musicals until four in the morning, poring over maps with the seriousness of UN delegates.

It's that last thought that really guts me. It sets off a vision in my head of the whole world, and each person Janie touched is a tiny light, and then Janie's light just—poof—winks out. And then so do the others, like dominoes. And now I'm not just missing Janie for me. I'm missing her for everyone else. My parents, her boyfriend, the friends she'll never make and the children she'll never have. And nameless people all over the world. Faces that stare out at me from my walls, drawn with my sister's careful fingers.

Sometimes one bright spot in a sea of crap can be the thing that gets you through. My sister was that bright spot for so many people. And now that she's gone—what are those people going to do now? What am I going to do?

I don't understand how she could be so vibrant—so her—while she had this darkness growing inside of her. How did I not see it? If it was taking her over, shouldn't there have been some kind of sign, like her blue eyes turning gray? How could a tumor kill someone like Janie? It reminds me of when we used to read Harry Potter chapter by chapter before bed. The part where Hagrid is outraged, saying a car crash couldn't kill Harry's parents.

Well, a tumor couldn't kill my sister.

It's not dramatic enough. She should have been mauled by a tiger in Sudan or taken out by a rogue bullet in a Russian mafia showdown. Not that I wanted any of that to happen. But she's that kind of magical. And my life felt like it had been brushed with magic when she was in it. Any minute now, I keep thinking someone's going to say, "Janie's alive. She had to fake her death as part of a multinational conspiracy." Or maybe even, "Yer a wizard, Hope."

But none of that happens. And after I saw the body, I stopped waiting for it.

She wasn't supposed to be so still. Janie is motion. There's no potential energy. Every ounce of her is kinetic. Using everything she has right now. Never saving anything for later. Which is good, I guess, because she didn't get a later.

The lasagna I'm eating tastes suspiciously healthy, like maybe someone snuck in some eggplant or the noodles are made out of quinoa. Someone is knocking on the door, but I'm not going to get it, so they can just keep knocking.

"I'm leaving something for you." It's Spencer's voice.

And now he's shuffling away. Hang on, I'm gonna peek out. There's something wrapped in stupidly cheery napkins (side note: who thought napkins with tulips and daisies were a good idea?) that he's stuffed through the crack under the door. I guess I should go see what it is.

Okay, I'm back.

I snaked my way over, careful not to flip the lasagna onto my shoe rack, and retrieved Spencer's mystery gift. Written on the napkin in his messy boy handwriting were the words: In case you want dessert.

He left me cookies, Pam's Peanut Butter Blossoms, which he knows are my favorite.

I think I've changed my mind.

The food and stuff? Sometimes it can help.

FROM: hopetacular2000@gmail.com
TO: janie.m.birdsong@gmail.com
DATE: Apr 27, 11:18 PM
SUBJECT: grief

You're in a dark tunnel. In the distance, there's the faintest circle of light, so you know it's possible to feel good again someday, but at the same time, it feels like you'll never get there. All the steps are made with such painful slowness, that maybe you don't even want to try. Maybe you want to curl up in the middle of the tunnel and stay there. Maybe forever.

Hey Janie,

It's been two months, since, well, you know. I don't even know why I keep writing like this because I know you can't read it, but I could really use some sisterly advice right now, okay? If you were here, you'd know exactly what to do. But you're not here. I feel like that summer when you taught me how to swim without floaties, and anytime I started to sink, you'd be there, pushing me up, and I knew there was nothing to be afraid of. Now I'm in the deep end all alone, and I'm floundering. I mean, I really have no idea what I'm doing, and I am so, so afraid.

There are a million things you'll never get to do. That's the thought that consumes me. That you could have all these dreams and plans and then, poof, it's over. If I think about it for too long, my lungs won't let me take a full breath and my heart starts beating in my ears. It's better not to think about it.

So, I chase the things that keep my mind empty. Don't make plans beyond the next hour. Don't build fantasy worlds where good things happen to good people and sisters live. Real life is no place for a dreamer.

Sometimes I turn over all the picture frames with you in them. I squirrel away everything that reminds me of you in dresser drawers and the darkest corners of my closet, so I don't have to see it. And sometimes I take all the photos out and cry over them for hours because it hurts more not to look. Last night was one of those nights with the crying and the looking. Someone at the foundation sent us all this stuff of yours, and a bunch of information about the work you were doing and how great you were. Which is nice, truly, but it sent Mom into one of those moods, and she kept crying and hugging me, long past the point where it stopped feeling normal. So, I pulled away and said, "I miss her, too." And she smiled and touched my cheek and said, "I'll be okay. God made sure you'd be here to finish what she started."

And I know she meant it as a kindness, but it just felt awful. I ran upstairs and pulled out all my pictures from that trip we took to New Orleans. I needed to feel your arms around me so badly and hear you laugh. The lack of it was killing me by degrees. I needed more than just photos. I needed you. And the emptiness was more than I could bear.

So, I climbed through Dean's window.

I know. I know. I said I would never do it. But I did do it, and it's too late now for your lectures from beyond the grave.

I tiptoed out of the house in a T-shirt and my bare feet. The ground was cold, and it almost made me turn back. If it had been just a little colder, maybe I wouldn't have done it. If Dean had slept through me knocking on his window. Because I knocked like a coward or like someone who wanted the fates to decide what happened next. The fates thought it would be a good idea for Dean to show up at the window shirtless and with TV-commercial sleepy hair. Clearly, they are pro people getting laid, these fates.

Dean opened the window and ran a hand across his exhausted eyes like maybe he was too tired to be seeing clearly. "Hope?"

"Hey," I whispered. And then I climbed through the window and into his bed.

He reached out a hand to steady me. "I never thought I'd see you do that."

"I don't want to be alone."

And I was so stupid, Janie. I curled up against him under the covers like I didn't know what was going to happen. But I did know.

I knew from the first second he started kissing me. I could have said no so many times, but I didn't because I knew he would have stopped, and I didn't want him to. I wanted to feel something.

Is this what it was like for those other girls? They slipped through his window because their worlds were falling apart? Or maybe they really wanted to. Maybe for them, it was fun and powerful, an adventure and an awakening. Seems like that'd be nice. Maybe some of them just wanted to be next to someone.

That's been the hardest thing, Janie. I miss the closeness we had. Even when you were thousands of miles away without Internet, I still felt you around me. Like how a blanket fresh out of the dryer holds its warmth for hours if you snuggle up tight enough. I hated having you gone, but every time you came back, it was like our lives were one long conversation and we had just paused for a second to catch our breath. And now you're gone, really gone, and it's over.

I've never felt this alone. I don't know how to do it. Every time I write a letter to no one, it rips a hole through me. I knew Dean couldn't fill the empty spaces you left, but I was desperate. So, I let him peel off my clothes like layers on an onion.

And before you even ask, yes, we used protection. I may be stupid, but I'm not dumb.

And it was fine. Sometimes it was kind of awkward, but he was sweet, and it only hurt a little, and it really wasn't awful or anything. But what do you do with the feelings after? When they're too big and you're not ready for them? I think you talk to your big sister about them, only that's not an option for me anymore.

When it was over, he held me close and told me he loved me.

I nuzzled my head under his chin, and whispered, "Let me fall asleep first."

"What?"

"I don't want your eyes to close first. Let me fall asleep first."

"Okay." I could tell he thought it was weird, but what guy who just got to have sex is going to argue about something so minor?

So, I pulled my T-shirt back over my head, and snuggled up beside him. His big hand spanning my shoulder blades felt like safety. I closed my eyes as he was still staring into them, and, as promised, he let me fall asleep first. When I was in that space between awake and dreaming, I felt like everything might be okay. But when I woke up, I felt more alone than ever.

Could you please just come back? I need you, okay.

Hope

FROM: hopetacular2000@gmail.com
TO: janie.m.birdsong@gmail.com
DATE: May 17, 3:47 AM
SUBJECT: Questions I wish they'd stop asking me

Are you going to go to Emory like Janie?
Are you going to major in Biomedical Engineering like Janie?
Do you want to work for a foundation someday like Janie?
Do you like jelly on your chicken biscuits like Janie?
Like Janie. Like Janie. Like Janie.

Dear Janie,

It's over. First boyfriend, first time, first breakup, first everything—you can take them all and put them in a box of firsts, and I don't even care if you use those stupid Styrofoam packing peanuts or not because these aren't the kind of memories I want to keep for posterity. If I could blot Dean out of The History of Hope with one flick of my wrist, I would do it.

We did not have the most amicable breakup. Can you tell?

So, you already know I slept with him. (I know you know because I can feel you making the silent judgey face all the way from heaven.) And you already know it was a huge mistake. (But really, couldn't you have made a tree fall in front of his window or something?)

Anyway. So, we did it, and I didn't want to do it again, except sometimes I was just so upset and wanted to feel close to someone, so sometimes I would do it again. Turns out missing your dead sister is not a good reason to have sex with someone. And apparently Dean is not built to handle relationships that are mostly crying and only sometimes hooking up because a couple weeks ago we were sitting in his truck in the KFC parking lot, and out of nowhere he said, "I have needs."

And at first I was like, "What are you talking about?" Because I had no idea at all. He has needs. What, like, for fried chicken? Because we could've fixed that right then.

(Side note: The KFC parking lot is a TERRIBLE place to break up with someone. They can't go anywhere after, so you're both stuck with a catastrophically awkward ride home.)

And then he was all, "I know you're going through a lot, and I'm trying to be there for you, but we hardly ever go on dates anymore, and we never hook up, and . . . I have needs." He said it all slowly like he was talking to a child. Maybe that was the part that made me snap.

I started insta-crying, the tears flowing fast and thick. Dean was pressed against the door, as far away from me as he could get. "Can you not see that I am drowning in need?" I managed to get out.

"This isn't working for me."

Wait. This wasn't just a talk, this was The Talk. The one we don't come back from.

"What are you saying? You don't love me anymore?"

"Hope." He looked like he wanted to crawl out the window, but I wasn't about to let him off that easy.

"Well?"

He squirmed in his leather seat. "You're not giving me anything to love."

I didn't know anything could hurt that much, J. If telling someone you love them is a gift, then revoking that love is like cutting the tightrope out from under them. That's when the real falling begins.

"This was supposed to be forever." Wasn't it? Why does everything have to be over so quickly? Why doesn't anything last?

He looked at me like I was crazy. "We're in high school."

"How can you do this to me?"

Dean's voice was exasperated with a side of guilty. "I'm not doing it to hurt you. If I stay, it'll only make it worse. It would be like lying."

Something about the way he said it. "Are you cheating on me?"

A flash in my head—him after practice. Talking to a girl with long brown hair and hands that flew around when she talked.

"No." Did he say it too fast or just fast enough?

It didn't matter. We were still over. It didn't even matter that a few days later I spotted a girl with long brown hair tapping on his window. I didn't wait to see if she talked with her hands.

Because with every day that goes by, I'm starting to realize he could have been anyone. As first boyfriends go, he was pretty dashing, but no matter what, this was a relationship I was destined to destroy. Because right now I need more than anyone can give me. Right now, I want every relationship to be forever because the person I thought I'd have forever with is gone.

So, that's it then. We're done. In the words of Nellie from South Pacific, "I'm gonna wash that man right outta my hair." I just wish you were here to tell me approximately how many washes it will take.

Love you,
Hope

Jun 16

Hope's Triathlon Training Schedule (pre-Janie):

Sunday – Run 4 miles, swim 20 minutes
Monday – Off
Tuesday – Bike 10 miles
Wednesday – Run 6 miles
Thursday – Swim 30 minutes
Friday – Off
Saturday – Bike 20 miles

Hope's Triathlon Training Schedule (post-Janie):

Running and crying
Swimming and crying
Biking and crying

Hey Janie,

Things are bad. Well, they haven't been good since that day you were supposed to come home, and instead collapsed on an airplane, but now they're worse. I'm sitting in a tornado of papers right now, and I'm worried you're going to hate me, but I had to take control. I can't keep living like this.

See, after about a month of listening to me whine about Dean, Spencer decided it would be a good idea to kidnap me. It wasn't the scary kind of kidnapping—usually bringing your grandma along is a good indicator that nothing sinister is about to happen. But I'm still calling it what it was—a kidnapping. I was sprawled on the floor of my bedroom this afternoon, listening to every sad song in the world and cutting up pictures of Dean while hooked up to an IV drip of chocolate. And Spencer decided to bust in and demand that I get in the car with him, even though, hello, I was obviously very busy.

I figured we were going to get peach ice cream or something, and it didn't even occur to me to ask where we were going until I realized we were on 75 and getting farther away from Peach Valley by the minute.

"Um, where are we going?" I asked.

Spencer looked damn pleased with himself. "You'll see."

"Mimi, where are we going?"

"North Georgia."

"Mimi! You promised," said Spencer, just as I said, "What?! That'll take hours!"

"I'm sure Dean's head will be just as ready to get chopped off when we get back."

I glared at him and turned my whole body sideways toward the window. He may have dragged me on this adventure to nowhere, but he couldn't make me talk to him.

Janie, do you know how long an hour is to sit in the car with someone without talking? It's a really freaking long time. It is also, it turns out, my breaking point.

"So, where is it that we're going?" I directed my question at Mimi, keeping my head pointed straight toward the driver's seat like Spencer wasn't even in the car (we both know I'm an expert at a freeze-out).

"She already told you. North Georgia."

"Yeah. But why? Are you planning on taking me to a secluded cabin and dicing me into little pieces?"

"Lands sakes, Hope." Mimi put a hand over her heart, but you know she reads too much true crime to be really, truly scandalized.

"We're going to the Great Smoky Mountains National Park," Spencer said. Well, actually, he sighed it. I think he was annoyed at having to reveal his big secret.

"Again with my original question. Why?"

"Photinus carolinus."

"Bugs? You're kidnapping me and driving me hours away to the mountains to look at bugs?"

"They're not just bugs." Spencer made his mortally offended face. "They're—well, I don't want to ruin the surprise, but you'll see."

I kept up a steady stream of complaining as we drove along roads that were increasingly winding, and my ears started to pop as we pulled into a parking lot with what felt like thousands of other cars. Picture that time Mom and

129

Dad thought it would be a good idea to drive all the way to Kentucky, only worse. We meandered our way to the front of a line that seemed to be for a trolley. There was a big yellow sign at the front. If there hadn't been so many sweaty kids blocking it, I might have been able to see what I was in for. A guy wearing one of those fishing hats with all the lures herded two kids onto the shuttle, and I was finally able to see the sign.

"Fireflies!" I punched Spencer in the arm.

He looked appropriately startled. "What?"

I pointed at the sign and the words *Firefly Viewing Information*, which were now plainly in view.

"Would it have been so hard to tell me that?"

"I did tell you. Photinus carolinus."

"Hmph."

An old-fashioned trolley pulled up, painted bright red and green, with beige-rimmed windows. For some reason, I felt like I was about to go for a ride on the very hungry caterpillar. It made me smile for the first time since Spencer dragged me on this impromptu bug-watching trip. Spencer paid our fare—one dollar apiece, cash only, exact change. It was nearly twilight by the time we curved around the top of the mountain. I remember him tic-ing a lot on the way there.

"We're almost at the Elkmont trailhead." Spencer handed us each a flashlight with the end wrapped in red cellophane. "Be ready. We need to get a good spot."

"Why are they red?"

"Because we don't want to disrupt the fireflies or impair our night vision." Like, obviously. Like, this was Firefly-

Watching 101. "Keep it pointed at the ground and only use it to find me. Then turn it off."

"Where are you going to be?"

"Getting our spot!" And with that, he shot off through the crowd of fanny-pack-wearing tourists.

He raced around, darting through trees and tall grass, until he found the perfect place to set up a folding chair for Mimi and a blanket for us. I wasn't sure what made that spot any better than the spots thousands of other people were clustered in, but if anyone would know about finding the best spot, it'd be Spencer.

In the walk from the trolley to The Best Firefly-Watching Spot Ever, I received no less than eleven mosquito bites. It didn't matter that they could be biting any number of other people. Remember how Mama always used to say we must be made of sugar with the way the mosquitoes eat us alive? Anyway, Mimi passed me some lotion, and I flashed her a grateful smile. My gratitude did not extend to Spencer, who was two seconds away from clapping his hands together with glee.

"These better be some damn good fireflies," I told him.

"They will be," he replied, all confidence and honesty.

I sat beside him on the blanket, and we watched the last bits of sunlight seep out of the sky. Nothing was happening yet, so I stared at the thumbnail moon that seemed to appear out of nowhere. And I waited. I was thinking about complaining again when it happened. Fireflies. And not just a few, but thousands. All at once, in a ripple of light that fanned out through the trees. Like one little guy decided to shine, and then all the other little guys were trying to catch up so as not to be outdone.

And then darkness.

I held my breath, wondering if that was it, and then it happened again. The woods were on fire, every last insect lighting up at once. Except it wasn't really all at once, it was more like a pattern. A dance. Dominoes falling and a swaying constellation and fifty thousand fireflies playing a game of Telephone.

It was so beautiful, I stood without thinking about it. Spencer rose at the same time, like we were connected pieces of the same being. Maybe the bugs were rubbing off on us.

"It's like watching music," I whispered.

He didn't say anything, just nodded and took my hand, and we watched and we watched, and every six seconds, there was darkness, and every six seconds, the universe unfolded in front of us. As the waves of glowing lights swept across me, the tight, dark things in my chest loosened. Tears formed on my eyelashes, but I didn't wipe them away.

Spencer's hand in mine, it felt good to be tethered to someone. The power of what I was seeing might've whisked me away if I didn't hold on tight.

I emerged from the woods with the heady feeling that I'd been changed forever. And then I spotted a girl with hair the precise honey-on-whole-wheat shade that you had, J. I had seen something breathtaking, heart melding, majestic. And you were the only person I wanted to tell.

Spencer bounced along beside me. "So? Great, huh?"

"Yeah. It was really great."

"I knew it! I knew you'd love it!"

The good things I was feeling curled up at the edges and collapsed in on each other. Because what I saw felt life changing, but with every step back to the trolley and real life, I was hit with a crushing realization: Nothing had actually changed, and nothing was going to change. You're not coming back.

I pretended to sleep on the way back to get out of talking to Spencer. It's mean, I know, but I knew what he was trying to do with this lightning bug thing, and I just couldn't.

But Spencer was determined. He walked me home, and not just to my door, all the way up to my room. And I was yawning and stretching and dropping every hint, but he just kept pelting me with questions, and finally, I snapped.

"Damn it, Spencer. What do you want from me? Do you want me to say it's okay that my sister's dead and that it's okay your brother had sex with me and then dumped me just because some stupid-ass lightning bugs all light up at the same time? Because it's not. Nothing is okay. Nothing will ever be okay again."

He stood there, stunned. I had finally stopped the flow of questions.

As if to prove my point, I noticed your purple J practically blinking at me from the map across the room. The pin was still sunk into Samoa, but it might as well have been digging its way into my brain. I crossed the room in two angry steps and ripped it out of the wall. The anger licked at my heart, and it felt good. Strong. Better than feeling weak any day. I decided the other purple pins needed to go and tore them out, one after the other. (Please don't be mad.)

Spencer was horrified. "What are you doing?"

"She doesn't need them anymore," I said through my teeth. And then I was really fighting mad. "And neither do I."

I tore down the blues and yellows, too. Spencer tried to block me, but I was possessed. None of it mattered anymore. The places I'd been? All colored by memories of you. Painful. Better to be removed. This list of places you'll never get to go? It needed to come down right then.

There was stuff flying everywhere. I peeled away a map of New Zealand, and the picture behind it gave me a stab wound. It was a drawing of two little boys in Haiti holding hands after a storm. The first drawing you ever sent me. And I broke.

At least Spencer was there to catch me. I fell into his hug and cried into his T-shirt, and we stayed that way for a long time, him patting my back and whispering things that didn't quite come together in my head but comforted me just the same. My foot started to fall asleep, but I didn't want to let go, so I shifted my weight to the other foot. And then something happened. I felt Spencer, against me. I mean, we were hugging, so of course I felt him against me, but I felt something else against me. At least, I was pretty sure I did. And then he backed away all freaked out which pretty much confirmed it.

"I'm sorry." He barely managed to get the words out, and then he ran (literally ran) out of my room and down the stairs.

I don't even know what to do about him. Both right this second and in the meta sense. I know he wants things, and if I'm really being honest with myself, sometimes I think I might want them, too. But it's more like the shadow of a future want. I can't be anything to anyone right now, and I need him to get that. But I don't think he does, and I'm already sorry for how I know I'm going to hurt him. I'm sorry I ripped down everything we built together, too. I'm peering out my window right now, but Spencer's already safely inside his house. Dean's light is on, and I wish like anything it wasn't because I have to go outside to throw all these boxes and papers in the trash. His window is only a few quick steps away, and I don't know how strong I can be. What if I can't help myself?

Taking your things off the walls makes me feel like I can breathe for the first time in months. Like your ghost isn't suffocating me. I can't purge the memories, but this is the next best thing. I feel whole and empty at the same time. I've scrubbed my heart with fire, and now I get to find out if it was worth it. This is me taking care of myself. This is me saying good-bye. I love you, Janie, and I'll never forget you, but I have to stop the vigil.

Missing you. Every second of every day.

Hope

CHAPTER 11

What kind of freak gets a boner while their best friend is crying over her dead sister? There I was, patting her back while she cried into my T-shirt, wishing like anything I could siphon away all the terrible things she was feeling and inject them into my heart instead. And then her hip shifted just the right way against the inside of my leg, and little me was all, "Hi, Hope, how do you feel about sympathy boners?"

I backed away as fast as I could, but I knew she felt it. I could see it in her horrified eyes. And even though certain physiological responses are automatic, even though I wasn't thinking anything dirty while I was hugging her, she could see in *my* eyes every time I thought about her while I was alone in my bedroom. I just knew it.

And I wanted to tell her, "You're not just some girl I think about with the lights off. You're my best friend, and the coolest girl ever, and the most important person in the whole world."

But instead I choked out an "I'm sorry" and ran out of her bedroom like the creepiest mouth-breather alive.

The next few weeks go like this:

Hope sighting #1: After several days of careful hiding and James Bond–esque subterfuge, Hope and I nearly run smack into each other on the trail that cuts into the woods behind our houses. We narrowly avoid getting our limbs all tangled up kraken-style, but the embarrassment factor is still an eleven because neither of us seems capable of normal human interaction. After silence and making goldfish faces and seconds that feel like days, we both turn really red and walk in the opposite direction.

Hope sighting #2: We are both at the grocery store, me with Pam, her with her mom. They stop their carts, like, oh, yes, let's just chat away the entire day next to these artisanal cheeses and totally ignore the fact that we are causing our children LASTING PSYCHOLOGICAL DAMAGE. So, yeah, I'm tic-sniffing up a storm, and Hope and I are scuffing our feet and looking everywhere except at each other, but then I finally hit this wall where I just cannot read the same goat cheese label again or I will literally die.

I look up.

And she's staring right back.

I feel my face flush again, and she turns away, but she's got this tiny smile, the kind that escapes even though you're trying to keep it to yourself.

I start to wonder if maybe this is the good kind of nervous—the kind that might lead somewhere. I wave at her as we walk away, and her cheeks go red and the tiny smile comes back. I know what I have to do: I will finally stutter out the most embarrassing apology of all time (in my head, this plays out without me ever saying any of the words for boner, but with her still knowing exactly what I mean), and we'll finally go back to being friends. Maybe more than friends, if I'm lucky. Except . . .

Hope sighting #3: I'm wheeling my bike out of the garage when I hear voices coming from Hope's porch. I'm just about to say hi, apology speech at the ready, when I see who's sitting next to her on the porch swing. Bella Fontaine.

Yeah, that speech is gonna have to wait. Maybe I can ride by without them noticing me. That's probably the safest bet.

But it's like I can feel Bella's eyes hit me, singeing me up one side and down the other with her laser harpy vision. I know I shouldn't, but I turn and look over my shoulder at them. Bella whispers something in Hope's ear. Neither of them is smiling.

Hope sighting #4: Today is the day. I slip up Hope's porch steps, my thoughts one long string of all the best scenarios. You got this, man. You can do this.

But the moment she opens her front door, I can feel my plans crashing and burning around me. She isn't blushing this time. Her face has rearranged itself into all angles and hard lines.

"Hi." The word falls out of her mouth and rises like a barrier between us.

I manage to squeak out a hi of my own. And then I wait for the bad thing that is coming next because even though I don't know what that thing might be, the fact that it is bad, I am sure of.

"Bella told me about what you did," she says.

"Um . . ."

"She saw you digging through my trash."

I feel like I'm choking. Like metal bands are squeezing my throat, and I can't get any words past them, can't even swallow. I look at Hope, my eyes begging her to understand.

"Oh, damn, Spencer. You really did it."

Spencer. Not Spence. She's about two seconds away from crying.

She swallows hard, pulling herself together. "She said you

used to do the same kind of stuff to her. That you're, like, a stalker or something, and you get desperate when girls aren't interested. I didn't want to believe her, but then Tabitha Silverman said you did it to her, too."

I know I have to do something, and it has to be right now. I find a hidden reservoir of Hulk strength, and I pop all the bands, and the words come pouring out of me.

"It wasn't what you think. I mean, it was with Tabitha. I used to follow her home from the bus stop and put stupid notes in her mailbox when I was eleven, and everybody used to tease me about it. But with you, I was only trying to help. I know how hard it's been for you since Janie—" I pause, but now that I've started, it's easier to keep going. "Dean didn't get it. And I'm so sorry he didn't. Because you deserve someone who gets things."

I'm supposed to be explaining about the trash, but instead, everything I've felt for the past three years comes spilling out. A flash flood of feelings.

"I could be that guy, I promise. I'd be the best boyfriend you could ever have. If you'd just give me a chance."

The weight of what I've confessed settles on my shoulders, and I watch for her reaction with something that feels a lot like terror.

"I really need a friend right now," she says through the lump in her throat.

We're going to be okay. I exhale. "Of course. I'm here for you."

"Thanks," she whispers.

She closes the gap between us, slumping against me in a hug that makes me totally unsure of what to do with my hands. I hold them straight out behind her back, while her breath comes in sharp bursts that make her chest jump against mine. I tic-shrug a couple times, but she either doesn't notice or ignores it. I'm unsure how to classify the change in her behavior. Girls don't do this unless they like you, right? She's tucking her head into the place where my neck meets my shoulder—that's supposed to be some kind of sign, isn't it? She squeezes me closer while she cries, grabbing a fistful of my T-shirt in a way that makes me forget how to breathe. I give her hair some tentative pats, moving on to strokes once I feel brave enough, and that seems to be okay, too.

But when she finally pulls her head away, there are tears meandering down her cheeks in zigzag paths, and she looks as broken as I've ever seen her.

"Aw, man, I'm so sorry." Our bodies are still touching, our faces inches apart. I wipe her cheeks as gently as I can.

If we've ever been this close before, it has never felt like this. She closes her eyes, still shaking from the crying, and I know exactly what I have to do. I let my hands slide down to her arms, stopping at the spot just below the shoulder. And then I press my lips against hers, and the entire world melts away.

I do not expect her to jerk backward. Or to whip out of my embrace self-defense-style. Or to say, with a look like I've wounded her, "What are you doing?"

The world stops melting pretty quickly at that point. And the reality that it crystallizes into seems a whole lot harsher and more confusing than it did a couple seconds ago.

"I . . . I thought—" I grab her hand, trying to keep her from slipping away from me.

"Just—" She yanks her hand back like I'm a hot stove. "Just stay away from me, Spencer. I mean it."

My mouth might have fallen open. I don't actually know.

All I'm sure of is the hurt. An ocean of hurt. I am no longer a human, but a collection of gashes and scrapes and clinical incisions that sliced clean to the bone. I don't know how much time passes before she speaks again.

"I don't know what's going on with you right now, but I need some space." She waits for me to say something, but I can't make the words, can't even form a coherent thought. Not until she starts closing the door.

"Wait." But I already have so many exposed wounds, I can't bring myself to tell her about the maps. What if she thinks it's dumb? Or weird? Or worse, what if she doesn't care at all? "It's not what you think," I finally mumble.

She shakes her head slowly, arms crossed over her chest, keeping her safe, keeping me out. "I still think this is the best idea right now. At least until I work some things out."

She closes the door before I can say anything back.

Part Four
16 years old

A TAXONOMY OF SPENCER AND HOPE

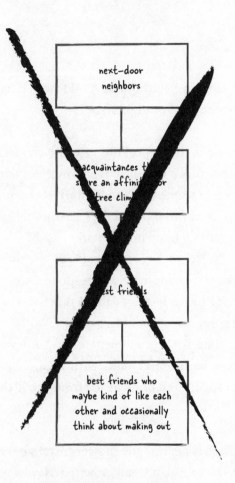

NOTHING

CHAPTER

12

Fact: Every morning, without fail, I do two things. I check on Lord Voldemort. And I weigh myself.

The first thing involves peeking into the terrarium on top of my bookcase as I rub the sleep from my eyes. Lord Voldemort (aka the coolest tarantula in the Western Hemisphere) burrows further into the tunnel of silk he's been building next to his flowerpot. I put my hand on the tank.

"Hey, Voldy. How's it going? I gotta go to school, but I'll see you later, okay?" He doesn't really respond, but I think at least one of his eight eyes winks at me. I just fed The Dark Lord a cricket yesterday, so he should be good.

Now it's time for the moment of truth. I walk down the hallway to the bathroom I share with Dean, hop on the scale, and wait for my fate to blink at me from the little rectangular screen.

146.

Water splashes against the shower curtain next to me, inter-mixed with the sound of Dean growling. He always sounds like a zombie when he's trying to wake up in the morning. I step off the scale and then back on just to be sure, but the display says the same thing: 146. So when you factor in eight to ten pounds for water weight, cutting to 138 should be no problem. The 145 weight class is way too close to my actual weight—*those* guys will probably be cutting from 160. They'll be giant. And there's no way I can cut all the way to 132 unless I want to remove a couple internal organs, so 138 it is.

Which would be fine. Better than fine. I could be killer at 138. But you know who else wrestles 138? Ethan Wells. The guy still hates me, and now I'm giving him the chance to kick my ass as part of a legit, school-sanctioned activity. We'll be paired off, every day after school, gunning for the same spot and each other's weaknesses. Starting today.

I step off the scale and debate weighing myself one more time, maybe trying to pee again first, when Dean drags open the shower curtain.

"Can you hand me a towel?" He shakes the water from his head like a dog.

"Sure." I pass him one without leaving my spot in front of the scale.

"It's not going to change," he says.

"I know."

"Not unless you want to spit in a cup or run a few miles wearing trash bags."

"I know that." We go to our separate rooms to throw on some clothes, which for me means going down the hall, but for him means going down to the basement. But when we pop into the kitchen at the same time, we pick right back up like conversations have pause buttons. "It doesn't even matter. It's not like I have an official weigh-in or something."

Dean smirks. "Then why are you freaking out?" he asks, just as Pam says, "Well, then, there's nothing to keep you from eating a good breakfast."

She sets a bowl of oatmeal and an egg-white omelet on my

place mat, which has a real cloth napkin because we are real southerners, and pushes me toward the table. "Eat."

"First wrestling practice is today," I say around bites of oatmeal. "And since I grew four inches and gained about twenty-five pounds since the end of last season, I won't be wrestling at 113 anymore. I'll be in 138 hell with your buddy Ethan." I tic-shrug. "Kill me. No, wait. You won't have to because Ethan will."

"Do you even know if Ethan's still at 138?" Dean shovels in eggs and muffins like they'll evaporate if he waits too long. Pam clucks her tongue at him as she slips my Tourette's meds onto my napkin.

"No. But I'm pretty sure. It's what he wrestled the last two years."

Dean used to wrestle, too, but he quit last year so he could focus on football and baseball. He hated the wrestler diet. Sacrificing to make weight. The complete and total abstention from alcohol during the season. Come to think of it, he hated pretty much all of it. Except the part where you get to knock people around, he liked that part. But he still gets to do that when he plays football.

My dad comes in carrying an unassuming black case. "Hey, Dean, check it out. We got some new fixed blades in."

"Oh, yeah?" Few things can tear Dean away from Pam's homemade blueberry muffins, but shiny new weapons are an exception.

Dad pops open the case of glittering knives. If you didn't know better, you'd think he was a serial killer. These are the knives from every scary movie you've ever seen—serrations across their spines, lethal blades, points that hook back like shark fins. Dad and Dean are throwing out phrases like "flat grind" and "through hardened," and I'm thinking the six inches between me and the edge of my dad's knife case feels like a canyon.

I lean over the table to get a better look at the knives. "That Camillus looks pretty cool."

Dean snorts. "That's a Gerber."

"Oh." I shrug like it's no big deal even though I suddenly want very badly to say something cool about that knife. "Well, it's got a mean gut hook," I try.

Dad studies the knife and smiles. "Yeah, it kind of reminds me of my old Bubba Blade."

"Hey. Hey, Dad." Dean's eyes are glowing at the mention of my dad's old knife. I think I know where this is going. "Remember the time Spencer tried to dress his first buck, and he puked all over your Bubba Blade?"

I roll my eyes. It's not my fault deer insides smell the way warm feels. "Hey, Dad. Remember the time Dean told the same annoying story every day for the past seven years?"

My dad laughs, but I can't tell which one of us he's doing it with. Probably Dean. He's still got the case turned in that direction and everything.

"Don't forget your medicine," Pam calls from the kitchen.

I swallow the pill with a big gulp of water. Even though they make me sleepy as all hell for a couple hours after, my new meds are totally worth it. No full-body tics. No twitches keeping me up all night (well, most nights). And, best of all, no mood swings.

I hurry to finish my breakfast and get ready in time to meet Dean at the truck. Rule Number One of sharing a vehicle with my brother: Dean always drives. No exceptions. Even though the license I got last month is burning a hole in my wallet, and it is technically *our* truck, which you would think means I get to drive it half the time. And my parents won't let me drive solo because they're worried that the meds drowsiness and my tics will get me in a wreck. The idea of me suppressing my tics until I get to a stop sign or red light completely freaks them out. Which, okay, they're parents, and it's their job to worry, but plenty of people with TS drive, and it's not like any of my tics impair my vision or make me jerk the steering wheel or anything.

The horn blares from outside while I'm in my room shoving stuff into my backpack. Rule Number Two of sharing a vehicle with my brother: The correct time to leave for school (or anywhere) is as soon as Dean is ready. He lays on the horn again, a good two seconds this time. I swing from the top of the stairs and land at the bottom with a thud.

When I slide into the cab beside Dean, he has a book cracked open on the steering wheel.

"What's that?" I ask.

"I got a book report due third period," he says, flipping a page.

"And you're just finishing the book now?"

"*Yeah.* I'll write it during first and second." He tosses the book beside him with a toothpaste-commercial grin. "And Monroe will give me an A, because it'll still be better than anything anyone else turns in." He faux-sighs. "We can't all be me."

"I kind of want to punch you in the face right now. Do you know I was up until freaking two AM trying to figure out *The Scarlet Letter*?" (Side note: I'm pretty sure you'd fall asleep reading that book even if you weren't on my meds.)

"Didn't you already get an extension on that?"

My shoulders hunch up like they're trying to protect my ears. "Some people need more time on stuff." Plus, tenth-grade English is kicking my ass.

Dean shakes his head. "Must be nice. Getting special treatment and shit."

"Dude—" I want to say a lot of things, but he waves me off.

"I'm sorry. I'm sorry. That wasn't cool. I'm just . . . I bombed my chem test last week. Whatever. I'm dropping my APs next semester. Senior year was supposed to be easier than this."

Dean, bombing a test? These things just don't happen. The idea of him not being able to hack it gives me this sick, happy feeling, but it's followed pretty closely by an I'm-a-total-dick feeling. "You sure you don't want me to drive so you can work on that?"

"Ha. Nice try." He cranks the engine and guns it to school so we can get a decent parking spot.

Dean parks the truck beside Ethan's. My phone says I still have five minutes before I have to go inside. At home, I am the lone blue fish sharing a little backyard pond with three orange fish. At school, there is an ocean of orange fish, and they're all swimming in a different direction from me.

Jayla skips over and knocks on my window with a huge grin. Having a girlfriend is awesome. Sometimes she asks me really complicated questions like, "Do you think I'm prettier than Hope Birdsong?" and if I don't answer fast enough, she gets really mad. But other times, she lets me take off her bra when we're in her den watching movies, so, like I was saying, *awesome*. I've barely gotten my door open when she laces her fingers through mine. She squeezes my hand, and my scales flicker to orange until she lets me go. I put my lips to hers, trying to drink up all her normal. She throws her arms around me and shoves her tongue in my mouth. I tic once, a small shoulder shrug, and she ignores it like usual.

When she pulls away, I see a flash of white hair over her shoulder. My eyes go from make-out-haze-halfway-shut to wide-freaking-open. I don't mean to do it, but I watch Hope cross the parking lot.

"Hey, so, guess what!" a part of me hears Jayla saying. "*Oklahoma!* auditions are today."

The good parts of my brain try to concentrate on my girlfriend. Her eyes lit up with excitement, mile-long eyelashes curling up at the ends. But the bad parts are multiplying like a virus, and before I know it, I'm staring again.

Hope is one of the cool girls now. Not the girls who sparkle through the hallways leading their jock boyfriends behind on leashes. The other cool girls. The ones who wear torn tights and think attendance is optional.

Most people think she's bad news. Angry. I can see the truth. She's so sad it hurts to breathe.

She leans against the wall of the school, one leg bent, high-heeled boot tapping against the brick. Her thumb pushes down on her index finger, and then each of the others in turn. Four little pops that her mom tells her will give her man knuckles.

" . . . thinking about singing 'Many a New Day,' but I really feel like 'Oh, What a Beautiful Mornin'' showcases my voice better." Jayla cocks her head to the side like she's weighing her options again.

Now that Jayla's moved, Hope is directly in my line of sight. The wind blows her hair across her eyes, and when she pushes the strands away, we're staring right at each other, and there's a beam of light holding us together, and I couldn't stop even if I wanted to. I gasp, but it's more like the air is being forcibly sucked out of me. And part of my mind can hear Jayla saying, "Are you okay?" but her voice seems so far away.

She touches my shoulder, and the light between Hope and me shatters. Wow. Was I really just doing that? First of all, Jayla could have noticed, like, ANYTIME. Second of all, I swear I'm not that big of a dick. This is something the old Spencer—the one who was stupidly in love with Hope—would have done. I look at my girlfriend—my beautiful, standing-in-front-of-me girl-friend—and cup her chin in my hand.

"Hi," she whispers.

"Hi." I kiss her, just for a second. "You are going to nail this audition. You're the best singer in this entire school."

She smiles, but it doesn't last. "The best girl singer," she says. "Justin Irby is the best boy singer. Maybe even best overall."

"Well, then, you'll be Laurey, and he'll be the main singer cow-boy guy."

"Curly."

"Yeah, him."

"I don't know." She twists her fingers together, and the smile she gives me isn't even a half smile. More like a quarter or an eighth. "I guess I just worry because Justin has blond hair and blue eyes, and what if Ms. Pickett doesn't want—" She stops and shakes her head. "No. You know what? I'm a freshman now. Maybe things will be different than they were in middle school."

"What do you—"

"Forget it." She smiles and kisses me.

I kiss her back until Dean flicks me in the back of the head.

"Get a room." He snickers like a third-grader. "Hey, Spencer, you're turning red. What, are you embarrassed?"

He flicks me again, and I yank the strap on his backpack, cinching it from its artfully low-slung position to somewhere up around his armpit. And before you know it, we're chasing each other around the car.

Jayla makes a big show of rolling her eyes at us before planting one last kiss on my lips. "See you at lunch, okay?"

She struts off toward the trailers behind A Building, her straight black hair bouncing against her shoulders, but I have to go to C, which means Dean and I will be walking directly past Hope. She's just ten yards away. And then three. Our eyes meet again, but this time it's a tiny beam of light. Like a strand of uncooked spaghetti. It would be really easy to break it. If I wanted to. Instead, I wave at her. My hand just shoots up and does it out of habit, before I can think about whether or not it's okay.

It's been so long since I've waved, or said anything at all. At first I think she's going to pretend she didn't see, but then her fingers lift just a few inches away from her leg. Just for a second. Maybe the mini-wave was one of those involuntary things. Maybe it was because she didn't want her friends to see. Dean sees.

"Why is that psycho bitch waving at you?" he says. Loudly. His voice carries across the sidewalk and bashes itself against Hope's boots.

She narrows her eyes, and the fingers fluttering by her side ball into a fist. She flips her wrist upward as we walk past. Gives him the finger.

Maybe she's angrier than I thought.

CHAPTER

13

Everything I've worked on in practice has led up to this moment. Ethan smells like sweat and my impending doom. We're only twelve inches apart on the mat. And that's only until Coach blows his whistle. I stand opposite him, hands ready. A muscle in his jaw tenses, and for a second, I'm twelve years old again and Ethan is a manticore, towering over me with flames for eyes and three rows of serrated teeth.

But then the whistle blows, and my body snaps into some sort of wrestler autopilot mode. The nervousness dissolves. My tics practically disappear. I am muscle memory and high-octane adrenaline. I am the sum of every wrestling practice I've ever been to.

We test each other out. *What if I go for his leg? What if I go for a sweep? What happens if I tap his neck down?* Everything is moves and countermoves, and then, oh shit, he rolls my neck and gets an underhook. He's got my leg. Before I can blink, I'm on my ass, and he's climbing the tree, inching toward my hips with a body made of cement. I lock my arms around him and try to resist, but I can only hold out for so long, and it's a takedown.

The guys go crazy. Ours was easily the closest match-up so far. I grab my water bottle and wait for the next session to start, and because we're playing King of the Mat, Ethan's wrestling again. He beats the guy just heavier than him, and then the guy just heavier than that guy, which makes me feel like less of a loser. Ty Mathers, last year's 152 starter, finally beats him, but since it was Ethan's fourth match-up and Ty's got at least ten pounds on him, it was pretty much a given that he'd get clobbered. There's no way you can win King of the Mat unless you're in one of the highest weight classes, but that's not the point.

I'm watching Ty and this guy from my English class go at it, when Ethan comes over and stands right beside me. I've spent all of practice trying to dodge him—stayed on the opposite side of the room during Coach's overly long welcome speech, during warm-ups and stretching. But when I weighed in, Coach made a comment about how much taller I'd gotten, and how was he ever going to find another 113 guy as good as me. And then a few guys later, when it was Ethan's turn, another comment: "Look at that. You and Spencer are only four pounds apart now."

Ethan's head snapped up, not unlike a spider whose web just got jounced by a fly. And since that moment, I've been getting these prickly feelings, like something is crawling up my back and into my ear. I'd be practicing moves with my drill partner, and I'd turn, and there he'd be, sizing me up. Like I was on his radar, and any time I did something too good—*ping*! Bloodlust activated.

Ethan doesn't say anything as he stands beside me. Just crosses his arms over his chest and glares straight ahead, all menacing-like, while he invades my personal bubble.

He clears his throat, and I nearly jump out of my skin. "You were better than I thought you'd be." His voice is gruff, and he doesn't take his eyes off King of the Mat. My brain struggles to process whether I've been complimented or threatened.

"Thanks?"

He nods. "You've got a good fireman's carry. But you need to work on your Radman Ride."

"Why are you telling me this?" It just slips out.

"The 149 guy at NC State is graduating this year, and I've got the coaches eyeing me for his spot. I guess I felt responsible for 138 or something."

I think about 113. How we don't even have any good prospects to fill my spot this year.

"I get that."

He glances around, almost like he's checking to make sure no one's listening. "Find me next practice, and I'll help you, okay?"

Ethan Wells wants to help me. Shock doesn't begin to cover it. "Yeah, okay. Thanks, man."

He nods and makes kind of a grunting noise before walking off.

I watch the rest of the match-ups, sometimes tic-ing, sometimes not, but all the guys on the wrestling team know about my Tourette's and are pretty cool. Except maybe Ethan, but honestly, now that I'm thinking about it, I can't remember the last time he made fun of me. Eventually, a King of the Mat is crowned—a gargantuan 195-er that everyone calls Zippy. Zippy does some gratuitous victory preening until Coach makes us go to the locker room. He's gripping a roll of masking tape in one hand and some markers in the other. It's time for the Just Say No speech. He clears his throat even though everyone is already paying attention.

"Signing this means you're serious. No drinking, no drugs, no smoking. Nothing that will pollute your body and jeopardize the season. You may wrestle one on one, but this is a team sport. What you do affects everyone. That's why we sign this together. An unbroken ring."

I remember when he did this last year. All the little hairs on my arms stood at attention, and I got that soaring feeling, like when you watch the climax of a good sports movie. I wanted to jump up and yell something. And then I wanted to wrestle the best match of my life. My dad would be so damn proud. Because Dean may have hunting and baseball and everything else in common with Dad, but wrestling is *our* thing. Especially now that Dean quit.

Coach starts the tape over the door of the locker room and winds his way around. Across one wall, around a window, and then back over the door, connecting the ends in a wobbly circle.

I grab a Sharpie and sign my name like I did last year. Then I hand it to the freshman behind me, smiling at the look of utter awe on his face. I want to tell him that I get it—that signing still makes me feel that way, too. Instead, I clap him on the back so hard his knees buckle. It's pretty much the same thing.

I grab my stuff and wait for Dean in the parking lot. About twenty minutes later he shows up fresh from football practice and throws his sweaty bag in the back of the truck. "How was practice?"

"Ethan beat me at King of the Mat."

"Coach let you guys do King of the Mat at the first practice?"

"Yep."

"Sucks. That he beat you, I mean." He pulls out of the parking lot, but he turns the wrong way.

"Where are we going?"

"Granger Packing Plant."

"Dude, you know I can't eat anything there. Just take me home first."

"I don't have time. It's senior-prank planning, and I'm already late because Coach kept me after practice."

"I'm not going. And anyway, why are you doing a prank so early in the school year?"

"Ethan thinks it'll throw off the administration. And unless you want to tuck and roll out of my truck right now, you're going."

"*Our* truck."

I harass him the rest of the way there, but it's no good. We are going to Granger Packing Plant. Dean has spoken. It is law. And during normal, non-wrestling-season months, that would be totally cool because Granger is this awesome place with peach orchards spreading toward the horizon, playgrounds and tractor rides, a catwalk hanging above the inside of the plant where you can watch the peaches getting sorted on giant conveyer belts. We used to go there for a field trip once a year in elementary school, and I was always struck by how the packing line seemed like a living thing, with a whirring, robotic heart, and arteries that pumped peaches to grocery stores and lunch boxes. But going today, when I'm on a strict diet, sitting in the restaurant/general store that is packed to the brim with peach cider, peach preserves, peach cobbler with peach ice cream spooned on top, will prove to be an exercise in extreme frustration. Or temptation. Probably some of both.

Basically, here's what I'm working with:

A TAXONOMY OF ACCEPTABLE FOODS
TO EAT DURING WRESTLING SEASON

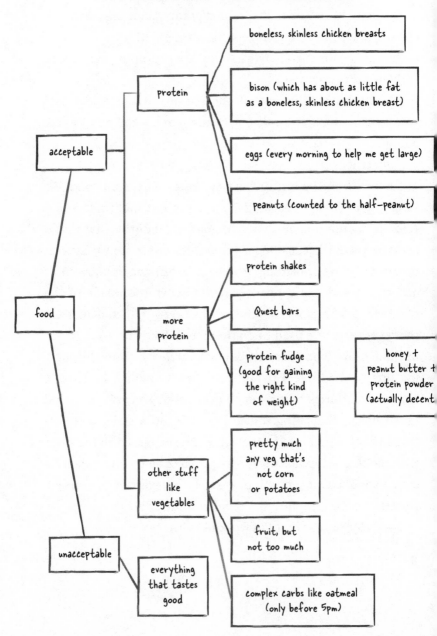

I trail after my brother into the giant building with the never-ending string of rocking chairs under its green-striped awning. Two ladies from Pam's Sunday school class stop us on the way in, just to say hi, how are you, how's your family. A bunch of senior guys and a few girls are already packed into three wooden tables. Dean gets peach ice cream and country-fried steak as a pre-dinner snack. I get a Diet Coke.

A few other underclassmen are sprinkled around the tables, people who are dating seniors or who, like me, got dragged here against their will. And Hope. She's curled up in a chair next to Mikey. I don't know what it is that makes me pick her out in a crowd of people, but sometimes I wish I could have it surgically removed. I'm still kind of freaked about what happened in the parking lot this morning, but I'm just going to lock that in the Behavioral Anomalies box and throw away the key.

Dean groans. "What's she doing here?" he whispers.

I don't know the precise details of their breakup, but whenever they see each other, they both get this look like they're about to explode, bits of anger flying everywhere like shrapnel.

"I don't know." I remember hearing she was hooking up with Mikey. Are they still together? Mikey whispers something in her ear, and she giggles. I guess that means yes.

Dean narrows his eyes. "Just so we're all clear, this is a *senior* prank." He looks pointedly at Hope. "I don't want to see any of y'all the night of the prank, and you better not tell anyone, either."

Hope whips a set of keys out of her pocket and swings them around her index finger. "You see these? They're the keys to the school. I swiped them off the table in the copy room, which means this prank wouldn't even be happening without me. Which means I'm going."

Gauntlet. Thrown.

She and Dean stare at each other for two long seconds. I get the feeling if I waved my hand in the space between their eyes, it would feel a lot like passing through a lightning bolt. Mikey's looking back and forth between them like he can see it, too, and says, "You brought Spencer."

They both turn to look at him. "What?"

"Spencer." He seems flustered. "He's not a senior, either, and you brought him, so back off my girl."

Hope flinches at the words "my girl," but when he slings his arm around her shoulder, she doesn't push it away.

"Yeah, but he's not coming to the prank," says Dean. "He doesn't even want to be here."

I nod. "Truth." Even less so now.

Hope pushes her chair back. Mikey catches her hand. "Where're you going, babe?"

She shrugs. "If y'all don't want me here, I'll go. I wouldn't want to bother *Dean*." She squeezes as much scorn into his name as she possibly can. And then she adds the clincher. "But I'm taking the keys."

Dean groans and rubs his hand down his face. Hope pauses, eyebrows slightly raised, lips pursed in a way that's almost sexy.

"Just. Don't leave yet," he says. "Will you sit back down while we figure the rest of this shit out?"

She plops down like it doesn't matter to her either way, but she knows she's already won.

Dean and Mikey shout across the table at each other, with Ethan occasionally jumping in. The three of them are the ring-leaders of the prank, but even though Dean likes to drink and cause minor trouble, he's more of a straightedge (parties just enough not to be a goody-goody, takes AP classes, but tears it up at baseball and football). Mikey, on the other hand, is apathy personified. So yeah, they get along greaaat.

The argument ends with Dean grudgingly agreeing that they can't pull off the prank without Hope's help. The best part: Mikey telling Dean not to get his panties in a twist, and Dean sulking in his peach ice cream. Plus, Hope's face lights up with this thousand-kilowatt triumphant smile. It's too bad she almost never smiles anymore. Hers are the best. I grin and sip my Diet Coke and decide maybe it wasn't such a bad thing coming here after all. Unfortunately, Dean notices.

"Hey, Spencer, you want some of my ice cream?"

"No."

"You sure? Not even one bite?"

He holds the spoon so close the smell of fresh peaches threatens to break me.

"You are an asshole."

Dean smirks with the kind of satisfaction that only comes from torturing your brother. "It's sooo good. Like even better than usual. It's all soft and creamy, like the kind Grandaddy used to make with his old hand-crank ice cream churner. And the peaches. Ripe, but mild. It's like they picked the perfect—"

"Dude. Shut up about the damn ice cream," Ethan says, smacking Dean's arm. That's when I realize Ethan isn't eating, either.

I nod at his drink. "Diet Coke?"

"Diet Fucking Coke." He clinks his cup with mine. "Only five more months to go."

It makes me feel at least 20 percent less crappy about losing to him today. Even so, I can't sit here and watch Dean devour any more soft-serve, peachy goodness, so I push my chair back from the table and go for a refill. My phone buzzes in my pocket—a text from Pam.

```
Hey Spencer,
Where are you boys?
xo, Pam
```

I'm typing a reply with one hand and not really paying attention as I jam my cup up against the ice machine. Someone's cup is already there. Someone's arm. Hope's arm, and it's touching mine. It's funny how skin just feels like skin until you see who it's attached to, and then it feels like terror or comfort or fire. Hope's knuckles burn against mine, and I have to jerk away before my entire arm bursts into flames.

"Oh." I hope she knows I didn't do that on purpose. "I'm sorry. I didn't—"

"It's fine."

We stare at the ice dispenser and back at each other. It takes decades.

"Well, here." I gesture at the machine, proud to have recovered the power of speech, though my voice feels rusty in my mouth.

She attempts a smile. "No, you. You were here first."

And then in a feat of unbelievable awkwardness, we both go for it at the same time. Again.

"Oops." I back up so she has tons and tons and tons of room. I wish the floor would swallow me whole.

She laughs. It's her nervous one, not the one that sounds

like music when things are funny but dissolves into snorts when things are *really* funny.

"Thanks." She presses the ice lever and shrugs her shoulders. "Sorry."

For getting in front of me for ice or for deciding we don't get to be friends anymore? I hold in a sigh. If we could just have some time to talk, really talk, maybe things could be different.

My shoulders let off a flurry of tics while Hope fills her cup with peach tea. I remember the first time she tried it. She went from "peaches and tea are not things that should go together" to "whoever decided to mix them is a genius" in one sip. She takes a sip right now, eyes closed in ecstasy, and for a second, I see thirteen-year-old Hope and sixteen-year-old Hope sharing the same body. They look at me, and young Hope slips away, and old Hope is left. She smiles, and it is so damn sad.

"Still genius," she says.

If I could say the magic thing, right here, right now, I could fix us. Hope leans forward, her face changing like there are big things sliding into place inside her brain. Her mouth opens.

And then it closes. And then she's turning to get a napkin, and I can feel the moment slipping away. So I just say, "Yeah, genius," and try to ignore the feeling that middle-school Spencer and Hope are yelling, "Noooo," and banging on the walls of the bubble that separates the past and the present because they both know we were supposed to be best friends forever.

CHAPTER
14

"Mikey is a dumbass," Dean says without ever taking his eyes off the TV screen.

"Yep." I make Robin follow his Batman up a ladder. This is probably the third time he's complained about Mikey during this PlayStation session alone, and I'm starting to wonder if it has less to do with prank stuff and more to do with Mikey's new girlfriend.

We're camped out on the carpet in front of the TV because the couch feels too far away at this critical juncture in the game, and because it's kind of an unwritten commandment that thou shalt never sit in my dad's monstrous recliner (that goes double during baseball season).

"It's like, the prank is going to be awesome the way Ethan and I planned it. And he keeps trying to add all this other stuff. And I'm like, 'Dude. Did you not see what happened in Clayborne? If you cause thousands of dollars worth of damage, it's a felony.' Four of the Clayborne guys might have to go to jail." Dean pauses so we can take out some of Two-Face's henchmen. "Flamingoes on the lawn. Blacking out the windows with window paint. All that stuff is going to look cool as hell, but it won't cause any permanent damage. I'm not about to lose my chance at a scholarship just because Mikey wants to do a bunch of crazy shit."

The sound of Dad's feet clomping down the stairs gives us

plenty of time to stop talking. He stands right behind Dean and crosses his Paul Bunyan arms. "We're leaving for the store in fifteen minutes. Get going."

Dean shoots a henchman directly in the head. "Make Spencer go."

"Yeah, I can go." I may not be into hunting, but Dad's always getting in crazy new camping gear, like solar phone chargers and bug-zapper rackets and stuff. I shrug. "It's been a while since I checked things out."

"You can come on Monday when it's less crowded," Dad says. He turns to Dean. "Saturday's our busiest day. I need you."

I keep pressing buttons and shooting bad guys, but suddenly the game doesn't seem as fun. My brother, on the other hand, is still 100 percent glued to *Batman: Arkham Unhinged*. My father steps directly in front of him, and Batman steps directly on an explosive and splatters into seventy-five billion pieces.

"Ah! Do you know how close I was to Two-Face?!" Dean unleashes a string of obscenities under his breath, which Dad pretends not to hear as he lumbers back upstairs.

I push my controller away. "I can help, too," I grumble to no one.

Dean pushes my head to the side. "Your Tourette's scares the customers." He stands up and stretches. "Ugh. I don't want to do this. For one freaking Saturday, I just want to sit around and play video games." He tosses the Player 1 controller in my lap. "Do you know how lucky you are?"

"Oh, yeah. I'm super lucky. Like, the luckiest guy on the planet." I slump against the coffee table.

He cocks his head to the side. "It really bothers you."

"I mean, *yeah*."

Dean's eyebrows go all serious—it's very out of character for him, but, hey, even wood lice are capable of empathy. "How come?"

He doesn't say it like it's a challenge. He genuinely wants to know. And yeah, sometimes I want to punch him in the face or I wish he would disappear, but at the end of the day, I know I don't really mean it. I'm glad he isn't gone forever. He's here and he's trying to understand, and that's something.

"Well." Where do I even begin? I don't usually talk about this stuff. "There's this thing we learned about at camp. The social model of disability?"

He shrugs. "I don't know what that is."

"It's. Well, it's like this. I have Tourette's syndrome."

"That part I know."

"But it's not my Tourette's syndrome that keeps me from working on Saturdays. It's our dad. Because I could go to the store, and like, if someone noticed my tics, I could just be like, 'Oh, hey, I have Tourette's syndrome.' Or if the tics got really intense, I could always take a break or something. But the barrier isn't me and my tics. It's—"

"It's Dad."

"Yeah." We both get quiet.

"Do you want me to talk to him about it?" Dean finally asks.

The thought of it sends a flash of fear through me. "No!"

He looks up, startled.

"I mean, maybe. I don't know."

"Okay, well, you let me know," he says.

"Dean!" yells my dad from upstairs.

My brother stands. "Hey, I gotta go, but uh, thanks. It was

good to . . . I mean, I'm glad we—" He pats my shoulder awkwardly. "Good talk."

He heads upstairs, and I just kind of stand there with my mouth half open. My brother gets it.

Really gets it. Someday I hope our dad will get it, too.

CHAPTER

15

Dean snuck out a couple hours ago, but I'm too nervous to sleep. He's told me so much about the prank over the last few days, I almost feel like I'm part of it, even if all I'm doing is waiting up and playing video games.

The call comes in the middle of the night. I hear the phone ring. Hear Dad's feet stomping down the stairs like he's trying to punch through the floorboards. The den door flies open, and he squints in the glow of the TV.

"Where's your brother?"

I hit pause on the controller and try to look as honest as possible. "I don't know."

He makes an angry noise through his nose like it's my fault Dean is gone and then stomps back upstairs. Normally, I do my best to stay away from my dad when he's pissed off, but then I hear Dean's truck creep into the driveway. There's nothing quite so satisfying as watching the perfect son get in trouble for a change, and I hurry upstairs so as not to miss a second of it.

Pam wobbles from left to right in a frantic sideways kind of pacing. Her lips recite silent lists of worries, and wrinkles I'd never noticed appear around her brown eyes. She always looks at least eight years older whenever one of us is in trouble. Dad's head is a red balloon on the verge of popping. That means things are bad. My body casually leans against the floral wallpaper while my mind claps its hands together with glee. The side door opens—it's the only one that doesn't creak—and Dean steps inside. When he sees the welcoming committee, his mouth falls open and everything in his face says, *Oh, shit.*

"Are you in trouble?" Pam twists her fingers while she waits for the answer.

"What? No."

Dad's head deflates.

"Yeah, so," Dean pastes on a smile, but his eyes are shifty. "I just came by to get some stuff, but then I'm going back to Ethan's house."

In the middle of the night. Riiight.

Balloon-head Dad is back. "You're not leaving this house for the rest of the night. Especially not to go pull a senior prank."

The cocky smile rips in half, and Minotaur Dean emerges. "You told them?" he hisses at me.

"I didn't tell anybody shit."

"Spencer. Language." Pam locks the side door behind Dean. "We got a phone call from the president of the booster club. Somebody tipped off the administration. They're going to the school tonight."

"We're lucky that people care about seeing you play football," says Dad. "There's nothing there that'll link you to the prank, is there?"

Dean's face goes pale. "I gotta go warn the guys."

My dad's lips disappear between his teeth. "You. Are. Not. To. Leave. This. House."

"You don't understand. I just came home because I forgot the flamingoes. Everyone else is still there setting up the prank. Ethan, Mikey, Joel . . ."

Hope. I remember Hope is there. "Call them," I say. "Call them right now."

Dean pulls out his phone and dials Ethan. We wait and wait and wait, but it goes to voicemail. "Fuck."

"Dean. Language."

He leaves a quick voicemail warning, then some texts, then calls a couple more times. There is no response. He swings his phone around like he wants to throw it against the wall. "He's not answering his phone. This is just wasting time, and they're all gonna be screwed. I've gotta go up there."

"No. What you *gotta* do is go up to your room and stay there." Dad's red eyes say it would be dangerous to argue.

Dean moves like he's going to leave again anyway, and Dad grabs his shoulder. Minotaur vs. Minotaur. Their horns clash like stags fighting over a deer, but we all know Dean's already lost. At times like this, I remember just how big my dad really is.

"You'll go to your room if I have to take you there myself."

Dean turns away from the door, but he's still angry as hell, a teakettle about to shoot steam, and it pops out of his mouth before he can stop it. "This is bullshit."

As soon as he says it, his face pales. We don't swear at my dad. Ever. (In front of him, yes. But at him, never.) He's old-school southern—the kind who believes in respecting your elders and belt whippings—and the way he looks right now, well, let's just say I wouldn't trade places with my brother for anything. Dad's hand lashes out, and for a second, I think he's going to smack Dean, but instead he grabs Dean's phone.

"Your room. Now. You can have your phone back tomorrow."

Dean goes. Neither of us argue that taking Dean's phone

hurts the wrong people. There's no chance of him changing his mind once he's made a Dad Decree.

I mutter something about my video games and slink back downstairs. I don't think it even registers with them. Dean's shadow hides me pretty well.

I grab my phone from the coffee table. I'm not friends with the seniors, but I can at least try Hope. I pull her up in my contact list and hit the call button. It feels like going back in time. Her voice makes me jump, but it's just the pre-recorded, leave-a-message message. I text "CALL ME! PLEASE!!!" and try calling a couple more times, just in case, but get the same thing. So, I text "LEAVE NOW. ADMINISTRATION KNOWS." Still nothing. Well, that's it, then. There's only one thing left to do.

Dean's door is closed, but I think I'd rather do this on my own anyway. I walk right past my spot by the TV and stop in front of the door that leads outside. I can still hear my parents walking around upstairs, so I guess this is my only option. I tic-sniff approximately eighty-seven times while I freak out internally over whether this is really a good idea. I take a deep breath and release it. Here we go. I turn the handle, and the hinges shout my escape plan to the whole neighborhood. I grab my keys from the hook by the door. Run to the truck. The blinds are down, but I could recite the scene behind them. Now is the part when they wonder if they heard what they think they heard. I crank the engine. And now is the part when they know.

The side door swings open. A silhouette—my dad's head in the porch light, blown up to full hot-air balloon.

I'm already gone.

I navigate through our neighborhood, and it occurs to me

that I'm driving by myself for the very first time. And it's nice. No one gripping the door handle and looking at me like I'm a time bomb. No one asking me if I feel sleepy. I focus on the road, and my tics hardly bother me at all. It also occurs to me that I'm breaking the teen curfew law, but at least there's no one around to see.

When I get to the school, there are three cars parked in the south lot outside the cafeteria, and I recognize all of them. My lungs relax a little in my chest. I got here first. There's still time.

I fly from my parking spot to the cafeteria doors, but something stops me. A circle of orange light that becomes Hope's hand holding a cigarette and a surprised scowl framed by waves of white.

"What are you doing here?" she asks.

"Somebody'scomingtheyknowabouttheprank." I pause to breathe.

Realization flashes in her eyes. "That's why you called before."

Something about the fact that she's still screening my calls hurts more than it should. I hope that she'll say sorry or thank you or something, but she takes her damn sweet time puffing one last puff before she lets the cigarette fall to the ground.

Whatever. I'm still doing what I came here to do. As I pass through the cafeteria doors, I hear her say something behind me.

I turn. "What?"

"Where's Dean? Your brother's a douche, but he wouldn't abandon his friends."

"He didn't. My parents won't let him leave the house. They got a call—"

"What's the narc doing here?" yells Mikey.

Hope shrugs.

The prank insanity taking place around me finally starts to sink in. The cafeteria has a huge row of windows, one glass panel right after the other, and they've been blacked out with paint except for where the letters S-E-N-I-O-R-S shine through, one giant letter on each window. It's spelled out everywhere, even in the gaps between the tiny paper cups of water that cover the lunch tables. It's everything Dean said it would be. And a lot of things he didn't. In the hallway that leads away from the cafeteria, there are guys blasting door handles with cans of shaving cream and spray painting lockers with every four-letter word in existence. There's no way my brother would have been cool with that. Mikey pops the lid off two huge buckets of what look like live crickets. This is bad. A Taxonomy of What Not To Get Caught Doing at School bad. The administration is going to annihilate them.

I remember why I'm here and yell, "People are coming! Y'all are gonna get caught!"

The guys debate the validity of this threat with a series of looks. Mikey stares at me, his face weirdly serious, and that's when I notice. His eyes are all red, eyelids hanging lazily, and most of the other guys look the same way. Mikey cracks first, busts out laughing—that prick. And then everyone else is laughing, too, and going back to their water jugs and paper cups and F-bombs.

Except Ethan. "Where's Dean?" he asks. His eyes are clear.

"My parents won't let him out of the house."

Ethan shakes his head. "He'd still let us know."

I run my fingers through my hair and sniff twice. Even my

tics are exasperated with these guys. "He *tried*. Check your phone."

"Why do you even care? You can't stand Ethan," says Hope.

"I just don't want anyone getting in trouble, okay? C'mon," I tell her. "We need to go before they get here."

Her eyes have a faraway look.

"Hope. I need you to come with me."

She's still not listening. They could be here any minute. I grab her hand and pull her toward the door.

She wrenches it away like I've burned her. "I appreciate that you're trying to help, but I can take care of myself."

I take a step closer, blocking the path that leads to Mikey. I sure as hell don't want her driving with him if he's high. "But—"

"You need to back off."

Here we go again. No matter how much I care, or maybe *because* of how much I care, I come off looking needy or creepy or desperate or all of the above.

Hope's anger sounds an awful lot like a sigh now. "Look, it's not that I don't—"

"Holy shit, you guys, stop!" Ethan's got his phone pressed against his terrified face. "Dean says the administration's coming. We need to go. *Now*."

"THAT'S WHAT I'VE BEEN TRYING TO TELL YOU!"

Everybody's running frantic. Toilet paper, paint, Post-its— all forgotten. Headlights flash in the windows on the north side of the cafeteria, and all hell really breaks loose. We sprint in different directions, scattering like geese after a gunshot. Everyone tears through the doors to the south lot. I'm praying the administration hasn't reached that one, too.

Hope stops like she's hit an invisible wall. "Shit. My phone."

"There's no time," yells Mikey.

He keeps running to his car—to safety—but she turns back. "I have to get it, or they'll know it was me."

I stop in the doorway with the feeling of being torn in half. She bends to get her phone and races back, like she's doing a gut sprint for Coach. I keep my eyes on the north lot doors. Stay closed. Stay closed. Stay closed. Another sixty seconds, and we could be in my car.

And then the unthinkable happens—Hope slips. The worst part is, I see it even before it happens, but I'm powerless to stop it. She's flat-out sprinting, her eyes on the doors and not on the discarded can of shaving cream that rolls into her path. My mouth forms words of caution, but it's too late. Her foot hits the can, ankle bending grotesquely. Her scream gets cut in half when her back hits the floor.

She's groaning, and I'm pulling her up by the elbows.

"Can you walk on it?"

She touches her foot against the ground, but buckles in pain.

"Mother scratcher." It comes out as a hiss.

I'd smile if we weren't dead.

"That's not gonna work." There's only one option, and I try not to think—just act. "Sorry about this."

"Wh—"

I scoop her up like she weighs nothing. But it's not nothing. This is complete sensory overload, and middle-school me is freaking out. *Calm down*, I tell myself. *You'll never be able to be friends again if you can't be around her without getting weird.*

She thrashes halfheartedly. "Put me down. I don't need your help."

I raise my eyebrows at her.

"Okay, fine. But just hurry, okay?" she says.

I get us to the doors, but maneuvering through them is tricky. Hope presses her head against my chest, her hair tickling my nose. Don't breathe. Don't you dare breathe. Her hair has hypnotizing properties, and, oh no, I had to. The human body needs oxygen, especially when it's carrying another human body. And, oh hell, she still smells like honeysuckles under all that cigarette smoke.

I remind myself of a few important things: 1) She staked your heart like a vampire slayer. 2) You wouldn't even be here right now if she hadn't screened your call. 3) You're really, really, REALLY happy with your girlfriend.

It helps. I make it to my car and get Hope settled in the passenger seat, and I'm no longer thinking about her as anything other than a friend, which means I'm safe.

Until a strong set of hands clamps down on my shoulders.

CHAPTER

16

The girl of my middle-school dreams is in my arms again, but this isn't exactly how it played out in my fantasies. For starters, my vice principal definitely did not make an appearance. And secondly, in my daydreams, Hope wasn't injured and she was in my arms out of free will instead of necessity. It's funny how almost getting what you always wanted can feel a lot like the eighth circle of hell.

Vice Principal Kahn doesn't seem to notice or care about the hardship he's putting me through as he has me ferry Hope around the cafeteria. A few notes about our illustrious vice principal:

1) Yes, his name is just like the bad guy from *Star Trek*, only spelled different.

2) No, this fact is not lost on the students of Peach Valley High, who are all pretty sure our vice principal is a genetically enhanced supervillain brought out of suspended animation for the purpose of making us miserable.

3) He looks nothing like Benedict Cumberbatch. Or Ricardo Montalbán (the REAL Khan, according to Mimi, who has told me way more than I ever wanted to know about his chest muscles).

Anyway, he doesn't believe our cover stories for being here (perhaps because they are totally in conflict with each other?). The streak of purple paint written across Hope's cheek like a confession tells him we can't be trusted. Plus, my face has a way of looking guilty.

At first he tries the usual Vice Principal Kahn tricks. He's one of those administrators who pretends to be all, "Hey, we're buds. Tell me anything. I know what it's like to be a teen. Here, bro, have a stress ball. I'm a cool guy, and we're just chilling." But really, he's super strict. Which would be fine, but own it, dude. Stop pretending to be my bro while you're nailing my ass to the wall. And while we're on the subject, please don't ever say bro again. Like ever.

When the Bros4Life act fails, the real Kahn surfaces and pelts us with questions.

Did we vandalize the rest of the school or just the cafeteria?

Who else was involved?

Where did they go?

We don't know. We don't know. We don't know.

The lies are heavy in my mouth, and Hope is heavy in my arms. What's going to happen to us? Suspension? I'm thinking suspension. Which will suck, but hey, we still have another few weeks of wrestling practice before our meets start, so at least whatever they do to me will be out of the way before then. I hope.

I tic-shrug (again), which is a whole lot weirder when you're holding someone.

"Sorry," I say, for, like, the fifth time.

"Spencer, it's fine." She shakes her head.

I'm glad it doesn't freak her out. I'm double glad she only flinched the first time. And I'm quadruple-gazillion glad I've got a case of the shrugs instead of the sniffs, because if I was walking around tic-sniffing her hair like some kind of stalker with a hair fetish, I might need someone to put me out of my misery.

I lean against a table for support, and Vice Principal Kahn finally notices.

"Sorry about that," he says. "I should probably call someone about Hope's leg."

She lifts her head, and her hair tickles my nose again. "My mom deals with this kind of stuff all the time. You can just call her," she says.

She has clearly reached the giving-up phase of our interrogation, and I think she's right. Let's just get on with the inevitable punishment. The fear and waiting is always worse than the punishment itself.

He leads the way to the office suite, and we follow behind him.

Well, I follow. Hope mostly leans against my chest like a living, breathing hot-water bottle. I think I'm sweating. Nope, I'm definitely sweating. I really hope she can't feel it through my shirt.

"We can talk more in my office," he says.

She springs up so fast, I almost drop her. "No!" She coughs awkwardly. "I mean, how about we just talk out here."

He touches his office door handle, and Hope fidgets in my arms like she wants to reach out and stop him.

Kahn pauses, his eyebrows raised. "Is there something wrong, Miss Birdsong?"

Her eyes go wide. He's got her. She can't say yes because it would be admitting she was part of the prank. But if she says no, then whatever's waiting on the other side of that office door is going to happen in three. Two. One.

He turns the handle while she winces. I expect something big, an explosion of shaving cream maybe or some perfectly timed glue and feathers. The cloud of colorful confetti that falls all around us seems mild by comparison. I notice an orange snowflake on the tip of Hope's nose, and that's when I realize— it's a penis. All over my arms, falling from the sky, dusting Vice Principal Kahn's hair like phallic dandruff. We are standing in our own personal dick blizzard, a whirlwind of wangs in pink, purple, yellow, and green. Hope is trying her damnedest not to laugh. I can feel her body twitching against my chest, but I can't help it. I snort. And then we both lose it, and I have to plant her in a chair, fast, before I lose my grip on her.

I shake my arms a little to stretch out. My muscles ache from holding her. I don't dare look at her, though, or there's no way I'll be able to keep swallowing this laugh. And I need to swallow it because Vice Principal Kahn is not laughing. He brushes the penises from his shoulders and hair with as much dignity as someone who is covered in tiny, two-dimensional genitalia can. Which is to say, none.

Then he looks at us, all tightly wrapped snickers, and he grins like, Guys, I'm totally in on the joke. "Sweet A. This was a good one. I was known to pull some pretty boss pranks in my time, too. What'd you guys do to the other offices? Are they even worse than this one?"

He tears out to check, and I glance at Hope, but she shakes her head no. We hear him open the other doors and find nothing. I'm not surprised he's the only one who got pranked. People actually like our other administrators. Why couldn't it have been Vice Principal Parks who caught us? She'd bust us, too, but she'd be so much cooler about it.

When Kahn comes back, he is *Star Trek*–supervillain pissed. We sit there while he doles out a lecture that stings like a beating, and then he calls our parents. I can hear my dad yelling into the phone from three feet away.

There's some awkward waiting until our parents arrive (really, they could have taken one car, now that I think about it). My dad busts in like a dog straining to break its muzzle. Pam, the muzzler, trails behind him, and Mrs. Birdsong behind her.

Dad points a massive index finger in my face. "We'll talk about this later."

He starts to say something else, but Pam shushes him into the office. The door closes in our faces. Which means Hope and I get to do even more awkward waiting, only this time we're on the outside of the office and our parents are on the inside.

And then it hits me. Me and Hope, alone, really alone, for the first time since June. She's taking off her shoe and sock, rubbing gingerly at her swollen ankle. Our eyes meet, and I give her a tentative smile, brace myself while I wait for her response. She smiles back. (Tentatively also, but, hey, I'll take what I can get.) I smile bigger and open my mouth, and I'm going to say—I'm going to say—it doesn't matter because her eyes go wide and she turns practically in the other direction. Whatever earth-shattering thing I was going to say dies in the back of my throat.

I glance over every now and again, but she's still just sitting there, body totally rigid, leaning as far away from me as she can get. Our parents talk to the vice principal in Charlie Brown voices that don't quite make it through the thick door. The seconds spread out like pancake batter on a griddle. Hope starts popping her knuckles. Sometimes I open my mouth, act like I'm going to give it another try, but I know I'm not going to say anything.

This is how it's been with us. One minute we'll be laughing over penis confetti and the ice will be cracking, and the next minute she completely freezes over. The worst part is, I still get my hopes up. Every time. I rub the heels of my hands against my eyes. Sometimes I don't know if I'll ever be able to fully forgive her.

After minutes that feel like hours, the office door opens again. Dad barrels out, looking, if possible, even angrier than when he went in. He opens his mouth, and there's a split second of the most awful anticipation, but then Pam gently lays a hand on his shoulder.

"We'll be outside," she says pointedly.

He makes a kind of gruff grunting noise. "We'll talk about this in the car."

I mouth "thank you" to Pam as he sweeps past me.

Hope's mom hoists her out of her chair, and Vice Principal Kahn stands in the doorway. He doles out his parting words to the three of us, since my parents have already left.

Nice Kahn tells us we're not suspended, because he doesn't want to peel off thousands of Post-its by himself.

Mean Kahn tells us to be in his office at six AM tomorrow morning. Sharp. Better get there at 5:45, just to be safe.

I walk outside with Hope and her mom. Their Jeep is in the parking lot, parked a couple lanes away from my truck. Oh, right, I almost forgot I drove here by myself. A smile starts to creep across my face at the memory of my first solo drive. And then I spot my dad in the driver's seat.

"Good luck," Hope says with a half smile.

I'm grateful, really, but it would mean a whole lot more if it wasn't coming on the heels of a freeze-out. I stand at the door to the truck, watching as Hope's mom helps her into the Jeep.

When I finally get in, I'm relieved to see my dad's head is neither red nor balloon-like, although his frown does look permanently stitched to his lips. "I have a feeling that's what got you into this mess in the first place," he says.

"Leave her alone." That's all I have the energy to say. It's enough to get him started.

"I don't have to leave anything alone. It was a dumbass move coming to the school. You heard us tell Dean not to go, and then what did you do? You went anyway."

Never mind that Dean was the one doing the prank in the first place. But I don't say that. These things go a lot faster if you keep quiet while he gets it out of his system.

He smacks his hand against the steering wheel. "Any fool idea pops into your head, and you just do it. Absolutely no self-control. None."

Even though I know his tirade is about the prank, a needle of doubt digs its way into my brain. *He's talking about your Tourette's.* Once I think it, I can't unthink it. It's a loop inside my head. All the things that make me feel like I belong somewhere else, and Dad's real second son is stuck shooting hunting rifles in a family of dreamers and pacifists.

"When I tell you something, it's for your own good. Sometimes I wonder what's going on in there." He thumps two fingers against his forehead. "Dean wanted to help them, too, but he played it smart. And now he's at home, and you're in trouble."

I put my head in my hands and let his rant wash over me

until I hear his thoughts instead of his words: *Why can't you be more like your brother? You'll never be as good as Dean. Or as smart. Or as athletic. Or as important.*

Dad's lecture seems to be winding to a stop, so I tune in again in case he asks me a question. Nothing turns his face red faster than me letting his pearls of wisdom fly out the window.

He's strangely quiet. Oh, crap, did I already miss something? But he doesn't seem angry.

"Pam was beside herself when you took off. She was real worried you'd get in a wreck." His voice is softer now, calmer. "Seems like you made it here in one piece, though."

I shrug. "Yes, sir." I really do hate that Pam was freaking out.

"Don't take this as me saying it was okay to take the truck by yourself without asking, *but*"—I can't even believe it, but I think I see a twinkle in his eye—"how'd it go?"

In spite of all the shit that went down tonight, I grin. "Great. It went great. My meds didn't make me too tired, and I hardly tic-ed at all, and even when I had to, I could hold off till I got to a red light." I wonder if this is the best time, but I just go for it. "I really think I'm ready," I say.

He claps me on the shoulder as gently as his Paul Bunyan hands allow. "I think you might be ready, too. I think it's time we let you try some trips to the store and stuff by yourself. After you're done being grounded, of course."

"Yeah, yeah, of course." I try to seem extra mature because shouting "This is awesome!" would probably not be the best plan right now.

Dad nods. "There's no better feeling than cruising down a stretch of road in your first car."

We stare out at the open road together, him grinning at memories I can't see, me grinning at ones I haven't made yet. Maybe wrestling doesn't have to be our only thing. Maybe this driving stuff could be our thing, too.

A happy silence hovers between us. I wonder if this is what it feels like to be Dean.

CHAPTER

17

Sometimes, you can tic so much it makes you sore. Turns out tic-ing that much while you're holding another person is enough to make you feel like you spent seventy-two consecutive hours in the weight room with Coach. It probably doesn't help that I only get about two hours of sleep before I have to get back to school. Dean drags himself out of bed to drive me because he knows he owes me.

5:50 AM—I wait outside Vice Principal Kahn's office.

5:54 AM—He arrives, and the waiting moves to the inside of his office. Bonus: There's now a thick silence. Which lasts until . . .

6:00 AM (on the nose)—Hope squeaks in. I can't tell which of us is more surprised by her newfound punctuality. Kahn shuffles a stack of self-esteem mad libs for a full five seconds before he starts throwing inspiration and discipline at us.

"I've spoken with Principal Gonzalez and others in the administration, and we've come up with a plan. I really want you to take this time to think about your priorities, get in touch with a better you. I'm always here if you need to talk." No joke, he balls his hand into a fist and taps it against his heart when he says this. "You'll be cleaning up the prank this morning. And every morning for the next three weeks."

What I should be thinking is, *Three weeks isn't so bad. I'll make Dean trade me three weeks' worth of yard work.* Instead, I'm thinking dangerously optimistic things about how three weeks is plenty of time to talk to Hope about all the stuff we've been avoiding.

"Three weeks?" Hope says. "Do you really think it'll take that long?" She wrinkles her nose.

"We'll find other tasks for you when you finish. And I'll be checking in on you, so don't think about skipping out." He directs that part at her. "You're a suspension away from getting expelled, and your mom hooked me up with her cell and told me to call her for any reason at all."

Hope groans. I half-stand because it feels like the conversation is over. Kahn's eyes pin me back to my chair, and I curse myself for making sudden movements.

"And, Spencer, you'll be missing your first wrestling meet of the season."

I'm on my feet before the words pass his desk. "What? You can't do that." Is he effing serious? The first meet is still three weeks away. The only reason he'd make me skip it is if he had carefully calculated which punishment could hurt me the most, which, being an evil supervillain, is probably second nature to him. I've been busting my ass to make 138, and now the first match is going to go to some other dude gift-wrapped. "You're not making her skip anything."

I shoot a mental apology to Hope for bringing her into this, but I'm not sure she receives it.

"She doesn't do anything to skip." He shrugs like it couldn't be simpler, the bastard.

He's taking away *everything*, and he can't even be bothered to acknowledge that it's a big deal. "So I'm being punished for being involved? That's bullshit."

Kahn sucks in air through his teeth, a cockroach hiss, and I know I've crossed the line. Hell, I can't even see the line anymore.

"Look, I get that missing the meet will suck for you, but unless you can provide me with some names, this is how it's gonna be, dude."

I shake my head. "I'm not telling you anything." Dude. (The hell with yard work. Dean owes me a kidney.)

Nice Kahn has left the building. "For your attitude, I'll be extending the morning detention. Let's go for an even month."

Hope's posture goes from cool-delinquent-slouch to debutante-strapped-to-a-yardstick. "For Spencer?" she clarifies.

Big mistake.

"For both of you. Actually, it should probably be five weeks for you since you're not missing an activity."

"FIVE weeks? Are you serious?"

"I'm happy to shorten your sentence if you tell me who else is involved."

"Five is good."

Hope's mouth twists like she's trying to eat her cheeks from the inside. Neither of us is dumb enough to say anything else. Kahn has us start with the water cups on the cafeteria tables because they'll interfere with lunch. It really was one of Dean's more genius prank ideas. Cover the cafeteria tables with hundreds of tiny paper shot cups. Filled with water. Nobody can eat lunch until they dump the cups out, one by one. Plus, they left spaces between the cups to spell out *SENIORS*. Our vice principal demonstrates how we are to walk them to a sink near the tray wash, pour out the water, and throw the empty cups in the trash. Because we clearly couldn't have figured that out on our own. Then he's gone, and it's just me, Hope, and a forest's worth of paper cups.

For a moment, I stop entertaining ways I'd like to torture our vice principal. The dangerously optimistic things begin to creep back into my brain.

"Where do you want to—" I turn, but she's already stalked off in the direction of the closest table. "Start."

I can see steam curling out of her nose, and I know it's useless. We're still not talking. Nothing has changed, except that now, in addition to shutting me out, she's possibly severely pissed at me. She could also be pissed at herself. Or Kahn. (Would definitely give her some rage solidarity on that one!) But as someone who spent three years being her best friend, I am pretty well versed in the fine art of interpreting her stomping. Well, half-stomping. Stomping with her right leg plus limping with her left means she is actually walking kind of like an ogre (a very cute ogre).

This isn't how it was supposed to happen. This was going to be the start of all the things that came after. I had this whole Hope and Spencer BFF Reboot hypothesis going. There were signs. That little wave she gave me when I was walking into school. And that thing she said about peach tea. Those things meant something. Didn't they?

Hope picks up two cups of water with the most indignant, most obnoxious, most infuriated and infuriating sigh. Well, I guess I did get her two extra weeks of early-morning hell. No. You know what? Screw that. I wouldn't even be here if it weren't for her. I storm over to the nearest table and grab two cups, then stomp them over to the sink and dump them. If I hadn't tried to warn her, if Ethan and Mikey and all those other losers had listened the first eighty-seven times, I wouldn't be getting up at the crack of fucking dawn. I wouldn't be cleaning up a prank I didn't even do. And I wouldn't be missing the most important thing in my life.

I think about what it's going to be like to watch that first meet and not wrestle, and I sling my cups into the trash can like I'm trying to break the damn thing. I picture Vice Principal Kahn and his stupid lectures and I sling the next batch harder. Mikey's face. Hope's freeze-outs. All of them are cups battering the walls of the trash can.

I barrel over to a table for more cups, wondering who I'll dedicate this next batch to, when I hear the unmistakable sound of cups thwacking against plastic. And then I realize, Hope is slinging hers, too. Now that I've noticed, I can't not notice. I'm still thundering around the cafeteria, still throwing cups with the gusto of a closer in the final moments of a baseball game, but now I'm watching, too.

Hope power walks back and forth, faster with each trip, never making eye contact. Her shoes slap louder against the gray and white tiles.

Snatch up cups with as much venom as possible.

Slapslapslap across the floor.

Hurl water into sink and cups into trash.

Maybe we're dueling, armed with nothing but paper cups. Or maybe we are partners in our anger, composing a song of stomps and slams and water trickling down the sink. After a few minutes, she adds a loud, huffy sigh to our concerto. I answer back by launching my cups as hard as I can. Her steps falter, and I feel the tingling of her eyes on the back of my neck, but when I turn, she's getting more cups. So I do the same.

Grabbing more cups, and more, and more. We've only got a couple tables left now.

And then it happens. We both reach the trash can at exactly the same time. There's a second's hesitation. Do we toss the cups in gently now that we've caught each other? Our eyes flick from the now-almost-full trash can to each other. And we go for it. Slam down our cups like three-year-olds on a sugar bender, the last droplets of water splattering the wall in front of us. Hope raises her eyebrows, and one side of my mouth curls up in a sideways smirk.

I wonder if I should say something. Before I have time to worry about it, Hope stomps away. But I can tell by the way her shoulders are bouncing that she's smiling. I stomp off in the other direction. Only now I'm smiling, too.

CHAPTER 18

Everyone has seen the prank. Everyone knows I was involved. And everyone has something to say about it.

Paul: Hey, did you really do it? Everyone's talking about it. You're a legend, man. A legend. Hey, only next time tell me so I can be a legend, too, okay?

Ethan and Mikey (who seem to be forgetting I saved their sorry skins last night): If you tell anyone, we'll kill you.

Dean: I can't believe your punk ass is getting all the credit. You still haven't said anything, though, right?

The only person I haven't heard from is Jayla. I figured I'd see her first thing. Paul and I walk the halls looking for her.

"I can't believe you're missing the first meet."

"I know."

"This is the worst news ever."

"*I know.*"

(Everything you need to know about Paul: He's the kind of person where I can say, "Hey, isn't my Greenbottle Blue the coolest?! He's got this awesome turquoise-colored carapace." Instead of: "Hey, check out the big-ass spider I got for my birthday!" So, basically, the best kind.)

Then he reminds me of a missing critical item in my prank fallout list: "Have you talked to Coach yet?"

"Shit."

He snorts. "I guess that's a no."

"Shit."

"Yeah, it's probably going to suck."

When we finally run into Jayla, she's outside the chorus room holding court over a gaggle of other freshmen. They're fanned out around her, and she's shining the way she always does when she's in the spotlight. Then she sees me.

"Spencer!" She hops up and flings her arms around my neck. Like I'm so important. Totally worth jumping to her feet and interrupting her conversation for. She was the first girl to ever think I was worth noticing, period. Three months later, and it's still my favorite thing about her. "Where have you been? I've been texting you all morning."

I wave bye to Paul as he does the best-friend fadeaway. "I'm sorry. My parents took my phone. I've been looking everywhere for you."

"It's okay," she says. I can feel her smile against my mouth as she kisses me in front of all her friends.

The hive buzzes with snickers and oooohs, but the attention only feeds her grin until it blossoms into a giggle. Some people like to talk shit about Jayla, saying she's a drama queen and stuff. And yeah, she loves singing and being in plays and all that, and sometimes when she talks, it seems like she's performing for an imaginary audience. But they can call her an attention whore all they want, because you know what? My girlfriend is awesome. It never fazes her when my tics flare up in public and people start staring, because she's cool with being looked at. She always gives a big smile and a wave like they're staring at us because we're movie stars, and it totally calms me down, and I forget to feel like The Kid with Tourette's Syndrome.

"Hey, you think we could go talk for a minute?" I glance to the circle of freshmen at my feet as if to say "without your entourage."

"Sure!" She turns to them. "Spencer really needs me right now, but I'll catch up with y'all later, okay?"

She can't hide her excitement over the fact that she's about to know ALL THE SECRETS. Her hand finds mine as we make our way to an empty stretch of hall and lean against a window. It's as private as we're gonna get unless we go somewhere that might get us into trouble. People stare and whisper as they pass us. A couple guys salute.

"So. What happened? Everyone in school is talking about it!" Her eyes sparkle at my minor celebrity, and she leans closer. "Were you really there?"

"I'll tell you everything, I promise. But, first, did they post the *Oklahoma!* list yet? Did you get the part?" The way she's been grinning, she must have—

"No." And the grin disappears.

"Are you serious?"

"Justin Irby and this red-haired girl who's a junior got the leads. And I'm playing Ado Annie. Opposite Calvin Jennings. Because I guess Ms. Pickett couldn't handle the idea of any interracial kissing onstage."

I pull her into a hug. "I'm so sorry. That is not okay."

"Thanks," she says into my shoulder. Then she pulls away. "And just in case you're wondering, I *heard* the other girl audition, and I *know* I was the best."

"Hey, I'm not doubting you. I've heard you sing." I lace my fingers through hers. "Are you going to, like, appeal it or anything?"

"I don't know. I have to spend three more years in her drama program, so I really don't want to make waves this early. And I want people to know I deserved that role, but I don't want to sound like the bitter actress who didn't get the part. Or for people to say I'm an angry black girl. And, well, honestly, I'm a little scared."

"Of Ms. Pickett?"

She shakes her head. "Not her exactly. Just, people. I don't know what kind of backlash there would be. Sometimes the world doesn't feel like the safest place, you know?" She's quiet for a second. "But I did have one idea."

"What is it?"

She smiles, and it banishes some of the sadness from her face. "Maybe I could act like Ado Annie is the star of *Oklahoma!* Upstage Laurey a bit?"

"YES."

"You think?"

"Hell, yes. Sing circles around her. Dance the crap out of all your songs. Make sure everyone who's watching wonders why you didn't get that part."

She squeezes my hand. "I think I will. But, hey. Tell me about the prank stuff because we're running out of time, and gossip cheers me up. Did you do it?"

"Not exactly. I mean, I was there last night, kind of, but it was a senior prank. Someone called Pam and told her that the administration knew, so I came to warn everybody. And then right after I got here, Vice Principal Kahn showed up. Everyone else bolted, and I got caught."

"That is so cool. Not the part about you getting caught. The part where you pretty much saved all the seniors' asses. They must love you right now."

I think about Ethan and Mikey cornering me outside the bathroom. "Oh, yeah. Totally."

"And the cafeteria. Oh, wow, people are gonna be talking about this prank forever. I love how they blacked out the windows so it's all dark in there."

"Oh, y'all don't even know the best part." I tell her about Vice Principal Kahn and the penis confetti. Jayla laughs so hard she wheezes.

"That guy scares the crap out of me. People are gonna freak when they hear this."

Her face is flushed with gossip she can't wait to share, and I'm glad I could make her so happy. The warning bell rings, and we walk to art class together.

"Did you get in a ton of trouble?"

"Grounded for a month."

She groans.

"Pam'll probably give me my phone back after a few days, though. Dean never answers his, and it drives her crazy." My upbeat act falters. "No dates, though."

"Well, that's okay." She bumps her hip against mine. "We'll just have to get creative."

I have no idea what she's talking about, but the mischief flickering in her eyes makes me want to find out.

"And you can still wrestle, right?" She bites her lip.

I tell her about having to miss my meet, and she turns into a tiny ball of rage and does a hilarious impression of Kahn.

"I have to see him every morning for a whole month," I say. "Doesn't that suck? He had me carrying water cups to the sink for over an hour this morning."

"Yeah, I heard about that," says Jayla. And then she says the part I've been dreading. "I heard Hope was there, too."

"Well, yeah, but that's just because we both got caught so we have the same detention." Are we still in a hallway? Because it suddenly feels a lot like a sauna in here. The collar of my shirt tries to strangle my neck.

"So, you and Hope were the only two who got caught?"

"Yeah, but that's only because she twisted her ankle."

I can see the pieces fitting together in her head. "And everyone else ran, but you went back to save her?"

"Yeah, but you know me. I'd do that for anyone."

She smiles, and it looks just the way a Jayla smile should, but her voice is soft. "I know you would."

CHAPTER 19

Day Two of our painfully early, painfully awkward punishment.

Kahn has us scrubbing lockers. Well, first he has us listen to an excruciating lecture on proper locker-scrubbing technique (it turns out spray paint comes off with non-acetone nail-polish remover, but you have to wipe *that* off with soapy water or it'll take the paint off the lockers). Then, he has us scrubbing lockers. Hope grabs a bucket and gets right to it. She's still not talking, but she's not stomping, either. Sometimes I think about saying something. And by sometimes, I mean every five minutes because this is so. Freaking. Awkward. I'm serious. This silence has hands and they're choking me.

I dunk my rag in the soapy water and think about saying, "Man, this sucks." But I don't.

Hope scrubs at a four-letter word, and I contemplate telling her how glad I am that they never got around to releasing the crickets. Those would have been a beast to track down. I don't say any of that, either.

When I go to rinse my rag, I decide I can't take it anymore. I'm going to say something. Anything. Nothing could be worse than this silence.

I open my mouth. Give myself a second to clear my throat. And then another second. The problem is, I keep thinking about what I'll say. And then I practice it in my head. Approximately 2,367 times. And once you've said something in your head 2,367 times, it doesn't sound cool anymore. Hell, it doesn't even sound like words anymore. And then I'm back to clearing my throat, trying to think of something else.

Maybe I should wait until she turns around. Yeah, that's it. If she turns, it's a sign that I should say something. So, I wait. And I wait. And then I wait a little more. I mean, she'll have to turn eventually, right? But she doesn't.

Well, if she's not going to turn on her own, maybe I could do something to help her along. I let my rag fall into the water with a splash that echoes down the empty hallway. She flinches. My heart forgets to beat. Her shoulders start to twist around! And . . . it's just so she can reach the next locker better.

I know it doesn't *really* mean anything. That I could still say something. But I go back to scrubbing lockers, because I don't have the guts.

Day Three

Is even worse.

We have to pick up all the penis confetti in Vice Principal Kahn's office. By hand. I asked if we could have a vacuum or broom or something, and was told that this way is better because it builds character.

Neither of us says anything today. With Kahn hovering over us, and the fear that the slightest misstep could trigger a lecture, there's no way we're risking it. At one point, though, he blows his nose, and it sounds like a foghorn, and we can't help but smile at each other.

Day Four

We're peeling an ocean of Post-its off the outside of the

administrative suite. I'm standing on a ladder and ripping off the highest ones, while Hope works on the bottom ones. It's really pretty cool looking when you stare at it from a distance. Two whole walls blanketed in bright, bright, bright Post-its spelling out *SENIORS*, with a different font color and background color for each letter. It almost looks like pop art. I wrench off a row of Post-its in rapid succession. It would be easier to appreciate their artistic potential if it wasn't 6:15 in the morning.

I peek down at Hope to see how she's doing, and suddenly her face is tilted up, looking back at mine, and I whip my head back to my Post-its like, *No, I wasn't looking at you. I'd never even dream of looking at you, like ever. Especially not right now when you're reaching for a Post-it, and it's making your shirt pull away from your jeans, and there are entire square inches of skin showing.* And then it gets worse—there are back dimples. I wait for something to happen, like me falling off this ladder. But I'm good. No weird butterflies or sweaty palms. No heart palpitations. See? I can be around her and be normal. I don't have to totally freak out and make an ass out of myself. I mean, yes, there was that thing with our eyes in the parking lot when I was talking to Jayla, but I'm counting that as an anomaly. Because back dimples, well, that's about the highest form of temptation, right?

Learning to be around her as friends and only friends—it just takes practice is all. It's like my brain has formed all these little "I love Hope!" connections, and now I have to rewire everything so that my brain knows I love Jayla, not Hope. And honestly, I don't know if I ever loved her. Can you really love someone who you put on a pedestal? It's different with Jayla. Real. Reciprocated. So, I just have to keep practicing being around Hope so I can develop an immunity. It's kind of like she's a virus.

Hope shifts, and the back dimples disappear. I start on another column of Post-its. They keep my hands busy, but my mind can roam anywhere it wants, which is maybe or maybe not a good thing. Isn't this what I wanted? To be alone with her? So why can't I make something happen?

I'm at the part where I sigh and give up for the day. Except this time I don't. I don't know what makes this moment different, but before I can second-guess myself, I hear my voice say, "Man, it sucks to be up this early in the morning. I could really use some caffeine."

Holy shit, I did it. I want to clap my hand over my mouth and shove all the words back in, but it's too late for that. All I can do now is watch her and see how she responds. If she responds.

Hope squints up at me. She does this nodding/shrugging thing, and says, "Yeah." Then she goes back to her Post-its.

Well, that went great.

You'd think the silence wouldn't be so bad now that I've punctured it, but it swells against me like it's going to sweep me off my ladder and out the north lot doors. I keep pulling Post-its, and she keeps pulling Post-its, and I'm thinking there's going to be silence for the rest of our shift when:

"Ow!"

The sharpness in her voice startles me, but thankfully it's not a fall-off-your-ladder level of startle. She's hunched over, inspecting one of her fingers.

"You all right?"

"Yeah, paper cut," she says. And then it's almost like she's embarrassed about the intensity of her reaction because she hurries to add, "But, like, the super deep kind where you can see both sides of your skin around it."

"Yikes." Yikes? Did I really think it was a good idea to say *yikes*? Kill me now.

She puts her finger in her mouth and sucks on it, and I have to turn away because it's kind of sexy. Her putting on socks would be kind of sexy.

Okay, so immunity to back dimples: check. Immunity to finger sucking: still pending.

I hop down off the ladder. "Is it bleeding?"

I reach for her hand, but her face has gone tight. "It's fine."

"Do you want me to see if the office has Band-Aids or something?"

"I said I'm fine, okay?" Then she flips her hair over her shoulder like it's a shield against my weirdness.

Okay, cool. I offer to do something nice for you and you act like I'm some kind of creeper who asked if I could have your toenail clippings. That's just awesome. It's like I can't even approach normal human decency without her thinking I'm about to go all "Can You Feel the Love Tonight." And you know what? I'm not going to let it slide this time.

"Hope," I say. Period, not question mark.

"Yes?"

And she's turning and wincing and shoulder-hunching like, *Here it comes, he's about to do it again.* And I'm so dang frustrated that before I can stop myself I say, "I don't like you."

Her head whips up. "What?"

Ooops. "I mean. I don't mean I hate you or something, I just mean I don't like you. I know I used to, and I know it made things weird, but it's over now, so maybe things could be normal again."

"Um, okay." She shrugs, and I feel like the biggest tool in all of the southeastern United States.

Way to go, Spencer. Way to take the fragile friendship that was maybe forming and just step on its neck and kill it with your brutally honest confession of un-love.

The bad kind of silence is back, a brittle thing that suggests every baby step we've made over the past few days is about to splinter into a billion pieces. It's so awful that when Hope gets up and heads in the direction of the girls' bathroom a few minutes later, I'm relieved. My lungs feel like they can open completely again, and I take a few deep breaths.

A little while later, I hear her footsteps tapping their way back. She brushes against the ladder on her way to her spot, but I'm not going to look down. Not until I hear the unmistakable *crack-hiss* of a can of Coke being opened. Hope tilts back a can of Cherry Coke, and it looks mouthwateringly good. Then I notice there's another can, resting on the first rung of my ladder. It's a Coke Zero. Hope doesn't drink Coke Zero.

I climb down and grab the can, waiting for her to stop me or say it's hers or tackle me off the ladder or something. But she doesn't. So, this is mine—I mean, she definitely bought this for me. The warmth of possibility rushes through me and a feeling of "Hey, maybe all isn't lost after all." I realize I've been staring sappily at my Coke can for entirely too long, so I hurry to say, "Thanks."

Hope shrugs, but she doesn't look pissed or anything. "Sure."

Part Five

17 years old

A TAXONOMY OF EVERYONE YOU'LL EVER MEET IN HIGH SCHOOL

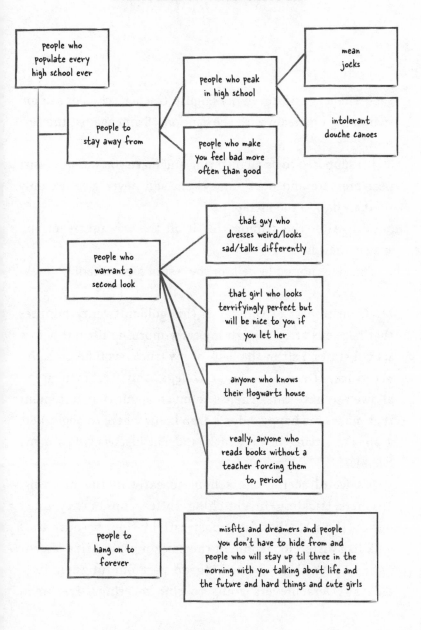

CHAPTER 20

Fact: There is a poster in my English teacher's class of salmon swimming upstream with the caption, "Swim against the current."

It's supposed to be all inspiring and make you want to resist peer pressure and buck the system and never give up, only there's a flaw in the metaphor.

Fact: After the salmon trek it all the way upstream and spawn, they die.

This does not bode well for the rest of high school.

My favorite part of the day is this golden twenty minutes that happens after I finish my early-morning lift but before school starts. I sit in the back of my truck—you heard right, MY truck. (Dean is away at college, and freshmen aren't allowed to have cars. There's so much about that statement that makes me happy, I don't even know where to begin.) So, yeah, I'm sitting in my truck, and I'm just waiting for my friends.

It's weird seeing the school so early in the morning. Teachers trickling in clutching coffee cups. (They must put on their teacher faces post-caffeination, because they look like different people in the early-morning fluorescent light.) Football guys finishing up part one of their two-a-days. Overachievers going to club meetings. Freshmen getting dropped off early because their parents have to get to work. There's this new kid who I'm pretty sure fits in that last category.

He reminds me of a puppy I took care of that summer Hope and I volunteered at the animal shelter. The little guy was deaf and blind, so the only way it could navigate its surroundings and figure out stuff about the world was by running in a circle, and then a bigger circle, and then an even bigger circle. High school is like that. Running around not understanding and waiting to run into things.

"Hey, cutie." Jayla hops up into the truck bed next to me. "You watching that new kid again?"

I grin sheepishly. "Yeah. I think that's probably what I used to look like."

"Freshman Spencer?"

"Yeah."

Jayla eyes the kid like she's making a serious appraisal, but her smile is sly. "I bet you were cuter."

I close the six inches of space between us and put my arm around her. "You were definitely cuter."

She glows, absolutely glows under the compliment. "You think?"

"Oh, definitely. I remember the first time I saw you. At that party."

"Ohmygosh, Justin's party!" She wrinkles her nose. "With that awful punch."

"I still maintain the secret ingredient was cough medicine."

"Or dish soap."

"And you were standing on a coffee table doing a dramatic reenactment of Ursula singing 'Poor Unfortunate Souls,' and every guy in the room was watching you, and no one was underestimating the importance of body language."

"I don't know about that," she says, but she's grinning as she scoots closer to me.

"They were. They were all thinking, 'How can I get this amazing girl to pay attention to me?'"

She smiles because this is the part where she picks up the story. "But there was this one guy who was not at all enraptured by my performance. In fact, he looked like he was looking for something."

"I was one hundred percent enraptured!"

"You were looking for something. I remember because it's what made you different. I had to jump off the coffee table and follow you, because you were so interesting. And, okay, I might have heard a couple stories about what a good wrestler you are."

"I remember you came right up to me and asked me what my name was."

"I grabbed your arm and made you talk to me."

"I thought you might have been flirting with me."

"Um, that is like saying, 'I thought you might have been hungry' to a guy who just pounded the entire McDonald's value menu, but sure, okay." She traces my hand with her fingers, looking suddenly serious. "Hey, what were you looking for that night?"

"Oh, um. I guess I don't remember." I'd been looking for Hope so that I could apologize. Someone told me she was going to be there, but then I met Jayla and forgot. "It's crazy—I mean, funny. It's funny." I promised myself I wasn't going to say stuff like "crazy" and "lame" ever since we learned about ableist language at camp this summer. "How we both remember that night so differently. I guess it was just so hard to believe that someone like you could be flirting with someone like me."

Jayla pulls my face toward her and kisses me. "It shouldn't be hard to believe," she says. She moves to kiss me again, and this time I can tell it's going to be one of those kisses that makes me wish we could hide in the back of the truck all day, but just as her lips touch mine:

"Okay. Okay. Not all of us have smoking-hot girlfriends, and not all of us appreciate being subjected to PDA this early in the morning." Paul climbs into the truck with us and makes shooing motions. "C'mon, I just ate eggs over easy. I don't need to see your spit all over her face."

Jayla rolls her eyes (lovingly). "We need to get you a girlfriend."

"I know." Paul rubs his hands together. "So, who are we thinking?"

He and Jayla dangle their legs over the edge of the truck bed and banter over his prospects as various girls get out of their cars and enter the school building. It is a serious business. It also happens approximately every other day.

They stop for only a second when Hope thrusts a small plastic-wrapped loaf in between them and yells, "Homemade Nutella Banana Bread!"

She climbs up beside them. "You guys have your intense faces on," she says. "Are we searching for the love of Paul's life?"

"Are we ever doing anything else?" I ask. I tic-sniff a few times, back to back to back.

"You're just grumpy because you can't have any banana bread." Paul polishes off his first slice and grabs a second. That kid is like an animal or something. If he doesn't eat his weight in high-calorie food daily, he'll starve. I, on the other hand, am already being careful to get a jump on wrestling season. I'm planning to wrestle 138 again, but my body seems to want to be bigger than that.

Hope is busy pointing out that Abby Stevens has a whole new confidence about her since she got her braces off.

"Confidence is sexy," agrees Paul. "I should get some."

Jayla bumps him with her shoulder. "It *is* a lot easier to get a girlfriend when you're actually willing to, you know, talk to a girl."

And then a Jeep full of sophomore girls pulls in right next to us, and the three of them lose it, and they're talking over each other so much I can barely make out what they're saying. I end up watching the new kid again. He's been writing (drawing?) in a notebook, and then he jumps up like he forgot something and runs toward the north lot doors. And because I'm watching from a distance, I can see what's going to happen before the new kid runs smack into these two offensive linemen, Hudson and Jace. I don't actually know the new kid's name, but I usually call him Brony in my head on account of him being totally obsessed with *My Little Pony*. (As you might imagine, this doesn't help him out in the arena of Dealing with Guys Like Hudson and Jace.) The Rainbow Dash notebook. The figurines he keeps in his locker. The T-shirts/socks/backpack/wristbands and the jacket that has, I shit you not, a rainbow tail hanging off the back.

I cock my head to the side, a question forming in my brain as Hudson blocks Brony's path, and Jace, aka Mini-Ethan, circles him like a panther. "Do you ever feel like you'll never fit in?" I ask.

Paul bobbles the piece of banana bread he's holding (his fourth, not that I'm counting), and the girls stare at me. I wish I could click a button and have the words zip back into my mouth, fast as rolling up a tape measure.

"I didn't mean it like that. I just mean . . ." What am I even saying? Mostly things are pretty good for me now. I have friends. I have a girlfriend. I have wrestling. Junior year is my best year yet. But it's like I have to tell myself I have those things, because if I don't, I'll remember what it was like to have everyone else be one way and me be another. And the truth is I still don't feel like I fit. I've just gotten better at pretending that I do.

"I mean, like, when I'm not in this truck with you guys, you know?"

Paul nods. So does Hope. Jayla appears to have no idea what I'm talking about, but then realizes that she is the only one who hasn't nodded, so she nods, too.

Hope scratches the back of her hand. "When I used to wish I could fit in, I don't know. It was almost like I was hoping for it to be this magical thing, like I'd pull a sword out of a stone and beams of light would fall on my head, and *tada*. I'd fit. Um, but maybe it's more fluid than that."

"Yeah, and maybe it isn't about finding a way to make yourself fit," says Paul. "Maybe it's about finding the other people who don't fit the same way you don't fit."

I think about that for a minute. "I like that."

"Me, too," says Jayla.

They are all the best for not thinking I'm weird.

My eyes are drawn to Brony again. It's a train wreck, and neither Hope nor I can look away. Paul and I are both smart enough to keep our dorkitude well hidden, but Brony has no idea. If you let your freak flag fly, they'll massacre you. But if you're careful, it's almost like there's a secret society of revolutionaries dispersed among the normal kids at school. The trick is finding the others without getting your ass beat.

"Yeah. I like that a lot," I say.

But I'm snapped out of thoughts of revolutionaries because the Brony situation escalates. Jace takes his backpack, and Brony goes from chill-but-irritated to full-on-pissed.

"Give it back. You could break something," he says.

Which only makes him a more interesting target. The guys laugh. My legs must realize my plan before my brain does because soon I'm headed in their direction.

"Don't get your panties in a twist, Princess Celestia," says Hudson. Which, okay, for someone ragging a guy about liking ponies, you have to wonder how he knows the name of their fearless leader.

"Yeah, I just want to see what's inside," says Jace.

Brony jumps for the backpack, but the guy's only about five foot four, and Jace easily keeps it out of reach. But he's laughing so hard he doesn't realize he's letting his arm droop. Brony jerks the backpack away with a speed I wasn't expecting.

"Asshole," he mutters.

Hudson's head snaps up. "What did you say?"

Oh, man. This is not good. We're gonna be peeling him off the parking lot when this is all over. Hudson throws an arm out to block him, while Jace grabs him from behind in a choke hold. Brony's fingers curl around Jace's forearm, and I'm thinking I should really jump in and help the guy out, when he flips Jace over his shoulder and onto the pavement.

"Holy shit," says Hudson, just staring for a second before he remembers he's supposed to be ass-kicking right now.

He charges Brony, and the kid does this ridiculous submission move. I've never seen anything like it, even at all my wrestling meets. Jace is up now, and he gets in a good sucker punch to the face while Brony's tied up with Hudson. Then one of the north lot doors opens, and Vice Principal Kahn sticks his head out, and Jace and Hudson take off running.

Brony waits until they're gone before his legs go all wobbly and he crinkles to the asphalt holding his face. It *was* a pretty mean punch. And now I'm standing in front of him without any idea what to do next except to say, "Are you okay?"

He startles. He thinks he's about to get hit again.

"It's okay, man. I was just coming over to check on you."

I give him a hand up, and he takes it.

"Thanks."

I pick up his backpack, too, and I can't help but notice all the *My Little Pony* pins as I hand it over. "Here."

He kind of grimaces before slinging it over his shoulder. His shoulders tense like he's waiting for me to make a comment about the bag, but there's something else I'm much more interested in.

"How'd you learn to do that? Those guys were twice your size."

He smiles, and his cheek pulls a little funny on the right side where it's starting to swell up. "Brazilian jiujitsu. I used to go four times a week with my dad before we moved here. I got all the way to my blue belt." The lights turn off inside his face. "There's one about half an hour from here, but he's deployed now, so I don't know."

"That's really cool. The part about the jiujitsu, I mean."

"Thanks," he says, just as I say, "So, how much do you weigh?"

His eyebrows furrow.

"That came out creepier than I meant it to." I laugh, but he's still looking at me like I'm a weirdo. "I'm on the wrestling team. Freshman year I wrestled 113, but then I got too big, which is cool because now I wrestle 138." (Hopefully.) "But we're kind of screwed for the 113 spot. All the guys who tried to fill it last year sucked something fierce."

"Wrestling," he says, and his face kind of de-clouds itself.

"It'd be an adjustment, but you've definitely got the strength and the talent."

"Um. Yeah. Hell, yeah. I'll think about it. It would be good to . . . Yeah."

I give him all the details for practice next week, and it turns out he's between 115 and 120, which is definitely doable. We're still swapping stories about wrestling meets and Brazilian jijitsu tournaments when the bell rings.

"I better get to class," he says. "But thanks again—"

"Spencer," I say.

"Traven."

He heads across the parking lot with a bounce in his step that he didn't have before, and I'm bouncing, too. All the way to Coach's office, where I burst through the door with a huge grin on my face.

"I found your new 113 guy."

CHAPTER

21

Hope's already setting up the lawn chairs when I get home. It started out as a Halloween tradition. Her dad would get out his old projector and hang a sheet on a line between two trees, and we'd come home from trick-or-treating and stuff ourselves with Skittles and candy corn and, if we were really lucky, mini-Butterfingers, while we watched *The Nightmare Before Christmas*. Something about sitting on a blanket with fall leaves rustling underneath it and stars overhead while we watched a movie felt like a slice of magic. Our parents seemed happier, too, although that might have had more to do with the special apple cider they were drinking.

And this year, Hope and I were thinking, why have the magic on only one night? Why not make outdoor movie night an October-long thing? So, yeah, pretty much any night that we're free, we do it. And tonight we're doing it as a Jayla-Spencer, Hope-Mikey double date. Just as soon as Jayla and Mikey get here.

I pick up the sheet and help Hope attach it to the clothes-line. "Hey, sorry I ran out on you guys this morning," I say.

"No worries." She sweeps her white-blonde hair out of her face and behind her ear. "Was that guy okay?"

"Traven? Yeah, he's good. It was pretty amazing how he almost took those guys, right? I told Coach all about him. I think he's gonna kill it this season."

Hope smiles. "You have a way of seeing good things in people that other people can't."

I shrug, but I'm so ridiculously pleased. "I know he seems kind of weird, but . . . I like him." I think about what Paul said this morning. "I think he doesn't fit the same way I don't fit."

And really, if fitting in means messing with people who are different, I don't know that it's something I ever want. Having Tourette's, it's like I can never go through life unnoticed. I can't even walk into a room unnoticed most of the time. I've learned a lot about the ways people react when other people are different. Sometimes they react badly out of surprise or because they're so nervous they say the worst thing that pops into their head. But they're not bad people. Most people, anyway. There's a few who will go after someone who's different for the sport of it. Those are the ones you have to watch out for.

"Paul won't stop talking about him, either," Hope says. "It sounds like you guys are going to have a pretty great season." She stares out into the trees wistfully when she says this. Maybe because we're smack in the middle of cross-country season?

Hope doesn't run anymore. I used to see her leave her house in a T-shirt and running shoes almost every morning in the off-season, and then, after Janie died, all hours of the day and night. She'd be gone for so long, I'd worry she wasn't coming back. But she always did, sweat slathered and weak legged like an overworked horse. But after she ripped down the maps and stuff, nothing. Not as far as I could tell. I guess whatever she was running from finally caught her.

Hope's phone buzzes in her pocket. She pulls it out and whatever she's seeing sucks the wind out of her sails. She flops down on the blue-and-yellow quilt, and I flop beside her.

"It's an e-mail from my mom," she says as she scrolls. "Sounds like our mid-semester grades are up."

We both wince. I whip out my phone, too, because I need to know how I'm doing for wrestling eligibility. English, Chemistry, Spanish—all B's. All okay. I got a C in History. An A in Weightlifting and one in Art, too. But a D in Trig. Shit, I knew I wasn't doing so hot in that class. It's the one right after lunch, which means it's the one right after my second dose of meds, but I had no idea it was that bad. I'm a failed test away from one of Coach's responsibility lectures.

I wonder how Hope is doing. She's in Mrs. Ramey's class, too, even though she skips half the time. She has her phone out, still peering at her grades. And I don't mean to look, but then I'm looking, and, "An A? You're getting an A in Trig? Holy crap, you're getting an A in everything."

Hope scowls. "I'm getting a B minus in English. Mrs. Campbell hates me."

"I thought you were doing badly at school. You're never there." It slips out before I can help it, but it doesn't seem to bug her. She just shrugs.

"It's a Georgia public high school. It's not like it's—" She catches herself, kind of stutters over her words for a second, and then blurts, "My mom's been on me. Like about school and stuff. And it sucks. So, sometimes, I have to get away for a little while. Blow off some steam."

"Right." I jab a button on my phone with an unnecessary amount of force. It's not like I want her to be doing bad at school—she's my friend. But it makes me feel like such a loser that she skips every chance she gets and still does great while I'm busting my butt and barely making it. If it's so easy for her and so easy for Dean, what does that say about me? That I'm stupid?

I don't know why, but this confession starts pouring out of her. "I feel like I have to be two people. Before I was just Hope. And now it's like I have to be Hope-plus-Janie. Go to the same school. Do all the same stuff. Live the same life. I have to be everything for my parents and do everything, and sometimes I can't, and I lose it, and I call Mikey. He's good about helping me forget."

I don't want to push. I don't *want* to, but: "What would you want to do if you weren't being Hope-plus-Janie? If you were just being Hope?"

"I don't know." She says it like a reflex, and then she doesn't say anything for so long, I worry I've messed up. "We had so many plans. When Janie got married, she was going to pick me to be her maid of honor—even though she's got a million best friends—because she said there's no one in the world as important as me. But she never got to get married. And she never got to have kids, and it kills me, because she'd be the best mom in the world. She was always talking about how we'd take our kids and go on beach vacations together, and how even if we had to live in different cities, they'd be pen pals. And honestly, it used to kind of freak me out because I am SO not ready to start thinking about stuff like kids, but now? Now it's like someone took a sledgehammer to my future and plucked out all the pieces that involved Janie. And without those pieces, I don't know if I'll ever be able to put the future together again." She stares at the white sheet draped between the trees like she'll find the answers there. "I want those beach vacations," she says softly. "Do you know how hard it is to have someone that important not be around?"

I do, a little. But really, I just want to say something to make her feel better right now. I think about putting my hand on hers. Instead, I put my hand on the blanket next to hers. "You know if she could be here with you, she would. She'd never leave you on purpose."

"Oh, gosh, Spencer, I'm so selfish. Of course you know what it's like."

Hope has this terrified, I-just-gutted-my-friend look on her face, and I rush to fix it. "It's different, though. I get to know she's out there. That makes it a lot easier."

We're quiet for a bit, debating the universe's cruel game of Would You Rather.

"I'm fine with it now. I really am," I say.

Hope puts her hand on top of mine. "Spencer, do you—"

"Movie time!!!" yells a loud, unwanted, and most definitely male voice behind us.

Hope and I jump apart on the blanket. Mikey doesn't seem to notice. He's too busy pushing buttons on the projector like he's early man trying to make fire. I almost don't realize Jayla is with him until the leaves crunch under the weight of her leather boots. Her eyes are on the spot on the blanket where Hope's hand touched mine. Uh-oh.

"Is there any food?" asks Mikey. "I had the longest day ever at the shop, and I'm starving."

He's been working at Ethan's dad's body shop since he squeaked by with a diploma last May.

"Do you want to help me carry the snacks?" Jayla's voice is fast and pinched. "I went inside, and Pam said you were out here, and she made us snacks." Oh yeah, I'm definitely in trouble.

I don't even look at Hope as we leave, just to be safe.

As soon as we're out of earshot, Jayla asks, "What were you guys talking about?"

"Nothing. Just—" Her shoulders hunch. I decide to tell her the truth. "My mom."

This piece of information seems to completely change her mind. From what to what, I have no idea, but of the fact that it is changed, I am certain.

"Oh. I've never heard you talk about her before."

"I don't, usually."

I stop talking abruptly as we enter the kitchen and pick up a plate of veggie sticks and ranch and another of cake pops (guess which one we're going to eat first).

"The ones with the dark-chocolate coating are low sugar, low carb," calls Pam over the hum of the blender.

"Thanks, Pam," I say. When we're back on the porch, I sit down with the snacks. "I try not to bring her up in front of Pam. Or, well, my dad."

Jayla nods seriously.

"My mom's a singer, mostly country, but with a sultry, blue-grass kind of feel. Well, that's what Dad says, anyway. She left when I was five."

Jayla squeezes my shoulder. "That must have been really hard."

I shrug.

"That's so cool that she's a singer, though. Is she, like, a big deal? Would I have heard of her?" Her hands fly around in kind of a giddy way.

"I don't know."

"Can we go see one of her concerts? You should take me back-stage and let me meet her. I have so many questions for her, as a fellow performer."

"Um." I suddenly don't feel like explaining that I haven't seen her since she left. That I don't even know where she is. "If I go to one of her shows, I'll definitely take you."

Jayla claps her hands together. "Cool! Wow, a singer. I can't believe you never told me this before."

I stand up and head to the outdoor movie theater. "Yeah. Me neither."

Hope gives me a sympathy smile as I approach. I get the impression she heard all of that.

"We desperately need your help picking a movie," she says.

"We desperately need your help convincing Hope that *Phantom of the Opera* doesn't qualify as a Halloween movie," Mikey says. "I'm thinking *House of 1000 Corpses*."

"Yeah, no."

"I thought we were watching *The Nightmare Before Christmas*," says Jayla.

"We only watch that on Halloween night," Hope and I say simultaneously.

"Oh." Jayla crosses her arms.

"*Hostel*? *The Evil Dead*?" Mikey chimes in.

"We could watch *Rent*," says Hope.

"You made me watch *Rent* the last time I played World of War-craft all night and forgot we had a date the next day," says Mikey. "And, again, not a Halloween movie."

"Okay, *Little Shop of Horrors*, then."

"I will *die* if I have to watch another musical. What about *Paranormal Activity*? Oh! Or how about *Saw IV*?"

"They made a fourth one of those?" Hope's lip curls in disgust.

"You're right," says Mikey. "We should go with the original."

I remember that I'm supposed to be contributing instead of making A Taxonomy of All the Best Halloween Movies in my head. "We could watch *Hocus Pocus*," I say.

"Well, sure," says Mikey. "And since we're five years old, we could watch *It's the Great Pumpkin, Charlie Brown* after and make it a double feature."

Jayla, who has been watching this whole exchange like some kind of stone-cold Queen of the Vampires, uncrosses her arms and smiles.

"What's up?" I ask.

"I have the solution," she says smugly. "Four words. *Rocky Horror Picture Show*."

She throws the movie title like a gauntlet.

Hope's eyes light up. "YES."

"I've never seen it before," I say.

"So, that's a DOUBLE YES," says Hope.

Mikey throws his hands up. "I am not watching a movie about a—"

Hope puts a finger to his lips. "Oh, yes you are, and if you ever want to see the Halloween underwear I'm wearing, you're going to keep any and all hateful comments to yourself."

"But—"

She hands him a cake pop, and he stuffs it in his mouth.

"Fine," he grumbles.

Jayla tucks her legs underneath her and snuggles up to me, while Hope queues up the movie. Mikey looks like he wants to say something else, but instead eats another cake pop. Probably a good move.

The opening frames of the movie appear on the sheet in front of us. The onscreen trees seem to ripple because there's a light breeze. I bite into a cake pop, and it explodes in my mouth with caramel-cinnamon magic.

And the stars wink at us from overhead.

And my arm is around my girlfriend.

And my best friend watches movies with me again.

And today is the best of all days.

CHAPTER

22

Hope is a no-show today. Not that I'm surprised. She skips school a lot, and then it's just the three of us in the back of my truck (or four, because sometimes Traven joins us now). It's kind of the best, feeling like with each person we add to our group, high school sucks a little less.

The bell rings, and we shoot off in different directions. I hunt down a trash can so I can spit out my gum, and then I notice Hope in the crowd of people streaming through the north lot doors. She looks like she's been crying. When she spots me, she beelines over, but she just stands there, silent, in front of me.

"Are you okay?" I ask.

She takes a deep, shuddery breath. "Pumpkinspicelatte."

"I'm sorry?"

"I needed (hiccup) a Pumpkin (sob) Spice Latte."

"Oh." Hope isn't the type of girl who has meltdowns over first-world problems (usually). "Is this a Janie thing?"

She nods, and her eyes have the look of a drowning person.

"It's her birthday," she finally says.

"Oh, hey, you don't have to be at school today. You could go back home. I know the office would give you an excuse."

"No! I mean, I don't want to. I thought about it, but I decided I don't want to be at home today. Because if I do that, it's like the tumor wins. And I can't let it win on her birthday."

She's so fierce and sad at the same time. I should do something. Give her a hug, at least. We're friends, and that's what friends do. But we don't exactly have the best track record with hugs.

Instead, I say, "That makes sense." But it doesn't feel like enough.

Hope tries to wipe her nose on her sleeve without actually looking like she's wiping snot on herself.

"So, um, what happened with the latte?" I'm reluctant to ask in case it sets her off again, but I am pretty curious.

"Oh. Yeah." She laughs. "Do you ever feel like something really big and terrible could be happening, but if you could just get this one small thing to go right, you could be okay?" I don't answer, but she shrugs and keeps going. "Well, I thought if I could do this thing Janie and I used to do and go get a PSL, then that would be this little piece of happiness, and I could say, 'Today is going to be okay. I can get through today.'"

"Yeah. Yeah, I can see that. It didn't work, though?"

Hope's eyes narrow. "They. Didn't. Have. Any. Lattes."

"Oh, no. It's not time yet?" I remember her and Janie making a big deal about how they were seasonal, and you had to be on the lookout for them, and once I remember saying I could just look up when they came out, and they both shrieked "Nooooo!" while Janie explained how the not knowing was half the fun.

"It IS time. They didn't have any lattes. Like at all. Their espresso machines were down. And I was all, 'Whatevs, I don't even drink espresso.' But apparently that means they can't make any good drink *ever*. What kind of piece of crap Starbucks can't make lattes?! But the guy didn't tell me that, so I kept asking for stuff, and he kept saying they couldn't do it, and finally I was like 'I give up.' But it wasn't just about the latte. It was a very meta 'I give up,' Spencer. And of course the guy just looked at me like I was a weirdo. And it's like, I can handle that Janie's gone, and I can handle that it's her birthday, and that I," her breath hitches, "really miss her. BUT I NEEDED THAT PUMP-KIN SPICE LATTE, DAMN IT."

I pull out my phone. I may be having trouble with things like re-friendship hug protocols, but mapping the nearest coffee place is something I can do. "The next closest Starbucks is twenty-five minutes away. We can go right now."

Hope's head cocks to the side, and I can see her brain calculating whether this day can be salvaged after all. "Well, um, okay." She freezes and touches her hands to her cheeks. "Wait. Is my mascara all runny?"

She looks like the love child of a raccoon and a Hot Topic employee. "Um."

She snorts. "That's a yes. Hold on while I go to the bathroom and fix my face. I think I've scared enough Starbucks baristas for the day."

"I'll meet you at your car," I call after her, but first I pop into the office and drop a few words like "emergency" and "dead sister," because Hope's already on their watch list.

I still get to Hope's car before she does. When she emerges from the school building, you can't even tell she's been crying, and I don't know much about how makeup works, but things about her face look different. Like, the black rings are gone, and I definitely think she put powder or something on her nose.

"Thanks for coming with me," she says as she clicks the key fob to let us in. She's quiet for a minute, just driving, and then she says, "I remember the first time Janie took me for a Pumpkin Spice Latte. I was eleven, and Janie was all, 'Don't tell mom I gave you coffee.' It seemed like the coolest thing in the world."

She smiles, and I can see her seeing that moment.

"Oh. I almost forgot." She switches on the sound system, and some up-tempo hip-hop comes on.

It sounds familiar. "*Hamilton?*"

"*Hamilton*. It's become a crucial part of the PSL-run tradition."

"Oh, good," I say. "I'm glad we're not deviating from the protocol."

Hope's smile fades.

"What's up?"

"Well, if Janie were here, we'd be singing along at the top of our lungs, but it's not like you know the words, and maybe that wouldn't be—"

"I know the words." I make a big show of scoffing. The song "The Schuyler Sisters" comes on. "Well, maybe not every song, but I definitely know all the words for this one."

She gives me this look, like: *Jefferson, please.*

"I do! I . . . 'We hold these truths to be self-evident that all men are created equal—'" Hopes eyes shoot wide open, but I keep going, belting all the words, even busting out the correct dance moves before I throw my hand in the air and snap my fingers and yell, "Work." It's a totally fierce impression of Angelica Schuyler (you know, if Renée Elise Goldsberry was a seventeen-year-old boy with no discernible musical talent).

Hope's jaw is on the floor of the car. We may need a doctor to surgically reattach it. And then she starts giggling, and she can barely talk, and there are tears in her eyes again, only this time they're the good kind.

"Where. Did you learn. The choreography?" she manages to choke out.

I shrug. "Janie made me watch that #Ham4Ham clip just as many times as she made you."

"Factually impossible, but I'm still impressed."

I spot the Starbucks, and she pulls into the parking lot and lets the car idle for a bit.

"You know she had a chance to go see it? Like on Broadway and everything? She was in New York visiting a friend, and she totally could have gone, but she was all, 'No, it's cool. Hope and I have to see it together the first time because seeing each other's faces is the best part.'"

"That was really sweet of her," I say.

"Yeah, except it's not because now I have to go the rest of my life knowing that she never got to see *Hamilton*, and it's all my fault."

I have no idea at all what to say to that, but luckily Hope doesn't seem to care. She gets out of the car, and I trail after her to the front door, which she flings open.

In a voice that carries to the far corners of the coffee shop, she announces, "Please tell me you have lattes because if you don't, I am going to lose all hope in the universe."

The nearest barista is wearing extra-thick guyliner and a confused expression. "Um. This is a Starbucks."

"Yeah, well, apparently that doesn't mean as much as it used to." She hops in line, grinning now. "Spencer, you have to try one. We can get you some kind of skim-milk, no-whip thing." Her mouth makes a noise between a sigh and an "oh." "No whip." She pauses with her hands clasped together, a moment of silence for my whipped cream. "Well, it's okay.

It'll be okay as long as it has everything else. Coffee, pumpkin spice, magic."

"Magic? That's one of the ingredients?"

She fixes me with a look of utmost seriousness. "You are already on dangerously thin ice with the no-whipped-cream thing. Don't test me about the magic."

When we get to the front, she orders a venti for each of us, rattling off specifications for mine. I've always appreciated that about her. She might tease me about my diet, but she doesn't nag me to break it the way other people do. My shoulders let off a chain of tic-shrugs while we're waiting for our drinks. The new meds have been awesome—I'm definitely not tic-ing as much as I used to—but it would be nice not to feel so exhausted every time I take them. Thank goodness for caffeine. We snag a table by the window, and Hope scrutinizes me as I take my first sip.

"Well?"

"It's good," I say. And I'm not lying. Even without all the frills, I get it. "Very . . . seasonal."

She beams. "Right?" She makes a big show of taking her own first sip. Leans back against her chair, eyes closed and smiling wide. "Mmmm. Fall."

Complete. That's how she looks right now.

Her eyes open. "Cinnamon is the most perfect spice ever. Like, I'm pretty sure I could put a stick of cinnamon in my mouth and gnaw on it like beef jerky, and that would be cool." She takes another sip. "Oh. And in about twenty minutes when the aftertaste kicks in, your mouth is going to taste like cinnamon-flavored vomit." She shrugs brightly and bumps her cup against mine. "Cheers."

The prodigal son has come home for fall break. We're having all of Dean's favorite foods—fried okra, squash casserole, rib-eye steaks—while he regales us with tales of college. His classes are all great, and he's keeping fit in the off-season, and he's figured out which dining hall has the best Saturday-morning pancakes. Oh, but he hasn't figured out how to do his laundry yet, so does Pam mind doing that while he's here?

"Of course I don't. I'll have everything folded before it's time to go back to school," she says, beaming.

"Thanks. I've just been studying so much. We're learning a lot of stuff that's really different from high school. And, like, the people are really different, too. I've never met so many people who are different from me."

"You're having fun, too, though, right?" I say.

An observation about Dean's stories: They're a little too squeaky-clean.

"Well, sure. It's college." He side-eyes Dad before grinning at me.

Oh, yeah. I am definitely going to make him tell me the dirt later.

"Have you met any girls yet?" Jayla asks, her eyes all twinkly and sly.

Hell, yes, my girlfriend is on Team Find-Out-What-Really-Happens-in-College.

"A few."

"*A few*," says Pam.

"Well, I don't want anything serious. I'm trying to focus on school and baseball."

"S'good," Dad grunts around a mouthful of steak. "We don't want any distractions."

"Because women are merely distractions and not actual human beings," says Mimi, rolling her eyes.

"That's not what I meant."

"Hmph."

Jayla kicks my foot and smiles at me, like, *I love your grandma.* And I smile back, like, *I know, right?*

Dean drains the rest of his drink and makes a big show of stretching. "Pam, can you get me another glass of tea?"

Jayla fixes him with her best withering smirk. "And you can't do that yourself because . . . ?"

Dean pretend-scoffs. "I'm the second-best pitcher we've got. I have to protect my pitching arm."

"Lifting a tea pitcher is not going to strain you. You can fill up mine while you're at it."

She jiggles her cup so the ice rattles against the sides, and to my surprise, he does it. He goes to the kitchen and refills it, and when he comes back, he hands it back to her with a bow and a flourish. She laughs and keeps her chin high like royalty.

I think if Dean found a girl like Jayla, he'd be a whole lot happier. He needs a queen, not a groupie.

"So, what's new around here?" asks Dean.

"I found a new 113 guy, and he's killing it. He's pretty cool."

Jayla grins. "I'm pretty sure you're the only person who would use the word 'cool' to describe that kid."

"Yeah." I frown. "That's kind of why he's my freshman buddy."

"Only seniors get freshman buddies," says Dean.

"None of them wanted him. I don't know. I just, I feel like he could use some extra help, you know?"

"Well, I think that's wonderful," says Mimi.

"Yeah, that's cool," says Dean, and I'm so surprised I nearly put steak sauce on my squash.

We go over wrestling, other sports, town gossip. It doesn't take long.

"Hope's still dating Mikey," I say.

Mimi clucks her tongue. "I hate to see her with that tattoo boy, don't you? He looks like he smokes those marijuana cigarettes."

Dean and I snicker.

"And Ethan comes home from school every weekend to see Bella," I say.

Dean snorts. "Loser." Only he says it like a term of endearment. "Wow, it's crazy how nothing ever really changes around here."

"Yeah." And then I remember something did change this year. A big something. "Wait, no, something big changed at school this year."

"A new brand of tater tots in the cafeteria?"

"No." I glance around the table. Haven't mentioned this in front of Dad, and not sure why I'm doing it with Jayla next to me, but here goes: "People aren't allowed to have rebel flags anymore."

"Really?"

"Yeah, you can't have them on your clothes or on your car or anything. No Confederate flags anywhere on school grounds."

Dad's eyebrows furrow, but his lips stay sealed. Thank goodness.

"It's about damn time," says Mimi.

"I can't believe it finally happened." Dean looks stunned. Not that I blame him. I was pretty shocked, too, when I found out. When you live in a small town, it's like life moves more slowly. It's easy to think nothing will ever change, until *BAM*, it does, and it gives you hope for all the other changes that might be next. "I mean, good," he says at last.

Jayla is silent beside me. We've talked about the whole thing, but I hope I didn't make her uncomfortable bringing it up in front of my family.

My dad puts his fork down, and it clatters against his plate. Oh, crap.

"You know, that's a Constitutional right they're taking away." No, no, no. Please stop talking.

But he doesn't. "You should be able to wear whatever you want on your own shirt. That's freedom of speech." He sticks some okra in his mouth.

I'm trying to put words together, but Mimi is on him almost before he's finished speaking. "It's a public place full of minors, Frank. The administration's allowed to dictate what people wear while they're there. It's important that all the students feel safe." She nods at Jayla. Who I hope will still want to be my girlfriend by the end of this dinner. I put my hand over hers and squeeze. "Pass the squash casserole."

Dad snorts. "I don't see what 'safety' has to do with anything."

"I'm sure *you'd* take issue with folks wearin' 'Death to Whitey' T-shirts, wouldn't you?" Mimi says.

"Well, that's just not the same!" Dad says. "It's an important part of our southern heritage, and people are trying to erase that. First, they take it off the Georgia flag—"

"Wait a minute. You need to check your history," says Mimi. "The flag we have now is almost just like the original."

"But—"

"Come on, Dad," Dean cuts him off. "There's no way you believe that 'heritage' crap."

Dad doesn't respond.

"You really think it's okay for people to walk around a mixed school wearing reminders that people who looked like us *owned* other human beings?" Dean goes on. "THAT'S what the flag represents. Even if your Daddy's Daddy's Daddy fought in the war, a bumper sticker on your Ford is nothing more than a shout that your family was pro-slavery."

Dean is at least two feet taller than my dad by the time he stops talking. I wish I had been the one to lay it all out there for Dad like that, and not just because of the way Jayla is looking at Dean right now.

Not to mention, Dean's looking back.

Dad glances at Jayla, turns eleven shades of red, and starts stammering. "Well, I'm not saying slavery was okay . . . I was just talking about the Constitution. I don't want any trouble for anyone at the school—"

Pam pats his hand. "We know you're not a racist, honey. We see everybody the same."

I feel Jayla stiffen beside me.

Oh boy . . .

"Can I say something?" she says.

"'Course you can, sweetheart," says Mimi.

"Okay . . ." She looks at me. There's hesitation in her eyes, but I nod. "I don't mean you any disrespect, Mr. and Mrs. Barton, but I don't think racism is that cut and dry. People always think, 'Oh, this person's a racist, and that person isn't, and that's it. The End.' But it's not really that simple, is it? When you've grown up in a place where people are treated differently because of their skin color, certain ideas become a part of you, whether you want them to or not. I think the fear of being pegged as a 'racist' can actually make people act worse and treat people of color *more* differently."

"So true," Dean says. He winks at Jayla and she blushes. Which is pretty uncharacteristic of her.

Dad and Pam glance at each other. Not sure what that means, but I'm so proud of my girl right now for shutting them up, it's a struggle not to lean over and kiss her. Assuming she still wants to be kissed by a guy who pretty much sucked at speaking up right now. I have to make sure I do better next time.

"That sounds like something I heard on NPR," Mimi says, cocking her head to the side.

Jayla smiles. "We might have listened to the same episode."

Mimi is so aflutter, I think I might have some competition for who at this table is most in love with my girlfriend. Everyone else seems unsure what to do next now that we've established that A) my dad may or may not be a racist, but he definitely just said a lot of racist things, and B) Mimi and Jayla will probably be getting mani/pedis together in the very near future.

Dad doesn't continue arguing, and trust me, he can argue with the best of them. Instead, he quietly eats his okra, which I feel means he's at least thinking about what we said, even if he isn't ready to change his mind yet. That's not nothing.

I don't know. Sometimes I worry that being from here means I'll always be three steps behind the rest of the world.

After dinner I walk Jayla to the truck, but stop before I open her door.

"I'm really proud to be your boyfriend," I say. "If you still want to be my girlfriend?"

She nods like she's scared her voice won't work and throws her arms around my neck, and I hold her for a few seconds or maybe a few minutes or maybe eternity.

When I get back from taking Jayla home, I let the truck idle in the driveway for longer than I probably should. Eventually, I force myself to go inside. Pam, Mimi, Dean—they've all disappeared, leaving my dad alone at the kitchen table with his phone. Something about the way he pushes it to the side when he sees me lets me know he wasn't actually using it. Just waiting.

"Hey, buddy." I can't remember the last time he called me that. Heck, I can't remember the last time we were alone together. He looks supremely uncomfortable right now.

"Hey."

Did Pam put you up to this? Or was it Mimi?

"I'm sorry about tonight," he says.

I really don't have the energy or patience to hear whatever his excuses are going to be.

"I do a lot of things wrong. I feel like—like I'm not the dad you're supposed to have, and I'm sorry you're stuck with me."

My breath catches.

"You've always been different. Even as a little kid. I don't know what to do with you half the time, but I want you to know, that's not your fault."

"Okay." I whisper it because my voice isn't working.

"I'm so very proud of you, son."

And then he's hugging me, and I imagine it's what being boa-constricted feels like, but it feels good, really good, and I am definitely not crying into his flannel shirt.

Before I can fully suffocate, he pulls away. "About tonight. If you and your brother think that this flag rule is such a good idea, then I'll at least read an article on it. I don't want to make trouble for you and your girl. Also." He looks uncharacteristically sheepish. "Your grandmother might have given me a reading list."

"Um, well, that's great." And not at all surprising. "You can talk to me about it, you know. I want us to be able to talk about things."

He squeezes my shoulder—gently—which means it only kind of feels like a vice.

"Me, too."

CHAPTER 24

Four things I will never understand: dogs that are smaller than cats; trigonometry; people who don't like mustard on their hotdogs; bras. I'm running my fingers along the back of Jayla's lacy, ribbon-y death trap right now, trying to be cool as I search for the clasp. Her shirt is still on and it has some kind of elastic thing that goes all the way around because this definitely needed to be more complicated. I still can't find the clasp. I give up trying to be suave and run my whole hand back and forth across her bra. It isn't there. I mean, there is no clasp. WHAT KIND OF SORCERY IS THIS?!

Jayla's face is all squeezed up like she's trying not to laugh.

I make a pitiful face. "Help?"

The giggles burst forth. "It's a front clasp."

"Front clasp?!" Who decided those were a good idea?

She laughs harder.

"And you couldn't have brought this to my attention, oh, sixty seconds ago?"

"It was more fun this way." She pulls down the straps of her tank top.

"I'm so glad torturing me is fun for you."

"It's a little fun." She flips down the top of her shirt, unsnaps the infernal front clasp, and in 0.2 seconds, there are boobs right in front of me. I forget to breathe. There are a lot of things I would like to do right now, but my stepmom is upstairs making dinner, so I will only do, like, one-fourth of them.

"You're beautiful," I say.

She laughs. "You say that every time."

"It's true every time." It really is. Her skin is so flawless, I wonder if she actually has pores.

I'm just getting started on the one-fourth when I hear a floorboard creak. I jump back/adjust my shorts/sit up straight/wipe my face/look guilty as all hell. Pam is standing at the bottom of the stairs. Jeez, I didn't even hear her open the door. She's like a freaking CIA operative. I glance back at Jayla, who is currently wearing all her clothes and smiling like a model citizen. How does she do that?

"Hi, Miss Pam."

"Hi, Jayla. Are you staying for dinner?"

She shakes her head. "My dad's picking me up soon, and we're gonna go get Mexican food."

"Okay." Pam brushes her hands off on her pants but doesn't move to go back upstairs. Her eyes dart back and forth between us. "What are you two doing down here?"

"Running Jayla's lines for the play," I say way too fast and grab the script, like, see, here's proof she didn't just have her shirt halfway off.

Pam raises her eyebrows. It's how she reads minds. "I think you should run lines on the porch."

As she creaks back up the stairs, we hold in our laughter, but as soon as the door closes, it all comes out.

Jayla whacks me with the script. "You are so the opposite of stealth."

"I'm sorry. I can't help it. How do you always get your clothes on so fast?"

We grab our stuff and migrate to the front porch. I sit on the porch swing, and she drapes her legs over me, and this time we really do run lines. I read Teddy and she plays Tina, and we practice one of *The 9 Worst Breakups of All Time*. It's warm for October, which means we're wearing shorts, but we're not dying of heat stroke.

"This is nice," I say.

"Yeah." Jayla stops with the lines for a minute and rests her head on my shoulder.

"This play is really funny. But, um, I don't see a kiss scene."

Jayla lifts her head off my shoulder. "Yeah, they're just nosey kisses. That's probably why I'm allowed to play opposite a white dude this time." She rolls her eyes.

"Yeah, but." Do I even bring this up? "When I picked you up after play practice last time, you and Justin were still onstage practicing, and it started as a nose kiss, but it slipped into a real kiss."

She makes a face. "Whoa. First of all, we were *acting*. And yeah, Justin's a really good actor, and a lot of time he'll improvise stuff and make it more intense. But second of all, I love *you*. Not Justin or anyone else."

"I'm not worried about you. I'm just—" Worried about Justin. Justin with the lips that seem to "slip" and the eyes that I watched follow my girlfriend's ass all the way across the stage and down the stairs.

"Please don't ask me to hold back from doing what I love because it makes you uncomfortable."

"No, I would never." I squeeze her hand. "I didn't mean it to sound like that."

"Good. Because the only person I want to be kissing for real is you." She smiles. "But it would be nice to be able to do it without getting walked in on every time."

"Pam is the best kiss-interrupter in fifty states."

"Can you imagine what it would be like to be together and not have to worry?"

"Oh, I can imagine."

It's not that we've never been alone. There have been bits of time here and there, in the back of my truck, in Jayla's living room before her parents get home from work. But it's all sneaking around, which is fine for some things, but neither of us wants our first time to be like that.

"I've been meaning to talk to you about something," she says. She's breathing faster. It makes me breathe faster.

"Yeah?"

"Yeah. My parents are going to visit my grandma in Savannah next weekend." She swallows. "I'm staying home."

She's staying home. Alone. She'll be . . . Oh! "Do you want me to—"

"Yes. I'm ready. I think I'm ready." She moves her legs out of my lap. "I want it to be special, you know?"

I catch her hands and hold them between us. "It will be. It's going to be so special."

She leans into me, and I tic just as her lips are about to touch mine, and she smiles and kisses me anyway. I remember being terrified of this very thing before we had our first kiss. And thinking about not tic-ing sometimes makes me tic worse, so it got to where just thinking about trying to kiss Jayla for the first time would send me into a flurry of tics. It's better if I tic after we've already started kissing.

The sound of her dad's car pulling into the driveway makes us jump apart.

"Crap. I gotta go," she says. "Hey, are you coming with me to Ashley's birthday tomorrow?"

I groan. Ashley's dad is throwing her a huge sweet sixteen/Halloween party with a ballroom-size tent and a dance floor and drama. Parties like that don't happen often around here, so it's a really big deal. It's also sooo many people. Just not my thing.

"Do I have to?"

She puts her hands on her hips. "Yes."

I know she'll talk me into it eventually, so it makes the most sense to smile and get it over with. "Okay."

"Yay!" She squeals and gives me a quick hug, but nothing more because, hello, we are RIGHT IN FRONT OF HER DAD. I give him an awkward wave, and he returns it, and they drive away.

When I turn around, Hope is flat-out sprinting out of the woods behind our houses. She's wearing a T-shirt and her hair is up in a ponytail. I can't remember the last time I saw her like this. I almost do a double take.

She screeches to a stop beside me and promptly collapses on the grass.

"Hey. When did you start running again?"

"Today," she pants. "Can you tell?"

"No . . ." She lifts her head off the grass to side-eye me. "Okay, yes."

"I think I'm gonna go out for track this spring. Assuming I can figure out how to not suck before then."

Her arms are over her face, blocking the sunlight.

"That's awesome! I mean, that's really great." I try not to get too excited. She hates that.

She drags herself into a heel stretch. I want to say other things but don't.

"Hey, Hope, we're friends, right?"

She gives me a funny look. "Yes."

"Like, the kind where I can ask you for girl advice?"

"Yeah, totally." She's smiling brightly and being extra still like I'm a small animal she might scare away.

"Okay." I wait for what is definitely an awkward amount of time because I'm not sure where to begin with this. "So, Jayla and I are probably going to have sex next weekend."

Hope chokes and tries to play it off as a cough. (Having had Tourette's for nine years, I am an expert on letting one behavior flow into another so I can play off my tics, so it's clear to me that me talking about sex with Jayla nearly killed Hope.) She laughs. "Okay, so we're not easing into this."

"Sorry." Is this awkward? It's probably really awkward.

"No, it's fine. Um. So, what would you like to know? About sex. But you're not going to ask for tips or anything, right? Because that'd just be gross."

I thought I was embarrassed before, but now I know I wasn't, because THIS is the most embarrassing thing ever. "No, I wasn't—I mean, I wouldn't—I mean—" Oh, crap, do I NEED tips? Because I'm pretty sure I don't know anything at all, and despite Dean's propensity for bragging, I can't remember him ever saying anything useful. "I just want to make sure it's really special, you know?"

Hope's face softens. "Of course you do." She sits up on her knees. "Here's the deal. Most guys are good about first times during the *during*. It's the after they fail at."

"The after?" I am way more worried about the during. Apparently, *most guys* are good at that.

"Yeah. I mean, you both want to do this and you're both ready, right?"

"Yes."

"Then, it's definitely the after. Trust me," she says when she sees the doubtful look on my face. "I've had a lot of girlfriends confide in me about this. Most guys just—they don't act like it's a big enough deal. And it's a really big deal."

I throw up my hands. "I know it's a big deal. It's a big deal to me, too."

This seems to appease Hope, and she settles into a butterfly stretch. "Good. So, tell her that. After. Tell her what it meant to you. Tell her that you love her. Ask her how she's feeling. Ask her again because the answer might change. Even if she was never planning to wait until marriage, even if she acts like she's totally cool, give her tons and tons and tons of hugs, and maybe even some flowers or a poem or something. Because maybe she'll be like, 'Wow, I thought I was ready, but now I'm not so sure.' Or, 'I was definitely totally ready, but now my boyfriend is lying on the bed and staring at the ceiling like the words IJUSTGOTLAIDIJUSTGOTLAID are scrolling around his brain on a teleprompter. Does he even love me?' Or, 'I think I was ready, but now I'm feeling all these feelings, and they're so big that they scare me, and I don't want to be alone in this.'"

I don't say anything.

Hope doesn't say anything.

"Wow, this is a lot." I am now nervous for a whole new set of reasons.

"Yeah," Hope says gently. She reaches out her hand and pats

me on the shoulder. "But, hey, you're going to be great, okay? You're a really good guy, Spencer."

"Thanks. And thanks for being my friend, like, who I can ask stuff like this."

She grins. "No problem."

"If you ever need to ask me anything, you totally can."

"Oh, I will. Now that we're *friends*, and not just friends, I'm going to come up with all kinds of things to ask you about."

"I'm really glad we're friends," I say to the grass. I'm talking about something totally different now.

"Me too," she says. No boisterous grin.

I laugh and shake my head.

"What?" she asks.

"Nothing. It's dumb—I mean, silly."

"No, what? We're *friends*. You have to tell me."

"Oh, is that how it works?"

"One hundred percent. I have a copy of *The Friendship Code* on my desk right now. You are not permitted to laugh in my presence without revealing the cause of said laughter."

"Well, then. Do you know I used to have the biggest crush on you in middle school?"

She cocks her head to the side. "Um. I'm pretty sure everyone in the tri-county area knows that."

"What? No, they didn't."

She raises her eyebrows.

"Okay, fine. Maybe they did. I told you it was silly." I laugh again, but this time it feels like I'm forcing it. "Anyway, it was a really long time ago."

She sits up straighter. "I used to have a crush on you, too."

"Are you serious?" But. I mean. No.

"Yep. I used to talk alllll about you in these epically long e-mails to Janie." She shakes her head. "Poor Janie."

"But then why didn't we—"

"Sophie."

"Sophie? That girl from camp?"

"That girl from camp that you used to talk about. All. The. Freaking. Time. I thought she was your girlfriend." She shrugs. "And then by the time I figured out she wasn't, Dean happened."

"Yeah. I remember that part."

I still can't believe she used to like me. Hope *liked* me. If I had never mentioned Sophie, I wonder if things would have turned out differently. Maybe we'd be together. Or maybe we would have ruined everything.

"It's funny how things work out," I say. "You and Dean. Me and Jayla."

"You guys make a really cute couple." But she says it like her heart is dying a slow, quiet death. "I broke up with Mikey," she adds quickly.

Oh. Well, that explains it.

"What happened between you guys? Never mind. I'm sorry. It's none of my business." I can't believe it. I mean, they were together a surprisingly long time considering he's Mikey.

"No, it's okay. Friends, remember? It's . . . complicated."

I don't know what to say.

"Well, actually, maybe it's not. Mikey's fun, but it's really hard to talk to him about anything real. He sure was great for pissing off my mom, though."

I think about her mom, and about what Hope told me about having to be two people.

"Hey, Hope?"

"Yeah?"

"Dating Mikey and all that . . . stuff." I wave my hands around, searching for the right words. I don't want to seem like I'm judging. "Does it make you feel less like Hope-plus-Janie and more like Hope?"

"Not really." She thinks for a minute. "Not at all. But it does help me forget for a while."

I understand all about how good forgetting feels, but I also understand that it keeps you from ever getting anywhere. I think the conversation is over, but then she says, "Sometimes I think about ditching the Janie things. Doing more Hope things."

"I think you should. You should tell your mom to screw it. I mean, not in those exact words, because your mom can be kind of scary, but, you know, something. It's not fair for her to ask what she's asking."

"I know. And it's not that I don't want to do good things in the world and help people. I *do*. But, like, I don't think I can handle dealing with people who are really sick. I started shadowing a doctor in Warner Robins—a surgeon, the kind that Janie shadowed. And sometimes I have to sneak out of the room and throw up, and sometimes I cry all the way home. I think it's great that some people can do stuff like that, but I don't think I'm one of them." She hugs her arms to her chest, and she can't seem to make her eyes meet mine.

"But that's okay. Not everyone's meant to help people the same way. Maybe you'll be a lobbyist or take photographs or write."

"Yeah." The corners of her mouth turn up. "Yeah, I was thinking of taking a photography class next semester. If I dropped
AP Chemistry, I'd definitely have room."

She's still for a while, thinking it over. And then, "Hey, Spencer?"

"Yeah?"

"Thanks." She takes a step closer, and I think maybe she's
going to give me a hug or something. But then she looks scared,
like she forgot something or maybe remembered something.
It's hard to say.

"I better go," she says. "It's important to hydrate."

She jogs up the stairs of her house, and she doesn't look
back.

CHAPTER

25

♥

There's just one thing standing between me and the perfect Saturday: a mountain of pumpkins.

"You want me to do *what*?" I'm standing by the truck, keys in hand, ready for my day of doing everything and nothing. I'm going to pick up Traven and Paul, and we're going to the movies over in Warner Robins or to Sonic to get burgers or just drive around until I run out of gas. I don't even know.

Pam stands on the front porch, doling out bad news like second helpings of mashed potatoes. "I want you to drive over to the Akin Farm and pick up the pumpkins for the church pumpkin patch. It'll just be a few truckloads."

"A few?!"

"If you and Dean go together, it'll take no time at all."

"Dean already left to ride four-wheelers with Ethan." Like he would do manual labor during his weekend home anyway. I cross my arms over my chest. I'm fully aware I'm being an insufferable brat right now, but I can see my golden Saturday slipping through my fingers while Dean and Ethan ride four-wheelers into the sunset.

Pam sighs, and it's like her whole body sinks a couple inches into the porch. "I'm sorry. I hate that you have to do it by yourself, but they're counting on me. And they need the pumpkins there by three because the fall festival starts tonight."

My shoulders hunch. I'm going to say yes, but I'm not going

to be happy about it. Before I can find the words, a voice pipes up behind me.

"I can do it."

Hope? I turn. Yep, it is definitely Hope, and she is definitely volunteering as tribute.

"Oh, honey, you don't have to do that," says Pam.

"You don't. You really don't," I add.

She shrugs. "I don't mind. Seriously. It'll be fun."

Well, I wouldn't go that far. But I don't want to look like an unhelpful douche, so I throw on a smile. "Yeah. Hope and I will do it." Hauling pumpkins really isn't that bad, anyway.

Pam smirks at me. "Are you sure? I don't want to ruin your big plans."

Okay, I deserved that. "It's fine. We got this."

"Okay. Well, you two have fun." Pam is still grinning like a fiend as she heads back into the house.

Hope and I hop in the truck, and I crank her up. I drive us through town, and then down winding country roads that are so narrow you have to slow down and really squeeze when it's time to pass another car. Hope stares out the window at the cotton fields that spread in every direction.

"Thank you," I say. "You really didn't have to do this."

"It's fine." She side-eyes me. "It's been months since I've gotten roped into one of Pam's projects."

"Someday you'll have to train me in your project-avoiding ways."

When we get to the Akin Farm, the pumpkins are already organized on the front lawn. The Akin boys help us load the truck, so it really doesn't take that long. We make the first and second trips, and before I know it, we're on the third, and we're loading the last of the pumpkins.

I tic-shrug as Mrs. Akin presses a couple mason jars into my hands. "Thanks for your help. And please tell your mother thank you, too. She's done such a nice thing, organizing all this." She nods to the jars. "Can you give those to her? They're my Brunswick stew."

"Sure."

I tic-shrug a couple more times, but she doesn't even bat an eyelash. All the ladies in Pam's Sunday school think I'm "just so adorable," and they like to embarrass me by trying to fix me up with their daughters and granddaughters. Then, we do the super polite southern dance of "You're so welcome," and "Oh, no, thank *you*." And then we're off to the church.

We pass the billboard for my dad's store out on 75. You can tell a lot about a place from their billboards. For example, here is a taxonomy of the ones that dot 75 as it winds down through the southern half of Georgia:

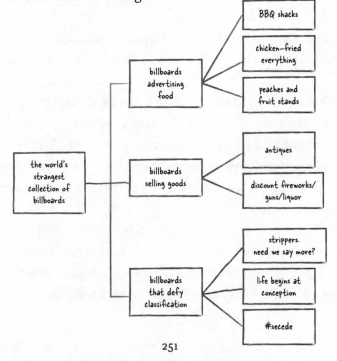

It kind of makes you wonder what the rest of the world thinks about us as they grab their French fries and gasoline on the way to Florida. Sometimes it's weird how it's possible to be simultaneously so proud and embarrassed to be from a place.

Pam is already at the church by the time we get there with the last of our pumpkins. She stands with her megaphone, a petite, motherly dictator, directing people on where to take cans for the food drive, and how to make a festive fall wreath, and where to put the ungodly amount of candy apples she spent all last night making. My mouth waters. Pam's candy apples are basically the best-tasting thing on the planet.

"Your stepmom is kind of a big deal," says Hope.

"Yeah. She's a legend around here because she prayed Jane Fonda into the kingdom."

Hope giggles. "Do I want to know what that means?"

"Jane Fonda is this old, famous lady—"

"I know who Jane Fonda is."

"Well, she used to not be a Christian, and like, everybody hated that about her or something. And Pam's Sunday school teacher said, 'Wouldn't it be so great if she *was* a Christian? Think of all the good she could do with her influence.' And Pam was all, 'I'm going to pray for that Jane Fonda. I'm going to do it every morning.' And now Jane Fonda is totally a Christian and uses her powers for good instead of evil, and Pam is famous."

Hope is full-on belly laughing now. "That. Was everything I thought it could be."

She checks the pumpkins on her side of the truck. It's almost time for the festival. If I'm lucky I'll have a few hours to do stuff with the guys before I have to get ready for Ashley's Halloween/birthday party. I don't have to pick Jayla up until right before—she said something about relaxer and an inch and a half of new growth and desperate times. Hope and I unload most of the last batch by ourselves, but it really isn't bad. A few families are already picking through the pumpkin patch, and a couple kids are watching us.

A little boy jumps up and down. "I think the best ones are still in the truck! Look at that one! I want that one! No, wait, I want that one! It's big as an elephant!"

I grin at him. "It sure is."

He laughs.

Half a second later, I tic. "Sure is."

He laughs again.

"Sure is."

He stops laughing and looks uncertain.

Damn it. I hate it when I scare little kids. "Sure is!"

The boy looks worried, and so does his mom. I don't think I've seen them at church stuff before. It occurs to me that I forgot to take my afternoon dose of meds. He hops over to where his sister is sitting on a giant lopsided pumpkin.

I touch his mom's shoulder. "It's okay. I have Tourette's syndrome."

She nods, but her eyes have shut down. As she goes to join her kids, I tic one more time, the loudest of all: "SURE IS."

The boy startles and peeks over his shoulder in fear.

His mom puts herself in between us like a shield. "Don't worry. He's just retarded," she says.

If she had said it two years ago, I would have wanted to disappear. Now I catch myself. There's nothing wrong with being intellectually disabled, though there is something wrong with A) completely not hearing me about the Tourette's syndrome, and B) using disgusting slurs. Some people don't know how to react to people who are different, I tell myself. And most days I'd probably take it upon myself to go over and educate her, but today I am just bone tired. So, I am going to unload a pumpkin, and then I'm going to unload another pumpkin, and before I know it, a string of moments will carry me away from this one, and it won't seem so fresh once it's a memory.

Hope seems to be following my lead, but then she's standing there, holding her pumpkin to her chest like she's frozen, and I know what she's going to do even before she does it. She sets the pumpkin down and traces her way over to the woman. I think she's going to give her a piece of her mind, but then she kneels by the little boy.

"He's not retarded." She cups her hand to his ear like she's telling him state secrets, but I can hear her stage-whisper from clear across the pumpkin patch. "Also, that's not a nice word, and you really shouldn't say it. He has Tourette's syndrome, and that just means he sometimes says stuff or moves a certain way, and he can't help it. He's also the nicest boy I know and one of the best wrestlers in the whole school."

The boy's eyes go as big as the pumpkins he's sitting on. "Sometimes my dad lets me watch wrestling with him," he says in this awestruck voice.

Hope nods seriously. "He's probably even going to go to state this year."

"Whoa."

"Right?" Her voice goes soft. "He's basically one of the best humans there is."

Her eyes catch mine, and the way she's looking at me, it's like there are little hooks pulling us together or like she's about to cry or like the me she sees is different from the me everyone else sees or like I'm imagining things because in the next second, she looks exactly like how she always looks.

Then she stands and narrows her eyes at his mother just slightly before she walks back to the truck. The boy can't seem to pull his eyes away from me for the rest of the time we're there. I have gone from boogeyman to hero in a matter of seconds.

I'm pulling another pumpkin out of the truck when Hope sidles up next to me. Puts her hand on my arm.

"You okay, Spence?"

"Oh, yeah, sure. I'm fine." I can't remember the last time she called me Spence.

"I'm sorry," she says. "I couldn't help myself."

I grin. "Can you ever?"

CHAPTER 26

Jayla's best friends, Emily and Sheree, are hanging out near the dance floor, but Jayla is nowhere to be found.

"Spencer!" yells Emily.

She and Sheree take turns hugging me around the neck.

"Nice costumes," I tell them.

"I don't know," Sheree says, tugging at her jacket zipper. "I feel like people are looking at me."

"A common side effect of painting your hair white and wearing skin-tight pleather," says Emily.

"Your Storm costume is freaking awesome," I tell Sheree. "Have y'all seen my girlfriend?"

"Nope," says Emily. "Have you seen mine?"

"Negative."

Emily rolls her eyes. "The hazards of dating leading ladies. Well, at least we know yours is at the party, because we came with her. Mine was 'almost done with her hair' half an hour ago."

"I'm sure she'll be here soon," says Sheree.

"Well, FYI, I'm not telling any of you what my costume is until she shows up."

Sheree and I exchange confused glances.

"Um, you're a fifties girl?" says Sheree.

I nod. "Your yellow skirt is kind of a dead giveaway."

Emily shrugs mysteriously. "Just wait till Caroline gets here."

I assess her costume one more time: yellow skirt, white tennis shoes with white folded-down socks, white shirt, yellow sweater. Her hair is in tiny braids, but instead of her usual long ones, these stop at her shoulders and curl upward in a preppy kind of way.

"I got nothing," I say.

This guy Ty, from wrestling, walks by dressed as a zombie, and Sheree's eyes follow him like she's going to say something. Instead, she sighs.

"You're never going to get together if you can't even talk to him," says Emily.

"Who, Ty?" I ask.

Sheree shakes her head fast, like: *Shut up, shut up.*

"Hey, Ty!" I call. He comes over, and we do a handshake/hug/back-slap maneuver. "What's up?"

"Nothing, I was about to go dance." He jerks a thumb toward the dance floor.

"Oh, yeah? Sheree was about to go dance, too."

"Yeah?" He takes in her knee-high boots and tight, tight pants. "Hey . . . Hey, you wanna go dance?"

Sheree seems to have forgotten how to speak, but Emily pushes her forward and that seems like enough. She walks off to the dance floor at Ty's side, turning around to mouth "OH MY GOSH" at us as she goes.

I'm about to brag to Emily about my cupid skills, when I realize that Caroline has finally made her dramatic entrance. Emily can't stop staring, along with pretty much every guy at the party. Caroline has on black leather pants and red high heels and a very small black shirt that shows off her stomach and shoulders. Her reddish-blonde hair is big-curly-sexy, and she looks . . . different. Hot different. She puts an arm around Emily. "Did you figure out what we are yet? She told me she wouldn't tell anyone till I got here."

"Holy crap, you're Sandy before and after."

Caroline flicks pretend ash off her unlit cigarette. "Tell me about it, stud."

She turns to Emily. "Are you so, so mad at me for taking forever?"

Emily is still staring at Caroline's outfit with her mouth half open. "Nope."

Just then, Jayla grabs me by the shirtsleeve of my Ash costume.

"There you are!" I say.

"Spencer, I need your help. That toxic wildebeest Bella Fontaine has been talking crap about Emily again, and she and all her basic friends are over there eating cake right now, so *we're* going to go eat cake right now, and I'm going to be all, 'Hi, Bella.' But in a way that lets her know I know *exactly* what she said. I can't wait to see her go all crazy-eyes."

"Um." That's about as far as I get.

I let myself be pulled closer and closer to the three girls, all of whom are dressed in what appears to be Saran Wrap. And I know it's not going to make a difference, but I pause before we reach them. "Are you sure you want to get into it with her? It's kind of like having a target on your back."

She laughs and waves my words away. "You see a target, I see a spotlight."

Jayla grabs a slice of cake for each of us, which involves her squeezing uncomfortably close to Bella. "Oh, hi, Bella. What are you guys supposed to be?"

Bella points to the sign taped to her body that reads, *We go bad October 31.*

"We're leftovers," she says, like: *Obviously.* Like: *How could you not get this.* "And you guys are those Pokémon people?" She pronounces it wrong.

"Ash, yeah." I'm dressed just like the Pokémon trainer, and Jayla is dressed as the sexiest possible version of his adorable, lightning-bolt-shooting little friend. I'll be sorting out my unnatural feelings for Pikachu all night.

Jayla looks like she's gearing up to give the leftovers a piece of her mind, so I jump in real quick. "Hey, sweetie, how about I get us some punch?"

"Thanks, baby, I'd love some." She smiles, and I kiss her on the cheek and whisper, "Go easy," and she smiles some more.

I wait in line for punch, and Hudson and Jace get in line behind me. I tic-shrug while I'm standing there, really big exaggerated ones that make people look.

Jace whispers to Hudson, "You think he does that while they're geting it on?"

They snicker, and Hudson whispers something back, but I can't hear it. I'm doing a pretty good job ignoring them, until I hear Hudson mutter something about "liking the dark meat."

I turn around and stare at them. And stare. It's not so easy when someone's looking you right in the face, is it? But then it's my turn for punch, so I just say, "Not cool." And walk off with a glass of something pink and sparkling that I hope Jayla will like.

I try to shake it off. I'll be fine. I have an awesome girlfriend, and if I made A Taxonomy of Everyone at This Party, I would totally be in the branch for people that fit in. I just need to find Jayla, and she'll make me feel normal again. Plus, our costume is like 80 percent funnier when I pop her onto my shoulder. But by the time I get back to the leftovers, she's gone.

I find her on the dance floor with Justin. The lights shine

down on them like beacons. He's spinning her and flipping her, and they look like the perfect couple from one of those musicals Hope is always watching. And then it's like I've called her into being by thinking about her because Hope appears next to me, dressed as a pretty badass zebra.

"Hey, are you okay?" she asks.

I shrug. "Nothing punch and cake can't fix. Except, since it's wrestling season, could you eat the punch and cake and then tell me in excruciating detail how awesome it is?"

Hope picks up a cake plate and wrinkles her nose. "You do realize this is super creepy, right?"

"Oh, totally."

"Well, as long as we've got that established." She takes a bite of cake, and we both laugh.

"Spencer? Are you over here?"

Jayla's voice announces her arrival before we see her. Or before she finds us. That's what it feels like. Because as soon as she spots Hope and me side by side at the cake table, her laughter dies in the back of her throat, and she says, "Oh."

And it is definitely the bad kind of "Oh."

Hope brushes nonexistent dirt off her black-and-white leggings. "Well, I better get back to the party. See you guys."

I will not be escaping so easily.

"I was looking for you," says Jayla. "It's a party. And there's dancing. I shouldn't be dancing by myself when I have a boyfriend." She shoots an irritated glance in Hope's direction.

"I wouldn't have even been talking to her if you weren't dancing with Justin."

She throws her hands in the air. "We were performing a dance from a musical."

"Yeah, with your arms all wrapped around each other like you're in love with him. Why do you always have to do stuff like that?"

"Because you won't do it with me, and I don't want to not dance." Her voice goes soft. "What I was saying before, about targets and seeing things differently? I was kidding around, but it's more than that. I feel like I don't get to shine as brightly when I'm with you."

And I go from angry to feeling like shit in 0.2 seconds. "I'm so sorry. I mean, that's not okay. At all."

"No, it's not." She wraps her arms around herself like she's cold, even though Ashley's dad packed the tent with portable heaters. "I've got everything against me in this world, and I've got so many dreams. I can't have anything else holding me down." She's blinking her eyes so fast, and it makes me realize I don't think I've ever seen her cry. "I love you, Spencer." She doesn't say "but," but I can hear it all the same.

"I love you, too."

"And I'm spending next weekend with you, not Justin." She wraps her arms around me and squeezes me tight. "Dance with me."

Next weekend. Everything that just happened seems stupid compared to that. I do really hate dancing, though. I love *watching* her dance. In the latest school musical or at a party or around her bedroom. She always has this light-up-the-whole-room smile on her face.

"What if I just hang out while you dance?" I ask hopefully.

"Yeah . . . nice try."

She grabs me by the hand and drags me onto the dance floor.

Part Six
18 years old

A TAXONOMY OF LEAVING

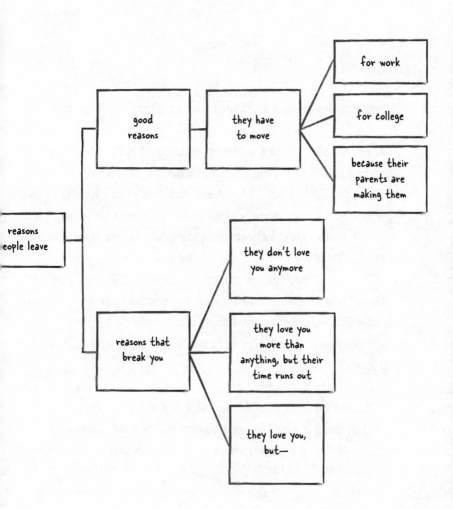

CHAPTER

27

Fact: Forever always ends up being shorter than you think.

Paul slides the last of his Magic cards into his deck and claps me on the back. "We're going, man. It's my last chance to see Eva."

That's right. Paul "The Perpetual Bachelor" Kravitz has a girlfriend. Unfortunately, she's moving to another state.

"What if I just stay here and look at all the pictures you guys take? It'll totally be like I was at the party."

"Yeah, no." Paul grabs one of my arms, and Traven grabs the other. "You're going, and I will force you to have fun if I need to. Senior year is supposed to be our year."

I gesture to our Magic card empire. "Are you sure you want to leave all this?"

"Yes. Have you *seen* Eva?"

Traven nods. "I've seen her. She is pretty hot, dude."

They drag me out of my house and down my driveway.

"It's just the next street over. You can always walk home if it's awful," says Paul.

I let them cajole me over to Ethan and Jace's house, but I stop on their front porch.

"But—"

"Dude, it's going to be fine," says Traven, as he opens the door. "Everyone in school is here. What are the chances you're even going to—" He stops walking. "See her."

Jayla is standing with Sheree and Emily just inside the front door. Our eyes meet. Our friends scatter. Which, super helpful—thanks, guys.

"Hi," she says.

"Hi."

Long, terrible seconds pass. I'm not ready for this.

"Well, I'll see you around, okay?" I go to leave, but she touches my shoulder.

"I hope you're doing okay. You're a good guy, Spencer."

She's wearing the pity face utilized by dumpers everywhere. I decide it is time for this dumpee to flee.

"Thanks. Um, you, too."

I squeeze past her, so I can find my friends. And that's it. Two years, and half my high school memories, just, *poof*, gone.

I look around the living room. Paul is already making out with Eva. Traven has completely disappeared. Dean, Ethan, and Bella are sitting on the couch drinking beer and catching up because Dean and Ethan just got home from college for Thanksgiving break today, which is nice for them, but honestly? They are totally being Those College Students Who Come Back to High School right now.

I try the kitchen. Still no Traven, but Hudson and Jace are in there trying to figure out what you have to mix with gin for it to taste good. I grab a two-liter bottle of Diet Coke because wrestling season is already a go. I tic-sniff a few times as I unscrew the cap, and just as I'm about to pour, my shoulder shrugs start up. I sigh and set the bottle down. We've been easing back on my meds all semester, because I'm older now, and maybe it'll be okay, and the meds make me foggy. Which means sooner or later my tics will probably get worse. But that doesn't mean that's what's happening here. I mean, this could be a completely unrelated bad-tic day. I sniff again.

"You okay, man?" asks Jace.

"Yeah, I'm good." I wait for him to make fun of me or start mimicking my tics or something, but he doesn't.

"I heard you and Jayla broke up," says Hudson.

"Yeah, that freaking sucks," says Jace. "That girl is hot as hell."

We all stare at my ex-girlfriend, who is currently in the living room talking to my brother.

"Thanks. Yeah, she's pretty amazing." I tic as I'm bringing my cup to my mouth and almost spill Diet Coke all over myself, and again, nothing from the peanut gallery.

I don't know if they've had some sort of empathy awakening or if they've decided I'm one of the guys now, but—

"That ass," says Jace.

"I bet she's really flexible," says Hudson. "Is she? You can tell us, man."

I give him the deadliest of side eyes. "Why would you even ask that?"

"Whoa, sorry." Hudson nudges Jace and says in a stage whisper, "Someone's still taking the break up hard."

But it's not even that. It's like, would they really be talking about Jayla like that if she was white? And it kind of makes me feel sick because I have this awful feeling that my friends and I do the same thing. Maybe I'm not as bad as Hudson and Jace, but isn't "hot" or "sexy" the first thing that pops in my head when I see her?

I think about saying something else, but they've already moved on.

"Dude, Hudson, check it. That *My Little Pony* kid is wearing leather pants."

Hudson leans into the doorway so he can see better. "What the fuck, dude?"

Jace laughs. "Oh, man, now he's talking to Ashley. You better watch out. He's gonna get a piece of your ex-girlfriend."

"That kid is going to be a virgin for the rest of his life."

My fingers clench and unclench at my side. They move on to doing impressions of what Ashley sounds like when she calls Hudson crying. Which apparently used to be every other day.

Okay, so that's a definite no on the empathy. I guess they really are being nice to me because they see me as one of them now. But instead of feeling good, it just feels gross.

I go outside and sit on the diving board with my feet skimming the pool cover. (Mr. and Mrs. Wells already closed it for the winter. Not that that's going to stop a house full of intoxicated high schoolers from ripping off the cover at three AM.)

I mostly alternate between staring through the wall of windows at the people dancing in the living room and reading an article on my phone about controlling the behavior of fruit flies with optogenetics. I am basically the coolest guy at this party and possibly in the entire universe.

I don't notice Hope walking down the brick pathway or standing behind me, but I do notice when the diving board jiggles, and she peeks over my shoulder at my phone.

"Whatcha doin'?"

I shove my phone in my pocket. "Nothing. Reading." I point at the window. "Thinking about how I don't fit in with the aquarium of dancing drunk people."

Hope smirks. "I'm pretty sure that's a good thing."

But my mind is in serious mode right now. I slouch lower on the diving board.

"Hey." She bumps her shoulder against mine. "You fit with me. You're the only person I know who knows we'll never be too old to climb pecan trees."

I can't help but smile at that.

"Who cares that you don't fit with the rest of them? The rest of them don't know how to make me laugh after Janie, and the rest of them aren't going to visit all seven continents or go to New Zealand to see the coolest glowworms ever or live in a great big house on a hill with trees that grow right up through the inside."

I raise my eyebrows, and she shrugs. "It's a thing. I've seen it."

I could get on board with that. "And a secret passage?"

"Obviously, a secret passage. It can lead to the library, which will be big enough to need those ladder things that you ride around on."

"Oh! And a dumbwaiter. I've always wanted to try to ride in one of those, too."

She nods. "And a hedge maze."

"YES."

"You see? We'll do things they couldn't even dream of."

She said "we." At first I thought she was talking about our separate futures, or maybe things we both wanted, but not necessarily *together*. But now that she's said it, I realize I want it. I want us to be a we.

She's waiting for me to say something. But, no. I can't like her. It wasn't all that long ago that we almost lost each other for good. It may feel like she likes me right now, but I'm probably just imagining it. There is no way I'm ruining things again.

"That sounds great." It's all I can manage.

"Yeah," she says, and her cheeks go pink.

I look back at the window. If I squint, I can just make out which one of the dancing aquarium people is my girlfriend dancing with another guy. Ex. Ex-girlfriend.

"Do you want to get out of here?" I say. "I kind of feel like walking home."

"Sure."

I don't want to fit with these people who make fun of other people. It's one thing when they're making fun of me, but being on the other side makes me sick to my stomach. I imagine a taxonomy of this party—I don't want to be on any branch that includes Hudson and Jace. Why did I feel like this was something I needed so badly? And how much life did I miss out on while I was beating my brains out trying to make them like me?

Traven pops outside. "Oh, sorry," he says, like he's interrupting something.

"No, you're good," I say.

"Oh, good." He literally sighs with relief. "Because some guys in there are being real assholes, and I kind of want to go."

Hope smiles. "We're going, too. To an asshole-free zone."

I walk home with my friends, and I don't even worry about who's doing what inside that house and what they might think about me. If it's a matter of us vs. them, I always want to be on the side of people who choose kindness over hate.

CHAPTER
28
♥

It's hot for November. And wet. The kind where it's as humid as it can possibly be without actually raining, and you wish the sky would just put itself out of its misery and wring out the clouds already.

And it does. A single cool raindrop on my cheek. Another on the back of my hand. I slam the door to the truck, and Dean and I race for the steps to the porch, even though it would probably feel pretty good to get caught in the rain. You can almost hear a hiss of relief with each drop that hits the ground. Sunshiny rain has always been Hope's favorite weather to run in.

"Pam, do we have any more SunChips?" yells Dean as he walks inside. He's been home for forty-eight hours and at least half of them have been spent eating.

"They're in the pantry." I hear the sound of my brother banging around boxes and jars. "Top shelf," she calls.

The rustling stops. "Oh. Right."

He walks into the kitchen eating a mini-bag of Harvest Cheddar (read: the inferior choice to Garden Salsa). I stare out the window. In the Birdsongs' backyard, outfitted from head to toe in running gear, is Hope. She tilts her face toward the sky and lets the rain fall on her cheeks. And it's hard to say from here, but I bet you anything she's smiling.

In the next second, she's off. Streaking up the dirt path that winds through the woods behind our houses. It kind of makes me want to go for a run myself, or maybe a bike ride.

I sniff-shrug-sniff in rapid succession.

Pam's head shoots up. "How are your tics doing?"

"Fine," I say quickly, even though I'm pretty sure it's not true. Ever since we went from two pills a day to one, things haven't been right.

"You getting the headaches again?" she asks.

"Yeah, but I got those the last two times, too." Headaches and a little bit of a heart-racing feeling, but the doctor said those are totally normal withdrawal symptoms, especially since the medication was originally developed to be a blood pressure drug.

I keep tic-ing (well, of course I'm tic-ing now that Pam's eyeing me like that), and she keeps watching. Yep, it's definitely time to go.

"I think I'm gonna bike around the neighborhood," I say.

"Not in that, you're not," says Pam.

"It's just a little rain."

"Yeah, right now." She taps the screen of her phone. "We're in for a thunderstorm. Maybe even hail."

"Hail? Does that even happen down here?" asks Dean, just as I say, "Are you sure? Hope just took off running."

There is only one logical course of action—I've got to stop her. I don't wait for Pam to protest. I run outside and sprint across the yard and up the path. Most of the leaves have been crunched until they're nothing but dust under my feet. The rain soaks my hair and T-shirt (which feels great) and my jeans (which feels absolutely disgusting). I run faster. The sooner I catch up to her, the sooner I can go home and change. I'm in good shape. I play a varsity sport. How fast can she be?

Damn fast. That's how fast. Leave-Spencer's-sorry-ass-in-the-dust fast.

I've been flat-out sprinting, and I haven't caught sight of her. Not even a flash of white hair. And now, for added fun, the water has dripped down my legs and into my shoes and socks. Whenever I take a step, it makes a double squelching noise. Once for my soggy shoes. Once for the mud that doesn't want to let me go. I try to avoid it, but my jeans are stiff and heavy, and I'm not exactly a master of dexterity right now.

"Hope!" I probably should have thought of this before, this whole yelling her name thing.

"Hope!" There are tree roots and briars grabbing at my feet and fallen branches to leap over. The rain's coming down so thick, I can barely see the path.

"HOPE!" And then my foot punches through some loose dirt and into a hole in the ground, and I fall with a splat into three inches of mud.

Well, that's great. Just great. I can't find Hope anywhere, and I'm soaking wet and covered in mud, and ow, fuck, I just tried to move my foot and something feels really wrong.

This is all kinds of bad. If it keeps me from wrestling . . . No. I don't even want to think about it. Let's worry about the things that are important in the present. Namely, I'm all alone in the middle of nowhere and who knows if I can walk right now. I wiggle my foot out of the hole. It looks like a place where a tree died and the roots and everything rotted out. I take a tentative step. Okay. Okay. It hurts, but I can do it. That probably means it's not broken. I try another step.

"Spencer?"

I freeze. Hope stands in the middle of the path, her eyebrows crinkled in confusion, her hair more blonde than white now that it's soaked with rainwater, and—

Oh, crap. Her shirt is soaked with rainwater, too. And it's white. It clings to her body in see-through patches, and her sports-bra thingy underneath is hot pink, and okay, I can't look at her anymore.

"What are you doing out here?"

I keep my eyes carefully trained on her face. "I was looking for you. Pam says there's gonna be a thunderstorm with hail and stuff, and we saw you run into the woods . . ."

"Hail? In South Georgia?"

I shrug.

As if in response, hail starts falling all around us. Hard little chunks that tear through the trees like bullets and land with soft thumps in the leaves below.

"Mother scratcher," Hope hisses, rubbing her arm. She pulls her hand away to reveal a dime-size pink welt.

We look at each other, and I know we're thinking the same thing: If we try to make it home, we'll get slaughtered.

I shift my weight and have to put my hand against the tree to steady myself. Twenty yards past that tree is another tree. Well, we're in the woods, there are trees everywhere, but I mean a tree I actually recognize. Dad's tree stand—the one where he and Dean hang out—is at the top.

"C'mon," I yell.

I take her hand and nearly pull her down in the mud with me when I try to run.

"What are you doing?" She looks kind of annoyed, not that I blame her.

"My dad has a tree stand over there. We can wait it out."

Hope cups her hand to her brow. "Yeah, okay."

Then she slides an arm around my waist.

"But—"

"Don't pretend you don't need my help."

I think about protesting again, but she glares me into silence. Somehow we walk/tumble/crash through layers of vines and undergrowth and make it to the ladder under the tree stand. I apologize about a billion times. But now we have to make it up the ladder. And did I mention we are still being pelted with hail?

I climb up first, with Hope spotting me. At one point, I slip, and she has to grab my butt to keep me from knocking us both to the ground. I mostly try not to think about it. When I finally feel the boards of the platform, I could cry, I'm so happy. I roll myself onto the deck with Hope's help and crawl inside. It really is like a grown-up tree house. The roof isn't tall enough to stand up, but it keeps out the hail and most of the rain. I lie on the floor panting.

"That. Was awful."

Hope laughs. "Maybe you shouldn't try to rescue me so much. It doesn't really work out for you."

I scoff. "This was an excellent rescue. We're safe, aren't we?"

"Oh, sure. It was, um, super manly. Especially the part where I had to push you up here by your butt. Very gallant."

"Thank you." I cross my arms over my chest and sit up so I'm leaning against the wall.

Hope sits next to me, and because the tree stand is so small, she has to sit rightnext to me.

"Glad to know my skills are appreciated," I say. "Meanwhile, if you could stop putting yourself in life-threatening situations, it would make my life a whole lot easier."

"Are you kidding? There's no way I was passing this up. It's perfect running weather. I mean, before it started hailing."

"Ha." I take off my socks and shoes because they're still so squishy and gross. I wish I could take off my pants, too, but that would probably be awkward.

Hope fusses over my ankle, which is A) swollen, B) already turning purple, and C) still hurts like a mofo. Then, she settles back in beside me, and we're shoulder to shoulder, but that's okay because we're friends. I just need to be cool with it. I mean, if I scoot away, that would only make everything more obvious.

"Do you ever have a day that feels like a metaphor for your whole life?" she says.

"Um." I honestly don't know what she's talking about.

She smiles. "So, that's a no." She twists her shirt to wring some of the water out of it, but despite the trickle of droplets that hit the floor, she still looks like a cat that just had a bath. "I was just thinking about how I ran out into the storm because I'm so worried I'll miss something. I'm so scared all the time because there are so many things I want to do and see, and what if I don't get to?"

"Hey, you'll get to. Of course you will. I don't know anyone who's as driven as you."

She shakes her head. "But she didn't. And I want to do a lot of things, Spence. A lifetime wouldn't be enough time, and that's, like, a Mimi lifetime. But what if I don't get that much? Janie had so many plans and now she's just gone. Why do people have to die? It's so horrible."

I don't know what to say, so I press my shoulder and hip against hers like I'm trying to send her messages. It seems to work.

"I'm sorry. I know that normal people don't spend tons of time thinking how sad it is that people die, but sometimes it's all I can think about. I think about never reading one more book or thinking one more thought or having one more kiss, ever again, and it's so terrifying. Sometimes, I just sit and think about what it would be like to not be able to think anymore. What it'll feel like when I'm gone."

"I don't think it's weird to be scared of that," I say. I chew on my lip and think about it for a while. "Do you believe in heaven?"

"Yeah." Her eyes go a little desperate. "Yeah, I have to, because I have to believe I'll see her again."

I nod. "Me, too."

Neither of us says anything for a while.

Hope brushes her hair out of her face. "Did I tell you I've been e-mailing with her boyfriend?"

"Oh, wow, I didn't know that. What was his name?"

"Nolan."

"Right, Nolan." I think I remember meeting him at the funeral.

"We're actually going to visit him in South Africa for a whole week. Like, Mom, Dad, all of us." She smiles at the thought of it. "We're leaving in a few days. Oh. That reminds me. I'm supposed to ask you if you'll check our mail while we're gone."

"Sure. So, uh, what's he like?"

"He's . . . interesting."

I snort, and Hope laughs.

"No, I don't mean it like that. It's just. Her other boyfriends were a lot like Dean, and this one was more of a—" She blushes. "Well, he's different."

I guess I'm not surprised to hear Janie's boyfriends were like Dean. The Deans of the world get the girls. It's like a law of nature.

"I guess I'm realizing that maybe my sister didn't have everything all figured out. Maybe she was still figuring things out, too." Hope shivers and rubs her arms. "Anyway, thanks for listening to all of that. I could never talk about this kind of stuff around Mikey. That's kind of why I broke up with him."

"Oh, yeah?" I try not to sit up straighter or anything, but she almost never talks about them breaking up. "What kind of stuff?"

"I don't know. Honest stuff? Maybe that's not right. I'm not pretending when I'm happy. But sometimes I'm not happy. I felt like I could never be serious around Mikey—but at least I could be angry? And I can't be sad *or* angry around most people."

Is it wrong that it feels so good to hear her say that about Mikey? Oh, she's looking at me expectantly. This is the part where I'm supposed to say something. "That has to be really hard."

She shrugs. "It's okay. I think as long as you've got at least one person you can tell all your stuff to, that can be enough."

She holds my hand and rests her head against my shoulder. But it's okay, because friends can do that, right? And our fingers are cupped and not interlocked, so it barely counts.

"Thanks for being my friend. Again. I'm glad you didn't give up," she says.

She's talking really close to my face, but it's okay. I think friends probably do that, too.

Then she leans in like she's going to kiss me. Okay, if the past has taught me anything, it's that friends definitely do not kiss each other. Like, ever. Like, it causes a friendship apocalypse, in fact. So, even though our mouths are so close together, and her eyelids are halfway shut, and I can feel her breath against my cheeks and see the rain dripping from the ends of her hair—

She kisses me.

Lightly on the lips and just for a second. Atomic bombs go off in little thought bubbles over our heads. And then we're staring at each other, watching the fallout on each other's faces. Her eyes are saying everything I'm thinking: This can't be a one-time thing. It has to happen again.

Now. It has to happen now.

I lean forward again, and her lips are parted this time, and I can see the smallest crescent of tongue inside her mouth, and I want so many things.

But before we can kiss again, she says, "I can't."

My mouth opens and closes. Did I misread everything? *Again?* I don't understand. She kissed me first.

"No, it's not that." She squeezes my shoulder like that's supposed to tell me something.

It doesn't work. There are hummingbirds where my lungs should be. "I'm sorry. I thought—"

"It's okay."

I cup my hand over my mouth. "Oh, gosh. I'm so sorry."

"I wanted to." She takes a deep breath. "I want to. I—well, there's something I need to do first."

I'm so scared this is all going to disappear. "But after?"

"After."

It feels like a promise.

Hope helps me up my back porch, and I watch her walk into her house, waiting until that last flash of white hair disappears with the close of a door. Then I tear (read: hop clumsily on one foot) upstairs to my bedroom. Rip open my blinds. Hope's window is right across from mine, and if I see her it means, well, I don't know, SOMETHING. I need to know, is she dancing around her room? Is she brushing her teeth repeatedly?

There she is! She's walking to the other side of the room! She's—oh, holy crap, she's looking out her window, too, and she just saw me. I flip to the side, my back against the wall. I'm huffing and panting. I can't believe she saw me. It's so embarrassing. Hey, wait. She was looking, too. SHE WAS LOOKING, TOO. I peek back, and she's still there. She gives me a wave before she pulls the blinds shut.

I clutch my heart. That smile. That wave. I float over to my bed and fall spread-eagle onto my back.

CHAPTER

29

A recap:

- Hope and I have kissed.
- Neither of us has a boyfriend/girlfriend.
- I have no idea what to do next.

Naturally, my next move is to involve Paul. I follow him downstairs to his basement to play foosball, which I'm pretty sure is a homeopathic therapy for relationship problems. I move slowly, gingerly, careful about how I apply weight to my ankle (which is, thankfully, not broken or even sprained, just like, badly bruised or something).

"I don't see why you're freaking out," he says. "Based on everything you just told me about what happened in the tree house—"

"Tree *stand.*"

"Whatever. You should be totally fine."

"Ah, but then there's two hours ago."

He swivels his little wooden man back and forth, trying to get the ball out of a corner. "What happened two hours ago?"

"I saw her when I was leaving the house, and I was like 'Hey, Hope.' But she seemed really flustered, and she was all, 'Hey, sorry, I can't talk right now. I have to meet my dad so we can pick up some stuff for the trip, and I'm already late.' And I was all—"

Paul jerks one of his handles and the ball shoots across the table and hits the back of my goal with a *thwack.* "Terminator!"

I raise my eyebrows.

"Sorry. What?"

I roll my eyes, but I'm laughing. "She was leaving, and I was all, 'Oh, okay, well what about . . . ?' And then she smiled and squeezed my shoulder and said, 'Later. I gotta go.'"

"Huh. 'I gotta go.'"

"But it wasn't necessarily a bad 'I gotta go.'"

Paul is more skeptical. "Is there any such thing as a good 'I gotta go'?"

"I don't know." He scores. Again. "You're not helping!"

"Helping beat your ass at foosball."

"Ha."

I could ask Dean—he has tons of experience with girls. My desperate brain tries to forget for a second that Hope is included in that "tons of experience." I shudder.

Paul is pretty unhelpful, despite his recent influx of experience in the girl department, but getting creamed three times in a row at foosball has a surprisingly positive effect on my mood. I'm definitely not freaking out anymore (well, not more than a little bit) on the drive home.

I keep coming back to Dean. What if I don't tell him it's Hope? If I just say "a girl." I'd still feel pretty gross, though. Maybe I should just ask Hope herself. Yeah, or at least say hi. Make sure she's okay.

I get out of the truck and stand on my front porch, keys in hand, debating.

Then I see Hope leave her house. She's walking this way! This is even better! But before she can get to the stepping-stone path that leads to the porch, she veers off like she's going to the side of the house. I run to the edge of the porch. No, she IS going to the side of the house. She kneels in front of Dean's window. Wedges her hands in the space where he keeps the window permanently cracked.

This isn't happening.

She didn't just open his window and slip into his room. And I am not hopping the porch railing and trailing after her like some kind of pathetic stray dog. I hear the creak of her landing on his bed. He hears it, too, because he turns from where he's digging through his closet, and his face lights up. I freeze because I don't want him to see me. I freeze because the girl I love, the girl I thought might finally feel something back, is on my brother's bed, and it turns me to stone.

They don't seem angry at each other. She's saying something, but I can't hear what. And then he says something back, and her arms wrap around his neck, and he pulls her against him by the waist like they've done this a hundred times. Because of course they have.

I can't watch anymore.

I don't know what to do with myself. I go to my room and lie on my bed with the knowledge that Hope is still in my house right this second doing who knows what with my brother. I don't understand how she could kiss me one minute and want him the next. I keep turning over all the information in my head, trying to organize our feelings and classify what we are to each other, but there is no solution. I can't make any sense of it. Unless. I don't even want to admit it to myself. Unless the kiss in the tree was an anomaly. Because Dean always gets the girl. That's the pattern, right? Of course, Hope would pick him over me. Again. Anyone would. Everyone does. These are things I already know, but they hurt more this time than they ever have before.

"Spence?" She's in my doorway.

Hope is in my doorway, and she's smiling so big (of course she is), and then she's sitting beside me on my bed. I'm reminded of that time in my attic. I know how this plays out. Except I don't think I can handle another dose of her pity/happiness cocktail.

"Hi," she says. Again with the smiling. She's practically bouncing.

"Hi." My arms are crossed over my chest, but it's like she can't even detect my sourness.

"Sorry I had to run off before." She grins again. Her face is going to hurt tomorrow if she doesn't cut it out. "But I'm here now."

Now. As opposed to where she was five minutes ago.

The smile train finally stops. "You seem really bummed out. Are you okay?"

She tries to arrange her face into an expression that is appropriately sympathetic. It bugs me how much she fails.

"No. You know what? I'm not okay. I'm sick of you stringing me along for the past five years. And I'm *really* sick of seeing you screwing around with Dean."

"What are you talking about? I—"

There is searing rage tunneling through the space where my heart used to be. I'm not about to listen to her excuses.

"Just stop. I am done with you and your bullshit. Congrats on being one of Dean's girls."

Hope is curling up and dying on the inside, I can see it on her face. Which is good. Because now maybe we're even.

She stands there and stares at me for a good five seconds.

"I can't believe you," she finally says. Her voice cracks, and she's gone.

I think all our chances are gone, too.

CHAPTER 30

There are a lot of good reasons not to go hunting with Dad and Dean today:

1) Sleep. I like it. Getting up at the ass-crack of dawn on a non-school day is not my idea of a good time.

2) A certain incident involving a certain Bubba Blade and an uncertain amount of vomit.

3) I don't want to accidentally punch my brother in the face.

4) It's not like they'll notice whether I'm there or not.

It's always been like this. Even when we go camping. You'd think us being crammed into a tent, the only three people for miles and miles and miles, would bring us together. Fresh mountain air and manly bonding and all that shit. But they're always off hunting. Or strategizing about hunting. Or sharing war stories about The Hunt. And I'm hunkered over my magnifying glass trying to check off more bugs in my beat-up copy of *The National Audubon Society Field Guide to Insects and Spiders*.

But none of these are the most important reason I'm not hunting today. No, no, no. That would be:

5) Today is the Wednesday before Thanksgiving, which means Dad's intensity will be dialed up to an eleven, and if he doesn't shoot a wild turkey, he'll come home from today's hunting trip with a store-bought turkey and a magnum of shame.

≷ ♥ ≶

When I wake up Thanksgiving morning, there's a burlap sack with a freshly shot turkey sitting on the kitchen island, and all is right with the world. The conquering heroes emerged victorious from yesterday's hunt, and now's when I feel like I can really contribute. I have a particular set of skills, and while those skills do not include hunting, they definitely include eating. And Thanksgiving is the one day during all of wrestling season for which I make an exception.

I spent most of yesterday helping Pam make pies—blackberry-apple, chocolate-pecan, pumpkin and cherry and coconut cream. This morning she started on the vegetables, and I worked on this sweet-potato thing topped with a crunchy brown sugar–pecan mixture. Mimi is making Brunswick stew, which isn't really a Thanksgiving thing, but nobody cares because Mimi makes a mean venison Brunswick stew. And if you want to go all traditional, you're technically supposed to make it with squirrel, but really, who wants to eat a squirrel? I think she's mostly making it so she could use some of the deer Dean shot yesterday, and even though I hate going hunting with Dad and Dean, I still think it's pretty cool how they never hunt more than we can eat.

"Spencer! Where have you been, my love chicken?" Mimi squeezes me into a hug that smells like her sugar-lemon hand lotion. And safety. If safety had a smell, it would definitely be sugar lemon. "Do you mind taking out the trash again?" she asks. "We seem to create extra on Thanksgiving."

"Wait, let me get these in first." Pam moves to dump some pie crust trimmings, but Mimi stops her.

"Oh, no, dear. Save those for the possum plate."

Some people compost. Mimi has a possum plate. Only Mimi has a heart big enough for the possums (or raccoons or flesh-eating Morlocks or whatever it is that comes to eat our food scraps in the middle of the night). It's really pretty impressive. Have you ever *seen* a possum? They make rats look positively cuddly.

Pam's face pinches. She clearly does not share Mimi's affinity for butter-faced marsupials. "Here." She deposits the floury scraps in Mimi's hands. "I'll let you take care of that."

Pam and Mimi are incapable of preparing a meal without sniping at each other (too many Mama Bears in the kitchen), and I'm not expecting a Thanksgiving miracle today, so I grab the trash bag and haul ass, but not before I hear Pam mutter something about vermin.

I'm just shutting the lid on the trash can when I hear: "Hey, Spencer."

My dad emerges from behind the woodpile, cigar smoke clinging to his clothes. I hope he knows he's not fooling anyone.

"Yes, sir?"

He brushes at the front of his jacket. "Listen, I've got a big sale going on for Black Friday, and I think we're gonna be short-staffed."

"Do you want me to help?" I try not to sound like it matters too much.

"The store'll be pretty packed . . ."

"Oh."

"I've been watching you work. It seems like you're a lot more comfortable with talking to people. Do you think you can handle it?"

He *noticed*. "Yeah. Yeah, definitely."

He grins. "Well, great."

I grin back. "Yeah."

"Well, I'm just gonna get a little more fresh air. I'll see you inside."

"Okay."

He's going to walk around the yard until the cigar smell goes away, but I'm so happy I don't even care. All the stuff I learned at camp and from meeting other people with Tourette's, figuring out how to explain it to people in a way that makes me feel the most confident—I never would have guessed those things would have helped just as much as my meds, but now I feel like everything is paying off. When I get back inside, Mimi is making sweet tea.

"Didn't Pam already do that?" I ask.

Mimi glances around and puts an arm around me conspiratorially. "That woman can't make sweet tea to save her life, bless her heart." She stirs faster. "I poured hers down the sink, and I'll have this in the fridge before she gets out of the shower. You got my back?"

I cross my arms like I'm really taking my time to think about it. Mimi looks scandalized.

"You know I've got your back."

"And I've got yours, chickadee."

She puts the new pitcher of sweet tea away, and I go upstairs to change into a polo shirt and khakis because that's something we do on Thanksgiving. I take a bag of ice, too, so I can sit on my bed and RICE (Rest. Ice. Compression. Elevation.) my ankle again.

RICEing is pretty boring. I stare at the ceiling for a few minutes, and then I attempt to re-read *Harry Potter* for the eighty-seventh time, while Lord Voldemort silently judges me for how I handled things with Hope.

"Dude, I know it was a dick move. You don't have to stare at me like that."

He bites the head off a cricket in reply.

I turn my body so I can't see him because eight eyes' worth of judgment is A LOT of judgment. I guess I get a little carried away what with the reading and self-loathing, because by the time I get back downstairs, Mimi is gone, and Pam is crying.

"I can't believe it," she says.

"Is it the tea?"

"What?"

"Nothing."

"The rolls." Pam is full-on sobbing now. "I let them go too long while I was getting ready, and now they're burnt to a crisp."

The rolls are the only part of Thanksgiving that's not made from scratch (well, that and the cranberry sauce—hello, my delicious, gelatinous friend). They're just these Hawaiian rolls we get at the store. No big deal.

I try telling this to Pam. "Don't worry. Those are like the least-important part of Thanksgiving."

"But they're your dad's favorite."

"Um." I am starting to feel completely and utterly out of my depth when Mimi swoops into the kitchen. Oh, thank goodness.

"Don't you worry." She wraps Pam in a hug. "I'll send the boys out to get more, and they'll be back before you know they're gone. You've made the loveliest meal."

Pam nods and cries and cries and nods. Mimi sends her upstairs to fix her makeup.

"That was really nice of you," I say.

Mimi acts mock-offended. "Well, of course it was. I'm a nice person."

"I guess I've always kind of thought you didn't like Pam."

Mimi puts her arm around me. "I didn't at first. But it takes a special kind of person to love someone else's children like that."

My grandma doesn't often let her soft underbelly show, especially where Pam is concerned. I kind of just stare at her, stunned.

"She still can't make sweet tea worth a damn."

There's the Mimi I know and love.

"Get your brother and get to the store."

Oh heck no. "I'll just go by myself."

"Oh, no, you will not. Dean, get up here!"

Dean and I haven't been alone together since three days ago when I saw Hope crawl through his window, I've made sure of it. I suspect Mimi has noticed and this is part of one of her plots.

My brother emerges from the basement with video-game haze in his eyes.

"Dean, you and Spencer are going to the store to get more rolls."

"Yeah, okay. I feel like I haven't seen you all break, man."

I start to protest, but she grabs him with one hand and me with the other and pushes us together. "You're going or you're not getting any pie." She pokes me in the back with her finger. "And *smile*," she whispers.

I really do try to smile during the car trip. It feels like my face is doing a bench press.

Dean makes small talk about college. Mostly about all the girls he's hooking up with. I stop bench-press smiling and consider punching him in the face. Luckily, we are already in the grocery-store parking lot.

"I'll get the bread. Don't bother parking," I say, and then practically tuck and roll out of the truck.

The rolls are easy to find and not sold out, which means I definitely have something to be thankful for today. I feel less thankful when I get back in the truck with Dean's ugly face. At least this time he takes the hint and stops trying to talk to me.

Then we get home, and Pam hugs us and tells us what wonderful boys we are and almost cries again. And then, The Eating. And it is some oh-so-wonderful eating. I almost forget how pissed I am at Dean. Almost. I still remember to "forget" to pass him the mashed potatoes until the third time he asks, and I also make sure to give him the stink eye and accidentally kick him under the table at regular intervals. But it's when we get up for second helpings of pie and I cut in front of him for a piece of chocolate-pecan that the shit really hits the fan.

"What the hell is your problem?" he hisses.

I peek over my shoulder to make sure the rest of the family is still at the table.

"I don't know what you're talking about."

"Um. You've been acting like a little punk all day, but okay, sure, nothing's wrong." And then he picks up my piece of pie (MY PIE) and starts walking back to the table.

And I am just so damn sick of him taking everything from everyone and never thinking about how his actions affect other people that I snap.

"YOU."

He turns. So do the heads of everyone currently enjoying Thanksgiving dinner (now with a show!).

I lower my voice. "You're my problem."

He rolls his eyes and grabs me by the elbow. "Spencer and I need to talk about something downstairs. We'll be right back."

He frog-marches me down and then sits on the couch. "Well? Let's do this, drama king." He takes a bite of my pie. Dean knows how to push all my buttons—he's the one who installed them.

"You're an asshole," I say. "I know you hooked up with her in your room this week, and you don't even care about her, and you're screwing around with all these girls at school, and you're an asshole."

"You said that already." Dean sets the pie on the coffee table, and at least has the decency to look ashamed. "And I really am sorry about that. I don't know what she told you, but I—"

I stamp my foot like a toddler. I am livid, and this rage fountain is coming out, sorry excuses or no. "How could you do this to me? How could you? Anyone else but her."

Dean throws his hands in the air. "That's what I'm trying to tell you. I didn't *do* anything."

The memories of that day flood back, and I let them. I take a fucking misery bath in them. "*Liar.* I saw her sneaking in your window."

My brother makes a stupider face than usual. "Wait, who are we talking about?"

And I say, "Hope," just as he says, "Jayla, right?"

There are three seconds of silence that feel like standing on the lid of a dormant volcano.

"Wait, *Jayla*? You had sex with Jayla, too?" *BOOM*.

"No, I *didn't* have sex with Jayla. That's what I'm trying to tell you. We walked home from Ethan's party together, and she said you guys had broken up, and you wouldn't even care if we hooked up because you were so into Hope. And out of respect for you, I asked her to put her shirt back on and took her home. Which wasn't easy because I actually think we'd be great together."

I can barely process the words that are coming out of his mouth.

"And just so we're clear, Hope was *my* girlfriend. You were the one pining over my girlfriend for years."

"I liked her first!"

"She's a person. You can't call dibs on a person."

He's right. But if someone you care about loves someone else, and it's in your power not to crush that? I mean, you shouldn't, right?

"I love her," I say quietly. "I've always loved her."

He sighs. "I care about her, too, Spence."

Her in his bedroom. Her after he dumped her. "You." I point my finger in his face. "You almost broke her." I snatch the plate with my motherfucking pie and sit in my dad's chair. "And she's the only one who gets to call me Spence."

Dean rolls his eyes. "She's not that great, man. I mean, yeah, she's fun and intoxicating and all that, but then something bad happens, and that's it. She's out. And it's all your fault. None of it's hers. It's just not worth it."

I'm up, and I'm fighting mad, and the pie is on the floor, and it's a damn shame there's a coffee table in between us. "Her sister died."

"I know. And that's really sad—"

"No, you don't know." I push him in the chest. "All you can see is how she relates to you. But she has her own life. Her own stuff. And she's amazing." I wipe my cheeks. Not that I'm crying. "But you'll never get to know it—about her or any other girl—because all you ever see them as is something to make you happy or inspire you or cheer you on."

I sink into the floor and rest my head against my knees.

Dean sits beside me. "I'm sorry. I didn't mean to talk about Hope like that." He pauses for a long moment. "And maybe you're right. Yeah, I've had a ton of girlfriends or whatever, but it's not like what you guys have. I get that." It hurts him a lot to tell me this. I can see it. "We didn't hook up this week, when she came into my room. She was asking for my blessing."

My brain is going to be mush before the end of the day. It's incorporating new facts and building new life knowledge like so many busy ants digging a network of tunnels.

"For what?"

He pushes me. "For you, doofus. She was asking for my blessing to date you."

Me. Blessing. *What?*

"I told her it was fine, and then we hugged it out. I'm really kind of surprised you guys haven't started dating already." He pushes me one last time before he heads upstairs. "It's probably because you're such a doofus."

How does it feel when it happens?

Like your heart is a firework and someone just lit the fuse.

Like all the colors in the world are brighter, and there are more of them, ones I would swear didn't exist yesterday.

And the air is filled with chances. They're just floating there like specks of dust. And I get the idea that they've always been there, a flurry of chances following me around, only now I can see them. Now I can take them.

I could do any bold, reckless thing, like hang glide off a mountain or talk to Hope.

Hope.

I have to see her.

I can't.

Because A) she probably hates me, and B) I'm probably not allowed. It's bad enough that Dean and I got up in the middle of Thanksgiving dinner to "brawl like heathens" in the basement. There is no way Pam will let me interrupt this meal a second time.

Turns out Thanksgiving dinners last a freaking long time when everybody keeps going back for seconds and thirds and fourths and just one last sliver of pie.

Finally, I feel like I can ask, "May I be excused?" Before Pam can answer, I add, "Dinner was really delicious. Thanks."

She smiles. "Thank you, sweetie. Of course you can."

I calmly get up from the table, calmly walk out the front door. But as soon as it's closed, I run/limp across the yard and up Hope's steps, and I rap that anchor-shaped door knocker for all it's worth.

No one answers. I knock again. It occurs to me that the lights are out and a car is missing from the Birdsongs' driveway. The trip. They've already left. I try calling, but it goes straight to voicemail, so I put my phone back in my pocket and sit on her welcome mat and lean my head against the door. I feel like I've swallowed a firework.

CHAPTER

31

I'm in trouble. I'm standing on the regulation, approved-by-officials-and-the-wrestling-gods scale, and I am 4.2 pounds overweight. I wish I could say going out in a blaze of trypto-phan glory was worth it, but really, I just feel guilty and kind of like a screw-up. I'm not the only one. Today's tournament is the first one since Thanksgiving, and even though we've had nine whole days to burn off the sins of one afternoon of pie-filled bliss, and even though they give you a bonus pound because it's post-holiday, people are struggling. Luckily, this is just the pre-official, how-am-I-doing weigh-in. The real weigh-in won't take place for two more hours. Which means now is the time we step away from the judgment of the scale and choose our poison: running, stationary bike, or laxatives. (I do not recommend that last one.)

Me, I'm a runner. I put on two pairs of sweats, a smaller pair that really hugs me, and then a normal-size pair. I add a knit cap and a hoodie, too. And now, dressed like the kid from *A Christmas Story* and with my stomach completely empty of breakfast or even water, I will run until I sweat off 4.2 pounds.

I wait for a minute to see if any of my teammates will be running with me. Jackson walks over. No surprises there—the dude always has trouble making 160. But then . . . Paul?

I look at him in disbelief. "You're over?"

I don't think this has ever happened before.

He rolls his head around on his shoulders. "I know. I know. I may have eaten an entire honey-baked ham for Thanksgiving."

"By *yourself*?"

"Well, my mom bought it for me, and she was like, 'Just take a slice whenever you get hungry.' So, I did. And then it was gone."

I mean, what do you even say to that?

"I'm only two over. I got this," says Paul defensively.

"Hey, I'm not judging. Just trying to figure out how someone your size put away an entire ham."

The three of us go outside and take off running, and because tournament days always feel a little bit like Christmas morning, we are all acting like really big dorks. We talk about Thanksgiving-food binges and video-game binges and staying-up-late-talking-to-your-new-girlfriend binges. Well, actually, Paul is the only one who has anything to say about that last one.

"I still can't believe you're dating a girl as hot as Eva," says Jackson.

"I know!" says Paul, with this ridiculous grin.

I force my legs to push harder even though my empty stomach is eating itself. My ankle twinges, but only a little. "I can't believe you had the balls to ask her out when she was leaving in a few weeks."

Paul puts a hand to his chest. "When you've got a chance at a girl like Eva, you have to seize the moment." He says this like he is some kind of expert on love, and between the three of us, maybe he is.

"And speaking of." He nudges me.

"What?"

"You know what."

"She's not even on this continent."

"Wait. *What?*" Paul is breathing heavy and sweating like a fiend.

"She's in South Africa." I don't have the breath to explain why. Running on an empty stomach is hard. Running on an empty stomach while talking is damn near impossible.

"No, she's not. I saw her getting out of their van on my way to school just now."

"She's back?"

Ohmygosh, she's back. I think about Paul and Eva and chances. I think about Hope. Every time I think it's really over, every time I think we've had our last chance, we find one more last chance to give each other. Maybe love means never running out.

I don't know if it's because I'm light-headed from the run, but a plan starts to take shape. We're not too far from our street. I could be there in a few minutes.

I sprint ahead and veer off to the left.

"Dude, where are you going?" yells Paul.

"To Hope's," I holler back. "I gotta seize my moment."

They don't say anything. Or laugh. I hear their footsteps behind me. Did they make the turn, too? I glance over my shoulder.

"We're coming with you!" says Paul.

It should feel weird, maybe, that they're coming. It doesn't, though. It just feels really good.

I bolt up the stairs of Hope's front porch like every second matters. I'm knocking on her door, and it is so, so urgent. Eponine barks shrilly from inside—dogs can sense these things.

Hope's mom answers.

"Hi, Mrs. Birdsong. Is Hope here?"

"She just ran to the store to get some stuff to make cupcakes to bring over to Ashley's."

"Oh." I shuffle my feet around on the welcome mat. It really didn't occur to me that she might not be here. My friends have caught up and are doing jumping jacks in Hope's front yard to keep their heart rates up. The weirdness? It has made an appearance. "Do you know when she'll be back?"

"I don't know. An hour, maybe?"

Crap. I can't wait that long. I have to get back before weigh-ins.

Mrs. Birdsong cocks her head in concern. "Do you want me to give her a message for you?"

"Oh. Um." I look over my shoulder like I can make her appear in the driveway through the very act of looking. (Spoiler alert: It doesn't work.) "No, that's okay. Thanks."

I jog back to the guys, and they give me some super manly back claps, and we head back to school. Okay, so I can't see her right now. But I can call her. Yeah, that's a great idea. Almost as good as seeing her in person. But maybe I'll wait until I'm not running full speed in three layers of sweaty clothes. Yep. That is probably a great idea, too.

We make it back in plenty of time. I would kill for a sip of water right now, but I have to wait. I think about waiting to call her until after the weigh-ins, too, so I won't have a creepy, parched voice or whatever, but in the end, I simply don't have the willpower. I whip out my phone and scroll for her name. My stomach flips when I press send. If that girl answers her phone right now, I'm going to marry her someday.

Except she doesn't. So I leave her a message. Which, honestly? Kind of sucks. Because A) this is just not the kind of thing you want to pour out after a disembodied beep. And B) I'm going to sound like a complete tool, I just know it.

But this is too important to wait, and I need her to know RIGHT NOW, so message it is.

"Hey, Hope, it's Spencer. Well, I guess you already know that. Anyway, I'm sorry. All that terrible stuff I said to you, well, I only said it because I saw you hugging Dean and got the wrong idea. I should have asked you what happened, and I didn't. I was pissed off, and I acted like a total dick, and I'm sorry. Really sorry. Did I mention I'm sorry? I really hope you can forgive me. Actually, I'm hoping for a whole lot more than that." I take a deep breath. Putting my entire heart on the line in three, two, one. "Because I like you. I really, really like you." Love you. I am head over heels in love with you. "And I hope you like me. I mean, really like me and want to date me and stuff." And by stuff, I mean spend every day together for the rest of our lives. "I understand if you don't. There's a lot that's happened. It's okay if you don't want to talk to me anymore." Except, no. Please, please, no. "So, okay. I want you. I'm in. And if you're still in, could you maybe come to my wrestling tournament today? If you don't show, I'll know you're not interested, but if you do? Um, well, that would be really great." And we can make out until the sun comes up tomorrow. "So, okay, I guess I'll talk to you later or something. Bye." Somebody kill me before I die of embarrassment.

I hang up the phone just in time for weigh-ins to start. I wait my turn to get officially weighed and also to get officially inspected for ringworm/molluscum/shingles because that is a thing that happens before wrestling meets (the mats—they're like petri dishes). I take off all my clothes because you never know when underwear could ruin everything, and then I step on the scale and close my eyes and think skinny thoughts and pray for 139.

The scale says 138.6.

I just lost 4.6 pounds in two hours. I made weight, people! But it's not just my body. Everything else feels lighter, too.

CHAPTER

32

♥

Bananas are the greatest. I eat two of them and pound a blue Powerade for good measure. Then I start in on the bagels and Powerade number two. Gotta replenish all those electrolytes I lost. Paul is replenishing right next to me without even bothering to chew.

My eyes flit from match to match. This is a pretty big tournament, so there are mats set up all over the gym. Sixteen different schools and at least half of them are 4A or better. Peach Valley's only 3A, and I'll be honest, we probably won't be winning this thing as a team, but Coach seems to think I've got a shot at 138. The bananas shift uncomfortably in my belly. Some guys get really, really nervous before a match—some of them even have to go throw up in a trash can—but not me. I mean, sure, I get a little jittery and have to take a giant poop half an hour before like clockwork, but I'm not *nervous*. I just eat a lot of fiber.

I alternate between watching my friends and yelling stuff, wrestling my own matches and checking my phone for Hope. Coach was right. Before I know it, I blow through my first two opponents, and I'm in the semis. If I win, I get a shot at being a champion. This season has been huge for me. I'm down to two doses of meds a day, and my doctor said I can push the morning one to the afternoon on match days. And yeah, I was hoping to wean myself off entirely, but my tics just got too intense.

It's cool, though. The pre-bedtime dose never bothered me anyway, and two doses a day is way easier to deal with than four. I'm not as groggy, which is definitely helpful when you're locked in a death match with another dude. Plus, I read some articles recently about how the differences in Tourette's brains might lead to more than just tics—that kids with Tourette's syndrome might have faster cognitive processing and response times, maybe even faster motor function. And now when I wrestle, I can't help but wonder if my Tourette's syndrome is giving me an edge. I feel like I have superpowers or something.

Fifteen minutes before my semifinal match, I start my warm-up protocol. I run in circles, do jumping jacks and somersaults. I gotta keep a sweat going because if you go into a match cold, you're done. I scan the stands while I do a few more jumping jacks. Mimi waves at me. She, Pam, and Dad are all here. Dean had to go back to school already (though he did stop by Jayla's first to grovel/see if there's a snowflake's chance in hell that she might be willing to go on a date with him the next time he's home). I kind of thought Hope would be here by now. If she was coming. I finally allow the thought to enter my mind—maybe she's not.

Whatever. I can't think about that right now. Can't let anything psyche me out.

The match ahead of mine finishes. I'll be up next, wrestling against a guy from one of the bigger schools in Warner Robins. Country boy versus city slicker, and the hometown crowd is loving it. I pull off my sweat suit so I'm just wearing my singlet. Get my headgear and mouthpiece into place. And just as I step onto the mat, I see a flash of white hair in the audience. I think Hope is sitting next to Mimi, unless she's some kind of mirage, but I can't think about it. I have to focus. The ref hands us our anklets, calls us to the center of the mat, and it's time.

The referee lowers his hand as he blows his whistle, and my body kicks into wrestling-robot mode, and I know I'm sinking an underhook and he's clamping down over it, but it's hard to really be aware of anything until it's all over, and we're standing side by side, and the ref raises my hand.

I could cry. I almost do. I am going to the finals. And Hope was there to see it.

My head whips back toward the stands, but the seat beside Mimi is empty. I look all around the crowd. All around the floor, too. But she's not here.

As soon as I sign the match sheet and take it to the head scorer's table, I make my way up to where my family is sitting. Pam wraps me in a hug.

"You were great, Spencer. Here, let me get you a Powerade."

She riffles through her cooler while my dad looks down at me like he's never been prouder. It all feels great, but I need to know if I was hallucinating. My eyes are question marks, but thankfully Mimi doesn't make me ask.

"Hope was here, but she had to run," she says. "Something about going to Ashley's."

Oh, right. Ashley Gray's. I remember Hope saying she and a few other girls go over there sometimes on Saturdays to hang out or something.

Mimi looks about as pleased and smug as it gets. "I'm supposed to give you this."

She hands me a folded-up sheet of paper. I open it.

I'm all in.

I want to do something dorky like clutch it to my heart, but

Mimi is still eyeing me. My smile kind of takes over my face, though.

"I knew it!" she says.

"It's nothing. This could be absolutely nothing." I say it like I believe it, because jinxes are real, and you have to be careful.

"Don't piss on my leg and tell me it's rain, Spencer Barton. I saw the way your face lit up just now." Mimi is nothing if not subtle.

The finals matches are starting now. Unlike the other matches, they'll be taking place on one mat in the center of the gym. No split focus this time. No one wants to miss a second. Except me. I want to run out of here and get to Hope as fast as I can because Lord knows what's going to happen if I delay by even a minute. She'll change her mind. A hot guy will materialize at Ashley Gray's and ask her to marry him and live on his island in South America. A tornado will whisk Ashley's entire house to an alternate universe.

I'm edgier than a cat in a room full of rocking chairs, and I just want this tournament to be over already, and I hate that by luck of the draw 138 is wrestling last. I need to get it together. Winning this would be major for me. Our team even has people on the sidelines videoing everything so we can put the best parts in our highlight reels to send to colleges.

None of my teammates are in the finals until Traven, and I sit up and pay attention. He and his guy are pretty evenly matched, but late in the second period Traven finally scores the first points of the match with a slick reversal. In the third, his opponent escapes, and Traven gives up a takedown in the final seconds. He looks wrecked, but he shouldn't be. The guy did awesome, especially for a sophomore. If he keeps it up, he'll win state when he's a senior.

The next two matches pass in a blur, and then I'm on deck. I'm dressed in my Peach Valley sweat suit. I've practiced for weeks. I am a lean, toned, certified lethal weapon. (At least, that's what I tell myself in the mirror every morning.) I am so hungry for a win I can taste it. I stuff my sweat suit in my gym bag and hop around so I can stay warm. It feels strange this time. Like the real battle is something that happens when this is over, and this is just something I have to get through. I shake hands with the other guy. I know he can't weigh more than 138, but I swear, he's huge. I hear Paul and the rest of my team screaming my name. And then I go for it. Because everything about this day is about going for it. There is no more holding back. There is no more being scared. There is only action and where it leads you.

I take a deep shot and go for a fireman's carry. He tries to drop his weight for a sprawl, but I pull him over me by his arm. He's fighting—off of his back, onto his belly—and I immediately sink a deep half nelson before he can clamp his arm down on mine. I drive my head into the back of his, pushing him forward with all my leverage. Reach around and grab his wrist with my hand. Good grief, his forearm is like an anaconda. I go for a knee whip and . . . he's on his back! I lock a Gable grip behind his head and squeeze. He flops with all his strength, and we're so close to the edge of the mat that I'm afraid he'll work his way out of bounds. I'm not sure I can beat this guy if he makes it off his back. I squeeze harder and drive my forehead right into his temple. And then I hear the whistle and the slap of the mat, and I know it's a pin.

My team floods the mat, and a dozen hands are pushing me

into the air, and there's a note under my phone that says *I'm all in*, and today is shaping up to be one of the best of my life. It's weird when you know that, but sometimes you do. Sometimes you have a day that is so epic that you know, even before it's over, that it's going to be one of a dozen that you remember forever.

There's yelling and congratulations, and I want to leave and I want to soak it all in. I'm on a stand, getting a medal, getting my picture taken, and then I just can't wait anymore.

I run over to Coach.

"Atta boy! You ready to celebrate?"

"Coach, I'm sorry, but I gotta go." I sure hope my face is showing how important this is.

His eyebrows snap together. "Well, sure. Is everything okay?"

"Yeah. I just. I really need to go now."

I run over and grab my bag and phone and keys and stuff. I start to tell my family where I'm going, but Mimi waves me off. "I've already explained everything."

"You don't even know what I'm doing."

She arches an eyebrow. "Are you going to Ashley Gray's to get together with Hope?"

How does she *do* that? "Maybe."

"I want a full report later!" she yells as I run away.

I push through the double doors and into the December air. I'm still wearing my singlet, but whatever, I can change in the car. Love doesn't have time for things like locker rooms.

I crank up the truck, and drive in the direction of Ashley's house. Luckily, I went to her sixteenth birthday party, so I know how to get there. Hope is going to be there. I am going to make it there before anything horrible can tear us apart. We are going to be okay.

It is only when I hit my first red light that this plan develops a hiccup. I open my gym bag so I can pull some clothes on over my singlet, only my clothes are not in there. Because it's not my gym bag. I was in such a hurry, I must have grabbed someone else's. The worst part—there are no clothes of any kind in this gym bag, unless you count a very large, very sweaty singlet. The guy must have already changed.

I weigh my options. Go back to the school and get my bag? Yeah . . . no. That's not happening. That is exactly the kind of thing the anti-Hope-and-Spencer fates want me to do right now. Go to Ashley Gray's wearing nothing but my singlet? I mean, I don't want to, but screw it. I'm doing this.

Ashley's house appears by degrees as I coax my truck up the hill on Moccasin Lake Road. They call it that because there's a lake at the end of the road where the water moccasins lay their eggs. In spring, you can almost see the water wriggling with all the baby snakes underneath. So, swimming there is probably not a good idea.

But today, nothing—not a lake filled with venomous snakes or a wrestling uniform that leaves absolutely nothing to the imagination—is going to keep me from telling Hope everything I've ever thought about us.

CHAPTER 33 ♥

I knock on the door with maybe too much force, I can't help it. A thin woman with short blonde hair and translucent eyelids answers. "Can I help you?"

She must be Ashley Gray's mom. I was kind of imagining Hope would answer the door, but hey, that's okay. As long as she's here. "Is Hope here?" And then because she looks so utterly flummoxed, I add, "Hope Birdsong?"

She frowns. "Yes."

The door doesn't budge.

"I'm sorry," I say. "I need to see her."

Mrs. Gray glances behind her into a room I can't see. Winces at me. "This really isn't the best—"

"Please. It's important."

I don't know if she can read everything on my face, but she sees enough to sway her into opening the door a few more inches. "I'll get her for you," she says.

But then she leaves the door open like I'm supposed to follow her. So I do. There's a short hallway, and I hear girls' voices coming from the other side of it. And then I'm standing in a dining room, only I can already see the girls in the living room because the house is one of those open floor plans, and really it's all kind of the same room.

"Hope," calls Mrs. Gray.

And now all the girls can see me. I wasn't expecting this

many of them. There's, like, seven (eight?) tucked into chairs, perched on couches and ottomans, sitting cross-legged on the floor.

Hope's eyebrows wrinkle in confusion. "Spencer?"

I weave closer, tripping over a stone statue of a bulldog wearing a Georgia jersey in the process. Their eyes zigzag right along with me, following my every move, and I become suddenly and uncomfortably aware of two things:

1) I am still wearing my wrestling singlet (and only my wrestling singlet). Normally, being on display in skin-tight green polyurethane in a room full of girls would throw me into worries about cold weather and shrinkage, except that,

2) They are all crying.

I mean, they aren't all full-on sobbing (though the one rocking back and forth on the ottoman is), but every last one of them has red eyes, and here and there I see a tear-streaked face or a fist clenched around a bunch of tissues. The last time I walked in on a group of women crying like this was when I caught Hope and Janie watching *Les Mis* with Mimi and their mom and a coffee table full of Girl Scout Cookies. I am as woefully unprepared now as I was then.

"Um, hi," I say. "I'm sorry. I didn't mean to interrupt. I just needed to talk to Hope, and . . ."

Everything I want to say is starting to feel like things that could wait, and I find myself wishing I could go back in time and wipe out this whole plan, or at least the part of it where I dash out of the tournament without putting on actual clothes. Lesson learned. Calling ahead is a good idea. So is asking permission. How come the guys in the movies don't come off looking like creepy stalkers because that is definitely what I feel like right now.

Hope jumps up from her place on the loveseat. "What's up? Is everything okay?"

"It's fine." I feel ridiculous. "Um, is there somewhere we could talk?"

"Sure. Um." Hope glances around and seems to realize what I've already figured out—they'll be watching us almost anywhere we go. She leads me back to the hallway by the front door. At least there's a wall. "Is this okay?"

"Uh-huh." I rub the back of my neck. "I'm really sorry. I didn't realize. I mean, I thought this was a sleepover."

"Oh." It's Hope's turn to get red-faced. "Yeah, I didn't tell anyone because I guess I was embarrassed. Not that it's anything to be embarrassed about—it's not." She takes a deep breath like she's trying to get her thoughts together. "It's a grief support group. With other girls who are going through the same stuff as me."

So, really, the worst possible thing I could have burst in on. "Well, that's great. I'm so glad you're doing that."

The smile that spreads across her face is shy/proud/genuine/relieved. "Thanks. It's been a really good thing for me. I've been . . . Well, it's really helping."

"That's so great." My smile back is giddy/dopey/oblivious.

"So . . . you're here."

"Oh, right. I just wanted to—well, I wanted—" I didn't think I could feel any more like an idiot, but barging in here to declare my undying love for her is starting to seem like the worst idea ever. My thumb traces shapes on the folded-up piece of paper I'm holding. I'm still going to take the flying leap. "I wanted to talk to you about the voicemail I left you. And about this."

I unfold the paper so we can both see the words. So I can

remind myself that they're real. Hope smiles, and this time it is sheepish/eager/knowing/sexy. My stomach flips. I could spend the rest of my life classifying her smiles.

"I want to talk to you about that, too," she says. "But maybe somewhere that's not here."

I glance back at Ashley's living room. "Yes, please."

I wave to the girls and apologize about eighty-five times, and then Hope hangs back to give some sort of explanation speech. I go outside and wait by my truck and rub my arms to keep warm. Hope stays in there a really long time. Long enough for me to make up stories in my head about how they're all inside laughing at me, and she's never coming out.

Ashley's front door finally opens.

"Hey," I say. "What all did you tell them?"

Hope shrugs coyly. "Let's just say, I think you have your own fan club now."

"Oh." I can barely get one girl to like me, let alone a whole room full of them. I stand a little taller. Puff out my chest a bit. "Well, that's pretty cool."

She rolls her eyes. "Stop it."

And then she goes to push my shoulder, but it's like her bare skin against my bare skin is too much because her hand kind of gets stuck there. We're frozen for a second, and then like an idiot, I look down at her hand because I want to see it touching me. She comes to her senses and pulls it away. But now that we've touched, I don't want to be not touching, so I reach out my hand and hold my breath and trace my finger down the back of her hand where it rests by her side. She lets me. Actually, she makes this little gasping noise that makes me very concerned about the fact that I'm wearing a singlet. I lace my fingers through hers, slowly. It's different from that time we held hands in the tree stand. Because that time I was trying to figure out if we were friends, and this time I know we're not.

"Should we go?" I ask.

"Yes," says Hope. But she doesn't move to get into the truck. "I drove here, so I should probably drive home, too."

"Oh." I don't know why this disappoints me so much. "Well, we'll see each other in a little while, then."

"Yeah," she says. She doesn't move to get into her car, either. "At my house?"

"Sure."

I stand there.

She stands there.

Neither one of us wants to let go of the other's hand. It finally occurs to me that the sooner we leave, the sooner we get started.

I squeeze her hand. "Soon."

"Soon," she echoes. She gives me another smile to catalogue, and we let our arms stretch as she walks away, our fingers tearing apart at the last possible second. Then we both laugh because we realize how ridiculous we're being.

"Bye, Spence." Hope laughs again and shakes her head and then she's gone.

CHAPTER
34

I should have kissed her. Or done something to make this feel more final. It's all too fragile, and we've had too many close calls. I didn't want to let her out of my sight, but we had to get home somehow. Maybe she feels the same way because her silver Civic tails my car like we're in a bad spy movie, and every time we hit a red light, I glance at the mirror to find her grinning at me.

Part of me wants to go right over to her house when I get home, but a bigger part of me wants to race inside so I can change clothes (and, if I'm really being honest, put on deodorant). The brakes screech when I park, and I take the stairs two at a time.

"HEY, I'M GOING TO HOPE'S. I'M JUST CHANGING CLOTHES. I'LL SEE Y'ALL LATER," I yell.

This was necessary as both Pam and Mimi are sitting in the living room pretending not to wait for me.

"You are not off the hook!" yells Mimi as I dash past them a second time (now, with clothes!).

"Okay!" Everything is exclamation points today.

I slam the door. Hope is waiting on her front porch.

"Hey," she says.

"Hey."

Oh, wow, this is really happening. She pulls out her house key, and I realize her dad's car is absent from the driveway. She unlocks the door. We go into her house and stand in her living room, which is something I've done about a billion times before. Everything is the same, and everything is totally upside down.

"So, that was an interesting voicemail you left me."

Right. That. I don't know why I'm so nervous. I know what she wrote on the paper. I know she held my hand in front of Ashley's house just as tight as I held hers. But I still feel like I'm walking into a minefield and one wrong word and *BOOM*. Everything we might get to be will disappear in a cloud of smoke.

"I—"

She crosses her arms.

"You're not going to make this easy for me, are you?"

"If you recall, I was the one that did this last time. And I got shot down."

I wince. "I recall. Sorry about that."

"No, hey, I'm just messing with you. Do your spiel." She drops her voice to a stage whisper. "If it makes you feel any better, my answer is going to be yes."

It does. "Okay, here goes. I want you."

Her eyes go wide. Oh, crap.

"I mean, to be my girlfriend. But other things, too." I don't not want her that way. "I want to see you every day, and kiss you every day, and I want us to know each other forever and build whatever life we dream up."

Hope's smirk has disappeared, and she looks like she might cry. "I want all those things, too," she whispers.

There's this moment when we're staring at each other, and it feels like the moment after a hurricane when everything has subsided and you know you're going to be okay.

She takes a step closer. "I've always wanted to know what it would be like to kiss you."

"Me, too." Wait. "We have kissed."

"Not like this."

She wraps one hand around my neck and pulls my face toward hers. She kisses me and the trees explode with flowers, tulips shooting up out of the ground like one of those time-lapse videos. Everything is more alive and turning/growing/reaching for her like she's the sun. It is all so much bigger than labels and categories and convenient little boxes, and it almost sweeps me away. When we finally pull apart, she looks as dazed as I feel.

"Nope. Definitely not like that," I say. "Not like this, either."

This time I'm kissing her, and it doesn't feel like flowers or magic. It feels like a storm. Bodies crushing against each other. Hands tangled in hair. Feelings so big they feel like explosions. We aren't dazed this time. We are gasping for air.

And now the floodgates have been broken on kissing, the moratorium has been lifted, and we give each other every kiss we've been dreaming about for the past five years. Kissing. Laughing. Laughing. Kissing. We roll around in the blissful newness of it all. Sometimes I tic, but we're both way too busy to notice.

Hope takes a break from the kissing and lays her head in my lap so she's looking up at me. "Why couldn't we have done this before?"

"Right? We have lost out on years of kissing. *Years.*"

Hope snorts. "Thanks a lot, past Spencer and Hope."

We're laughing, and then her face goes kind of serious. "I wasn't ready before."

I put my arm around her as my way of saying, *Anything you want to tell me right now will be okay.*

"There were times when I thought I was, but I don't know. I think we would have ruined it."

I think about what it would have been like to get together with Hope when I still practically worshipped her. "I think you're right."

"I needed a lot of time after Janie. I'm sorry if I hurt you, but that was what I needed. I just, I had to grieve on my own time line."

"You never have to apologize for that. I'm sorry for trying too hard and pushing you."

"You don't have to apologize, either. I know what you were trying to do, and I kind of love you for it."

Love. She definitely just said "love." We both turn red and find the wallpaper to be fascinating.

"Hey, want to see something in my room?"

"Okay." I turn even redder, which I didn't think was possible.

I follow her upstairs.

"Check it out," she says.

Her room looks the same—the empty walls, the overflowing bookshelf, the desk with the . . . Oh. There is a map over her desk. A small one, but that's how the best things start. I walk closer and touch it with hesitant fingers.

"Brazil, huh?"

She shrugs shyly. "I've been planning trips again. Ugh, but it would be a whole lot easier if I hadn't thrown away all that stuff after, um, you know."

Ohmygosh, it's finally the right time!

"Wait here!"

I can only imagine the series of expressions she's making as I sprint out of her room, but I don't even care. This is so going to be worth it.

I run inside my house. "HEY, I'M JUST GETTING SOME-THING OUT OF THE ATTIC. CAN'T TALK."

The attic is dark and spiderweb-y. It's been a long time since anyone's been up here. The plastic container is sitting right where I left it, though. I try to brush some of the dust off, but it's kind of a lost cause. Oh, well.

I pick it up and run back downstairs. "GOING BACK TO HOPE'S. SEE Y'ALL LATER."

"You are still not off the hook!" yells Mimi.

"Noted!"

And then I'm tearing across the yard and through Hope's front door, clattering up the stairs to her bedroom, setting the box on her desk.

"Open it." I can hardly contain my excitement. This must be what it feels like to be Santa or that guy who gives out gold medals for wrestling at the Olympics.

Hope appears . . . skeptical. She carefully lifts the plastic lid and then wipes her hands on her jeans before reaching inside. The maps and drawings are still there, perfect, protected, though I had to piece together some of them with tape.

She unfolds a map, slowly, silently. It's Haiti, and her eyebrows draw together in the middle. "But—" She pulls out another piece of paper, long and winding, with pieces of Scotch tape holding together all the places she wanted to visit. She claps a hand over her mouth. There are tears streaming down her cheeks, and her face is going all splotchy, and her nose is running, and she is the most beautiful girl I have ever seen.

"So, when you were—"

"Yes."

"But why didn't you—"

I shrug. "I didn't want to make things worse."

She's crying and she shakes her head, and then she's laughing.

"What?"

"I was throwing away my dreams, and you were *literally* picking them up."

I smile. "I guess I was."

She doesn't so much hug me as fall into me. I catch her. Hold her. Wrapped up in the magic of second chances and being together.

A TAXONOMY OF HOPE'S SMILES

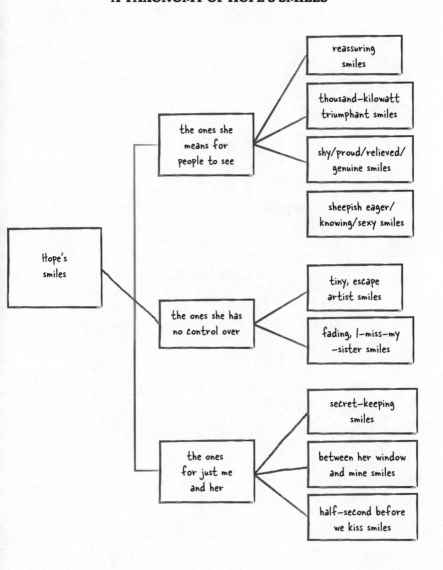

Epilogue

19 years old

THE TAXONOMY OF US

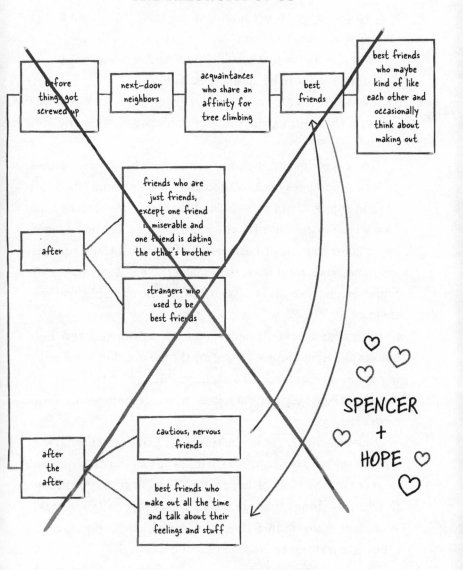

"SNEAK-ATTACK SELFIE!" Hope kisses me on the cheek and snaps a picture with her phone at the same time. I am 87 percent sure my eyes were closed.

Hope checks the picture. "Perfect!" She sends it to Paul.

"I am not so sure he appreciates those."

"Please. He lives for my Spencer-Hope selfies. And soon we'll be out of the country, and I won't be able to send him any. How will he cope?"

The suited-up guy behind us narrows his eyes at Hope's perkiness and goes back to shouting into his phone about idiots and supply chain issues. The lady beside me runs over my foot with her suitcase for the second time. The line is moving in slow motion or backward or not at all. Hope squeezes my hand, and the line doesn't matter. (Side note: When you find someone who makes even the TSA line tolerable, you keep them.)

We make our way through the line in centimeters and millimeters and nanometers. I trace my thumb over her hand, pausing at the black streak by her finger. She got it this morning putting the last big permanent *X* on our Countdown to Caribbean calendar.

When we finally get to the front, she loads her photography equipment onto the conveyor belt like it's a newborn baby. She bounces on the balls of her feet while we wait to go through the scanner thingy that probably shrinks your balls and makes your nose hairs radioactive. The equipment comes out the other side post-x-ray. Hope checks it obsessively.

"It's okay." I put my hand on her shoulder. "Your camera has not been replaced by a changeling."

She shoots me a pretend glare.

Three escalators, a tunnel, and a fifteen-minute train ride later, and we have successfully navigated the belly of Hartsfield-Jackson International Airport. We are at our gate, scanning our boarding passes, stowing our carry-on bags in the overhead compartment, and sitting with our seatbacks and tray tables in an upright position.

I tic-sniff a couple times and wipe my nose. "Are you starving? Because I am starving. I wonder what they're gonna feed us. I hope they've made great strides in airplane food since the last time I flew."

Hope stares at the seat in front of her. I don't think she's heard a word I've said. I put my hand on her knee.

"Are you okay?"

"She died on a plane," she whispers.

"I know." Hope puts her hand on top of mine, and I flip it over so she can lace our fingers together. "Are you scared?"

"I don't know, maybe. I'm sad, mostly. But it also feels like I can't catch my breath."

"It's going to be okay."

I bend over and pull my iPad out of my bag. Her dad told me this might happen. I grab my earbuds and hand one to her and keep the other.

"What are you doing?" Her voice has un-cried tears in it.

"We're not on a plane," I whisper. "We're in a magic portal movie theater that transports people from Atlanta to Belize City without ever leaving the ground."

Hope sniffs and gives me a skeptical look. "What's playing at this magic portal movie theater?"

I smile. "A musical."

Her skepticism grows. "Which one?"

"It has to be a surprise or the magic goes faulty."

She frowns. "This magic portal movie theater sounds very temperamental."

"Oh, it is."

We slip in our earbuds, and I hit play. The Columbia lady appears onscreen.

"What happens when the movie's over?" she asks.

I pat my iPad. "I've loaded this baby with enough musicals to get us all the way to Belize. *And back*."

She snuggles into my shoulder. The music begins. People start singing about five hundred twenty-five thousand, six hundred minutes, and tears stream down Hope's cheeks.

Her eyes flick over to me, and she mouths, *I love you.*

I mouth back, *I love you, too.*

Dear Janie,

It's been kind of a while now, huh? Sorry about that. Maybe you weren't worried though. Did you know all along that I'd write you again?

Things are a lot better now. Well, I'm a lot better. Mom and Dad could still really use some help. Can you work on that?

I graduated from high school last month. Every time I hit a milestone without you there, it feels so weird. Like there are two parallel worlds in my head: the reality one and the one where you're still here, pinning my cap so it doesn't mess up my hair, teasing Dad when he cries through almost the whole ceremony, composing an elaborate toast for me at dinner.

I'm organizing an art show for the end of August. You would like it. It's to benefit sustainable energy in developing countries. And I know you're probably laughing right now and thinking who in their right mind is going to pay to see my stick-figure masterpieces, but it's not my art. It's yours. Remember when I threw a fit and ripped down all your drawings and the maps, too? Spencer saved them. (More on him later.) He actually dug through our trash and flattened them out and pieced them back together and kept them in his attic until I was ready for them. Which, okay, that created a HUGE misunderstanding, but we worked it out (more on that later, too).

So, I had all these beautiful, soul-opening drawings of yours, and I was trying to figure out what to do with them, and I thought about hanging them up in my room again, but

I didn't want them to be just for me anymore. I wanted everyone to see how special you are. To look at the faces you drew and feel like they'd been poured inside another person. Mimi's the one who thought to do an art show. She's still pretty enraptured with the idea. "We're going to bring this town some culture!" she said. She arranged to pair the show with a wine tasting at a local farm. Miss Pam helped me plan the menu while Spencer was away being a counselor at his camp, and then when he got back, they both helped me make installations with all the pieces. Mom and Dad had some more of your drawings stashed away, and Nolan sent me some, too. He's coming in August, for the show. I think it'll be a good thing for him. For all of us.

And maybe, maybe, maybe if I take some photos I'm really proud of before then (because FYI, I do photography now! It's a thing!), I might think of adding a few of them to the show.

And speaking of Spencer . . .

Okay, fine, I wasn't speaking of Spencer, I was speaking of Nolan, and then I was speaking of photography, but you know you're desperate to hear about me and Spencer.

. . .

. . .

. . .

We're together now.

You're probably smiling smugly and thinking finally, and maybe if you were in my shoes, you would have figured all this stuff out sooner, but I don't know. Sometimes I feel like things have to happen at just the right time.

Anyway, we planned the best-ever backpacking trip

through the Caribbean, starting with Belize, and I'm on an airplane RIGHT NOW writing you this letter on my tray table, and Spencer is sitting next to me holding my hand, and the guy in front of us is snoring like a chain saw, and everything is so perfect and amazing and magical, I feel like I could burst.

I still miss you. I'll always miss you. But I know you're out there, sprinkled throughout the world like the pieces of some great puzzle. Lives you changed, things you did, adventures you had, in Samoa, Haiti, South Africa, Belize.

You're everywhere, Janie. So, that's where I'm going. Everywhere.

Acknowledgments

I'm so grateful to all of the wonderful people in my life who helped make this book possible:

My ridiculously talented and hilarious beta readers: Michelle Ampong, Dana Alison Levy, Kate Boorman, Kate Goodwin (basically, if you don't currently have a Kate, GET ONE NOW), Jamie Blair, Erin Brambilla, Janine Clayson, Christa Desir Debra Driza, Marie Marquardt, Nic Stone, and Jenn Walkup. This book is so much better because of you, and I'm so lucky to call you my friends.

To Ellen Rozek, I can't thank you enough for reading, and I was blown away by your insightful feedback. Robert Worthington, thank you so much for reading and answering all my questions. And to Jess Thom for incredibly helpful e-mail convos, for pointing me in the direction of all sorts of amazing resources, and for your life-changing Tourette's syndrome awareness work.

To this amazing writing community that I get to be a part of, especially these little pockets: OneFour KidLit, the incomparable LBs, the Not-So-YA Book Club, Yay YA!, and my Atlanta writer crew and retreat girls (especially my coplanners Gilly and Maryann!). To Little Shop of Stories, which is like my very own Hogwarts, and to all the librarians, bloggers, teachers, and book people who make Kidlit awesome. Special thanks to the woman I spoke with at a YALSA mixer in 2014 for sparking the idea for this book, and to Natalie Parker and Madcap Retreats, without which, I never would have finished on time.

To all the neurodiverse kids. I think you're the coolest.

To my agent, Susan Hawk. Thank you for making my dreams come true again and again. For being supportive and inspiring and for tirelessly believing in me and in this book—I couldn't have written it without you, plain and simple. Also, thank you for the best ever phone conversations (Side Banana forever!).

To my editor, Erica Finkel, for taking this book to places I never imagined, for figuring out the piece about spanning the love story across time (and for suggesting I watch *One Day*, even if it did make me ugly cry), and for being so fun to work with.

To Samantha Hoback, Alyssa Nassner, Kyle Moore, Melanie Chang, Nicole Schaefer, Trish McNamara, Mary Wowk, Elisa Gonzalez, Rebecca Schmidt, Susan Van Metre, Andrew Smith, Michael Jacobs, and anyone else at Abrams who worked on this book in any way. You guys are my heroes. Also, Libby Vander-Ploeg, thank you for designing a cover so beautiful and perfect, I still can't stop looking at it.

To my family, who is so wonderfully supportive and caring, and especially Mom, Mica, Bekah, Dennis, and Maxie for taking care of my kiddos so I have time to write books. I love you guys.

To Ansley and Xander, for being the best things in my world.

And to Zack Allen. Thank you for knowing all the things about wrestling, for Wednesday writing days, and for more things than I can put into words.